Daughter of the Dales

By Diane Allen

For the Sake of Her Family
For a Mother's Sins
For a Father's Pride
Like Father, Like Son
The Mistress of Windfell Manor
The Windfell Family Secrets
Daughter of the Dales

DIANE ALLEN

Daughter of the Dales

MACMILLAN

First published 2018 by Macmillan
an imprint of Pan Macmillan
20 New Wharf Road, London N1 9RR
Associated companies throughout the world
www.panmacmillan.com

ISBN 978-1-4472-9516-7

1 3 5 7 9 8 6 4 2

A CIP catalogue record for this book is available from the British Library.

Typeset by Palimpsest Book Production Limited, Falkirk, Stirlingshire
Printed and bound by CPI Group (UK) Ltd, Croydon, CR0 4YY

In memory of Maurice Allen,
a true Dales man

1

Skipton, Yorkshire, 1913

'Get on, Bess.' Sixteen-year-old Luke Fox snapped the reins across the back of the exhausted and sweating horse, which he had been told to take care of by Jethro, as he had handed the horse to him. All Luke could think was that he had to undertake the task of telling his mother that his grandmama was near death, as he swept his hair back out of his eyes. He was dreading having to tell her the news, but knew that it was a son's duty to do so.

The early summer's warm sun beat down upon him and sweat was pouring off both him and the horse as they reached their destination, Skipton High Street. He was breathless, exhausted and thankful that he had got there safely, as he fumbled with the reins while he tied the knackered steed to a safe hold along the setts of the High Street. The horse and trap had flown like the wind from his grandmother's home at Langcliffe to Skipton, a distance of twelve miles, to where both his parents were at work in the family business, Atkinson's department store. In a bid to tell his urgent news, he had driven the trap too hard and knew it, he thought, as he looked back at the sweating horse.

As he pushed through the shining glass-and-brass revolving doors, he was thrust into the highly perfumed shop floor of the sprawling and busy Atkinson empire. A young shop girl sniggered when Luke nearly stumbled, and then quickly corrected herself as she seemed to realize who the unsteady shopper was.

'Where are my mother and father?' Luke asked anxiously, correcting his apparel quickly and blushing at the shame-faced girl.

'Up the stairs, sir. Your mother is taking a fitting and your father is in his photography studio.' The shop girl pointed through the many rows of scarves and accessories that filled the ground floor of the most prestigious shop in the Dales.

Luke made his way past all the shoppers in their finery, who were intent on browsing the luxuries that Atkinson's provided, sniffing at the perfumes and inspecting the latest in fur goods. With his head down, he reached the bottom of the stairs, flushed and anxious to tell his news to his parents.

'Luke, what are you doing here?' James Fox stood at the top of the stairs and looked down at his son, as he pondered how Luke had got there and why he was on his own.

'It's Grandmama, she's dying! I had to come – Jethro couldn't find Ethan to come and tell you, and he couldn't

2

come himself because he had a horse foaling.' Luke had decided to be the bearer of the news instead of Jethro's son, the stable boy, Ethan, who had disappeared as usual, probably to wander and wonder at the surrounding countryside, a regular occupation of his. Luke's voice rang out up the stairs to his father, making the shop girls stop in their tracks and the shoppers shake their heads in acknowledgement of the bad news that Charlotte Atkinson, the owner of Atkinson's, was on her deathbed.

'Quiet, boy. Now tell me: how bad is she?' James came down and stood at the bottom of the stairs, before placing his hand on his son's shoulder to calm him down.

'The doctor says she'll not be with us much longer, and that Mother has to come home. He says Grandmama's had a stroke. Grandpapa found her this morning – she can't move!' Luke looked pleadingly into his father's eyes, secretly regretting now that he had been so hasty to become the bearer of such bad news and realizing just what his message meant to the family. He hung his head and wiped his nose with the back of his hand. He wouldn't cry; young men did not cry and show their emotions, although his grandmama was the mainstay of the family and he loved her dearly.

'Good man for coming to tell your mother.' James patted his son's shoulders. 'I'll go and tell her. Go and see to your horse. Take it to the livery stable at the Red Lion and ask for a fresh one to take you home, or ask for someone to take you both.' He looked around the shop floor, where the staff were trying to go about their jobs, while being aware of the family tragedy unfolding.

'I'll take Mama home. I can do it, Father, I want to do it. I'll get a team and leave my horse, then you can ride it home. I'll be outside, waiting for Mama.' Luke looked up at his father; he knew his horse was tired, but he wanted to finish what he'd started. To change it would mean wasting time, and his mother would never notice, if he didn't tell her. He wanted to be the one who took care of his mama, getting her to the bedside of her dying mother as soon as he could. Changing horse would cost precious minutes.

'Very well, I haven't time to argue. But see to it that you do change the horses. Your mother will be with you shortly.'

James watched as his son made his way out into the blazing early summer's heat. He quickly made his way up the three flights of stairs to the fitting room with the news that would change everyone's world.

He glanced around the fitting room at the young bride, who was flushed with excitement as Isabelle – the owner of Atkinson's and his wife, and Luke's mother – swiftly made adjustments to the beautiful bridal gown, while Isabelle's assistant held a measuring tape. The bride stood admiring her own reflection in the full-length mirrors that surrounded the walls of the room, as tucks and pleats were added.

'I'm sorry to interrupt, but I'm afraid I have some grave news. Isabelle, my love – our Luke is here! He's come to take you home. Your mother's been taken ill.' James took the box of pins out of his wife's hand and

4

placed his hand round her waist. 'Your father woke up to find her barely able to move this morning. The doctor says she's had a severe stroke.' James looked at his wife and watched as she struggled to take in the news. He glanced apologetically at the crestfallen bride-to-be.

Isabelle caught her breath and James could see tears welling in her eyes. She glanced quickly at her assistant. 'I'm sorry, I must go. My poor mama, I must go to her.' She looked again at the young bride for whom she had been taking a fitting, and then thrust the box of pins into the hands of Madge Burton, her new seamstress.

'Luke is outside – he's waiting with a horse and trap. I did tell him to change his horse for a fresh one from the Red Lion, as he insists he will take you home, so I hope he's done as I bade him. Take your parasol; the sun is so strong today. Don't worry about anything here. I'll see to closing the store and will be with you as soon as I can. And, Isabelle, be strong; be there for your father, as he will need you before this day is over.'

Isabelle could feel her body trembling as her husband helped her down the stairs and half-heard the bride-to-be complaining that she had been promised Miss Isabelle for her fitting, and that being left with her understudy was most unsatisfactory. Stupid woman, she thought. Had she not heard: her mother was dying! Her dear, darling mother, who had been there for Isabelle every day of her life; the least she could do was be there for her now.

The shop floors were hushed as Isabelle was escorted quickly past the concerned shop girls, the bad news spreading rapidly as they watched with empathy their employer join her son.

'Give my love to your mother, Isabelle, she's very dear to me.' The aged Bert Bannister caught Isabelle's arm just as she stepped out into the blazing sunshine. He was bent nearly double with arthritis and his steps were laboured, but he insisted on working a few hours a week, 'just to keep my hand in'.

'I will, Bert. I only hope I'm not too late, as she sounds seriously ill.' Isabelle smiled wanly at the concerned man. He had been her mother's prop, from the time when she first set up her chain of department stores. If it hadn't been for Bert, Charlotte Atkinson would never have dreamed of owning a string of shops. He had insisted that he would work for her until he dropped, but now it looked as if it was going to be the other way round.

James kissed his wife tenderly on her cheek. 'Give her my love – I'll be thinking of you all. I'll be home as soon as I can.' He watched as Isabelle stepped down the stairs of the busy store, unfurling her parasol to shade her from the ferocious heat of the early summer's day, walking quickly to the trap and horse with Luke, their son, at the reins. Once she had climbed in, he turned and went back into the store to give support to Madge and the disgruntled bride-to-be.

'I thought you were never going to come. I seem to have been standing here for an age, and the horse here is getting hotter and hotter.' Luke looked at his mother as she climbed up beside him in the lightest trap, which Jethro

6

had advised him to take, for speed. 'Even though I've changed the horse, it's not liking the heat and standing out here,' he added quickly.

Isabelle looked at her son and then at the horse, which she instantly recognized as Bess, Jethro's most relied-upon trotter. 'Luke, do you think I don't know my animals? This is Bess, from Windfell. You've not changed the horses, as your father asked. I love my mother dearly, Luke, but I don't want Bess to drop down dead on the way home. Now what are we going to do? My mother wouldn't appreciate the waste of a good horse, for the sake of seeing her on what could be her deathbed. You should have taken your father's advice, or perhaps borrowed a horse and carriage from the Red Lion, for we do have an account with them.'

'I wanted to take you home and look after you,' replied Luke, scowling.

'I know, but there's no need to kill the horse for the sake of it. We could have been with my mother sooner, if you had listened to your father. I suppose the doctor and my father are with her, but I should be there as soon as I can.' She continued looking at her son. He was so stubborn, but she understood why he needed to prove himself to her; he was only showing his love for her. 'Now, if you are not about to change her, just let her trot home at a comfortable pace, and then Jethro or Ethan will cool her down when we reach home.'

Isabelle sat back and said nothing more, as Luke trotted Bess and the trap down the High Street of Skipton, with a surly look upon his face. Local business people and shoppers tipped their hats in recognition of one of the wealthiest shop owners in Skipton and beyond, as they made their way down the heavily used road, passing the church and heading out to the Dales beyond. Once outside Skipton, Isabelle let her feelings begin to show. The more she thought about her mother dying in her bed, the more she wanted to urge Luke and Bess on, but she was right – it was no good flogging the poor beast. Luke had obviously done that in order to reach her, by the look of the sweating animal. She should have made him change it, she thought, as she regretted not being firmer with her son. She bit her lip and fought back the tears and gazed around her over the white drystone walls at the blooming meadows. They were filled with buttercups, clover and daisies, a sea of yellow in the bright summer's sun. How could anyone die on a day like this? she thought, as she looked up into the clear blue sky. It wasn't right that her mother might be taken from her on a day like today.

'Are you alright, Mother? We will get there in time.' Luke dared not glance at his worried mother as they entered the fast-expanding railway village of Hellifield, with the echo of Bess's hooves filling their ears as they passed under the railway line that meandered south into Lancashire. They were getting nearer to home; another few miles and they would be through Long Preston, and then it would be Settle, and home.

'I know, you are doing well.' Isabelle smiled at her youngest. He really should not have been sent for her. He was so like she was and, at sixteen, he'd never known any-one close to him die. He really knew nothing of life yet.

'Is Jane alright – is she comforting your grandfather?' She thought of her seventeen-year-old daughter and hoped she was bearing up. Jane worshipped her grandmother. In fact Isabelle sometimes believed Jane thought more fondly of her grandmother than of her, which was not surprising, given the similarities in their personalities, which were more than noticeable when they were together.

'Aye, our Jane was organizing tea and sympathy as I left. She was there for Grandfather this morning. You'd have been proud of her. As soon as Ethan knocked on the door of Ingfield, to tell us Grandmother was ill, Jane organized us all. She can be so bossy, can our Jane,' said Luke.

'She'll only mean well. She likes to take control.' Isabelle smiled at her son; there was a healthy rivalry between her children, with both being a little jealous of the other. She sighed as they reached the outskirts of Settle. How she wished she was standing on the steps of Windfell, instead of passing her current home of Ingfield House.

'Nearly there, Mother.' Luke took the corner sharply as he passed the River Ribble and the Christies' cotton mill, worrying slightly that the horse was starting to become flecked with sweat along its shoulders.

Isabelle looked up at the open scars of the limestone quarry half a mile down from Windfell and knew she was truly home. Her heart beat fast and she felt sick; would she arrive in time to find her mother still alive?

Turning into the drive, they saw Ethan waiting for their arrival. His father, Jethro, stood in the shadow of the stables. Ethan grabbed Bess's harness and then held his hand out for Isabelle to dismount from the trap.

'Thank you, Ethan. I'm afraid Bess needs your assistance more than I do,' Isabelle said apologetically.

'Don't worry, ma'am, you get into the manor and see how it is with your mother.' Ethan smiled at the worried-looking woman and then led the horse and trap to where his father stood, while Luke climbed down.

'Sorry, I was a bit hasty and asked a little too much of her,' said Luke, as he took his cap off his head and rubbed the sweat on his brow with it.

'Not to worry, we'll look after her now. You look after your mother, and pray for your grandmother.'

Jethro looked at the knackered horse and swore under his breath, as he unfastened the harness and led her into the stables. He knew it was partly the hot day that was to blame for Bess's exhaustion, but the lad had no feeling when it came to animals. He should have insisted that Ethan go. After all, Ethan had only been fishing in the nearby Ribble, but Jethro hadn't said so, as his son could be caught for poaching. But Ethan knew how to get the best out of a horse without breaking it, and he would have had sense to change horses at Skipton, with the day being so close and muggy.

'Ethan, draw me some water – let's cool Bess down. You pour and sponge her down with it over her withers, and then I'll scrape it off, and we'll repeat that until she's cooled down. The main thing is to make sure that she doesn't go into cramp.'

Ethan ran to the water trough outside the stables and

watched as Isabelle and Luke entered the manor. Coming back with loaded buckets, he stood next to his father. 'If I'd have brought the horse back like that, you'd have brayed me.'

'That I would, lad. But Master Luke insisted that he went for his mother, and they've enough on their plates today. There's a storm coming, in more ways than one. I can smell it on the air, and look at how those beech leaves are twisting and turning in a near-breathless sky – a sure sign that a storm is on its way. My father taught me that, when I was knee-high. Bess will soon cool when the storm comes, and hopefully she will be alright; unlike the mistress.'

Ethan glanced at his father. He knew better than to disbelieve him, but right now the day was as hot as the new oven in Windfell Manor. It was common knowledge that his father was part gypsy, and he was invariably right when it came to reading nature's signs.

Isabelle plucked up her courage as she turned the brass door handle of Windfell's front door, not knowing what to expect as she stepped into the hallway.

'Thank heavens you are here, Miss Isabelle, your mother is failing fast,' said Mazy, the housekeeper. 'Dr Burrows was praying that you'd be here in time to say goodbye before she departs this earth. Thank heavens it is Dr Burrows who has attended. Your mother has always trusted him despite his age – he should be retired by now.' Mazy was nearly in tears as she took Isabelle's parasol, and tried to smile reassuringly at Luke as he followed his mother up the grand, winding staircase. She shook her head before disappearing below stairs, where all the rest of the staff at Windfell awaited the impending bad news.

Isabelle opened her mother's bedroom door, with Luke close behind her. She looked around the room and at her mother lying listless in her bed, rasping for breath. Archie – her father, and the man Charlotte had loved all her life – sat by her side holding her hand, his face tired and full of pain as he felt each shallow breath that his beloved wife took.

Dr Burrows patted Isabelle's hand and shook his head as she went and sat down at the bottom of the bed, next to her stepbrother Danny, who smiled at her and put his arm round her as she started to cry.

'I'm glad you are here, Izzy. Mother would be happy that we are all here together,' he whispered.

Isabelle smiled and wiped back the tears that trickled down her cheeks. She loved her mother so much – how could she carry on without her?

'No, tears, our lass, she wouldn't want you to be sad.' Archie looked across at his daughter. 'She's had a good life; she'd be the first to say that.' He bent over and kissed her mother Charlotte on her brow and ran his hand around her pale face. 'She hasn't felt right this last week or two; she knew her health were failing and she hoped that she wasn't going to be bedridden.' Archie looked over at his dying wife. 'I'm right, aren't I, lass – that wouldn't be for you?'

'If I could do more, I would, but her heart is weak. She

will not make nightfall.' The ageing Dr Burrows looked at the heartbroken family around him and thought about his own mortality. He'd seen many a body in and out of the world, but the death of Charlotte Atkinson hurt him as if she were his own. She'd always been a fighter, and now the fight in her was worn out and he couldn't help but think he was heading the same way.

Isabelle touched his hand. 'Thank you, Doctor, we know you have done all you can; there's nothing more that can be done by anybody.'

Charlotte breathed in deeply, causing all the family to look at her. The beautiful grey-haired woman whimpered, held her breath for a second and then, with quiet serenity, breathed a long sigh and silently passed from one world to the next, as if she had just been given permission from Isabelle and from the Lord above.

Dr Burrows rushed to her side and checked for signs of life, as Archie broke down in tears, his head in his hands. He'd lost the love of his life, his darling Lottie.

'Don't cry, Grandad. You said yourself that Grandma wouldn't want us to.' Jane placed her arms around her grandfather, whom she loved dearly. 'You've still got all of us.'

'I have, child. But your grandmother was my very life.' Archie wiped his eyes and looked at the doctor, who shook his head, as no signs of life could be found.

Isabelle broke down and cried, while Danny hugged her. 'I've just lost my best friend as well as my mother,' she sobbed.

'Yes, me too. She may not have been my natural

mother, but she never treated me as anything other than as if I was. Harriet and all my family will miss her – we owe everything to her.' Danny thought back to when his father, Archie, had married Charlotte, his first love, after both had been left bereft following the deaths of their original partners, and both finding that they were very much dependent on one another.

'Are Harriet and the children at Crummock?' Isabelle blew her nose on her lace handkerchief and looked at her stepbrother.

'Yes, our Ben has the German measles, and Georgina sounds as if she's getting it too, she's so twisty and in a mood. Rosie stayed behind to help her mother, else she would be here with me.' Danny felt he had to explain why his side of the family were not with him, at the deathbed of the woman they owed everything to.

'It's alright, lad. Charlotte knew everybody loved her, and that's all that matters.' Archie looked up and across at his son.

Dr Burrows closed his bag and felt that his time with the family had come to an end, and they needed their privacy.

'I'm sure you want to be on your own now. I'll be back tomorrow with a death certificate, in order for you to bury Charlotte.' He shook his head. 'She was one hell of a woman, if you don't mind me saying so. She's going to be missed.' He stood up and shook Archie's hand and patted his old friend on the back. He looked around at the woman who, as a baby, he had brought into the world. 'Big shoes to fill, Isabelle, but she will have taught you well, if I know Charlotte.'

Danny stood up and opened the bedroom door for the doctor to leave, as Isabelle rose and hugged the old man, who felt like part of the family.

'Thank you for being here for her. It is what she would have wanted.' She hugged him tightly.

'You be strong. Your family – especially Archie – will need you.' Dr Burrows put on his top hat and left the grieving family to say goodbye to their loved one.

Thomson, the butler, met Dr Burrows at the bottom of the stairs. Guessing that his mistress had died if the doctor was leaving, he didn't say a word, but simply opened the front door for the sad-looking old man.

'Your mistress is no longer with us. If you can tell the staff, it will give a little ease to the family,' Dr Burrows said as he stood in the doorway. 'She's gone and taken the sunshine with her, by the look of this worsening day. It looks like thunder rolling across those back fells. I'd better get myself home.'

Both butler and doctor looked up to the darkening fells over Malham and listened as a distant rumble of thunder made itself heard.

'She always was too bright to last long, just like the day.' Dr Burrows tapped his hat and stepped out with his cane, then walked down the drive of Windfell Manor, with the storm winds starting to blow their way through the beech trees.

*

'I'm sorry to say that Mistress Charlotte has died. I've just seen the doctor out of the manor,' said Thomson to the staff as they gathered, looking sombre, around the table in the kitchen.

Lily, Charlotte's maid, sobbed. 'She was such a lovely woman. She never lost her temper, and I remember when she first came here – both me and her were not used to the finer things in life, so we learned our roles together.'

'Aye, and she gave me a chance, when I was nothing more than a filthy-mouthed nothing who couldn't stop swearing. I didn't deserve the chance she gave me,' sobbed Mazy. 'I'll have to go and tell Jethro. Ruby, when you've done sobbing, put some tea on for the family; they'll need a drink, if nothing else. Master Archie hasn't eaten all day.' Mazy made for the back door and ran across the yard to the stables, gazing up at the rain-filled skies.

Jethro and Ethan saw her coming and met her in the stable doorway.

'She's gone, hasn't she? I saw the doctor leaving.' Jethro looked as black as the clouds that were scuttling overhead.

'Aye, she's gone, bless her soul. We are all in tears in the house.' Mazy put her arm around her husband, for she knew how much Charlotte had meant to him.

All of them raised their heads as a huge crack of thunder broke directly over the house.

'That's Charlotte and God arranging the furniture in heaven,' joked Mazy as she looked upwards, with tears in her eyes.

'Then he'll have to bloody well behave himself, because

little does he know it yet, but Charlotte will have her own way and will be running the show by nightfall.' Jethro sniffed hard and fought back the tears.

'Aye, that she will. At least Master Archie will get a bit of peace now, for she did lead him a dance some days, but he must be broken-hearted.' Mazy hugged their son Ethan and rubbed his dark head of curls.

'He's not the only one – a finer woman I've never known. She was true to her word, was Miss Charlotte, and never let you down. The world's a sadder place without her. Come, Ethan, let's away and check this horse.' Jethro nearly choked on his words.

Mazy watched as her husband and son strode back into the shadows of the stables. The thunder rumbled above her. 'God bless you, Charlotte Atkinson. You've left more than one broken-hearted man down here, if you did but know it. My Jethro worshipped the ground you walked on.'

2

The curtains at each house along the winding small streets of Austwick were pulled in acknowledgement of the passing of Charlotte Atkinson. Villagers lined the cortège route and bowed their heads, removing their caps and bowlers as the family passed them in the carriage on the route to the church – a route that Charlotte had taken many a time, in good times and bad.

'Look at the people!' Isabelle gasped to Danny. 'There are so many attending, they are even standing outside the church gates. I hope it doesn't rain, for their sakes.'

'It doesn't surprise me. Our mother knew everyone, and everyone knew her. What did you expect, our Isabelle? After all, she was one of the most powerful women in the district.' Danny looked out of the carriage as it pulled up at the church's gates.

'It isn't about the power, lad; it's that she was loved and always tried to do right by people. She could have made or broken half of the families in this district, but she showed each one the respect they deserved. If you and Isabelle both do the same as you go through life, then you'll earn just as much respect as your mother.' Archie stood up and waited for the coachman to open the carriage door, then looked out at the ancient market cross on the small green next to the church. The cross he had chased Charlotte around, when they were children. Where had the days gone?

The vicar stood at the church entrance and shook hands with the family, before nodding to the undertaker to follow him into the building. He was nervous as he looked around the packed church, which was full of dignitaries, family and those who had come to pay their respects to the once-humble farm lass from Crummock. He had never taken a burial service like this and expected not to have to do so again; not for a while anyway, he thought, as he looked over at the fragile Archie Atkinson as he started the service.

The vicar held a good service, knowing Charlotte and her roots in Austwick and the Craven community well. He remembered all her close family members, and spoke of her life without belying the heartache that had made her the strong woman she was. He gave his final blessing as the family gathered around the grave, and watched as those who wished to said their final farewells to the woman they loved and respected.

'I'm glad that's over.' Harriet linked her arm into her husband Danny's, and looked round at their daughter

Rosie. 'Are you going to the funeral tea with your father or are you coming home with me?'

'Would you mind if I go to Windfell with Father? I'd like to attend, if I may.' Sixteen-year-old Rosie looked at her father, hoping that he would back up her request.

'Of course you can come with me, Rosie – and you should come as well, Harriet, despite Ben and Georgina having German measles. You know you have no excuse not to, really,' said Danny quickly. 'The housemaid is quite prepared to see to their needs while you are there. I heard her say so this morning,' he growled at his wife.

'Well, you heard wrong. Ben's over the worst of it, but Georgina has such a fever that I fear for her. Measles is known for making a child's heart weak, and I've known some children have fits because their temperature is so high! Do you think I'd risk my children with a common maid, when your mother is dead and there's nothing further that can be done for her?' Harriet's face was full of fear, remembering the hurt and pain she had suffered over the death of two of her previous children, the twins Daniel and Arthur. She had always blamed herself for putting her work at Atkinson's before their needs. 'Have we not been through enough, losing two children? I will always blame myself for not always being there when they suffered. I should never have listened to your mother and Isabelle, when they assured me that the nanny would look after them while I worked at the store.'

'Harriet, there was nothing we could do to save the two offspring we lost. It was the diphtheria to blame; the disease moved quickly and, even if you had been there with them, there was nothing you could have done. The doctor told you that, and he said you were beyond reproach. You cannot keep blaming yourself for their deaths, nor keep fearing the worst every time our children have a sniffle. Nor blame Isabelle, or my mother. No one knew that day how quickly the disease was going to strike, and how bad the weather was going to turn,' Danny whispered quietly.

Rosie stood back from her parents. She was slightly tired of hearing her parents row, something they now seemed to do on a regular basis.

'I've not got a problem with Isabelle; it is she who has a problem with me. Did you notice that she hardly spoke a word to me in the church? She just doesn't understand that my children come first,' said Harriet.

'That's because she couldn't speak – out of respect for the dead. Perhaps you should be the one to show a bit more respect. After all, my mother did a lot for us and our family, despite what you think. Don't forget that Crummock was hers, and we will have to wait and see how the land lies after the funeral.'

Danny looked worried. What if Charlotte had left Crummock to Isabelle? Harriet would not be happy with that. To her, Isabelle had it all and enjoyed a life of ease. Isabelle being made the landlord of Crummock would be the last straw.

'I'll curse if your mother has left Isabelle Crummock. She's had everything on a plate since the moment she was born. Her mother set her up in business, and even then she was too busy chasing after worthless men, leaving me

21

to do all the work.' Harriet looked as black as thunder as she pulled on her leather gloves.

'You left the business because you wanted to bring up our family. You've only yourself to blame. Mother bent over backwards for you when Rosie was born, following the deaths of our first two. She was always there for you, and fully understood your decision to stay at home and be with Rosie and the rest of the family, as they came along. So stop blaming everybody else for your lifestyle. Besides, you want for nothing; we've a good living – it's a bit rough in winter, but we've all we could wish for.' Danny was tired of hearing the constant moaning of his wife. She had been broken-hearted at the deaths of her two eldest, but so had he. Harriet tended to forget that and withdraw into herself, blaming everyone and anyone who challenged her view on life.

'My children are everything to me, which is more than can be said for Isabelle. Just look at Luke – he doesn't seem to have an ounce of sense in him; and as for Jane, well, she's been brought up by your mother and has every one of her traits, the bossy little madam.'

'Aye, she's a fair lass, is Jane. My mother taught her well.' Danny grinned and looked across at his niece, who was standing next to her mother Isabelle, joining in intently a conversation about some subject that she had an opinion on.

'It's a shame you don't have as much interest in your own lass, Rosie, and a bit more time for the two at home.' Harriet looked across at her husband. She was fed up with her lot in life, and sick of hearing Charlotte's and

Isabelle's names on everyone's lips. She was the one who had helped to start the Atkinson empire; or had they all forgotten? She too had put in many hours designing and sewing, initially in the first little shop at Settle, but then the business had expanded and her family had become her main focus. It was then that she had decided that running a business was not for her, and that her heart lay with her family and home.

'Get yourself home, Harriet. Henry from Sowermire next door to us is about to leave, so get a lift with him back up to Crummock, before you say anything else that you might regret.' Danny scowled at his wife. She had a caustic tongue in her head, when she was that way inclined. Better that she went home before she caused any bother. He watched as she made her way through the mourners, catching Henry at the church gate as he climbed into his trap. At least she had the sense not to argue with Danny there, but he knew he would be in for an onslaught on his return home.

'Well, that's your mother seen to, Rosie. Let's away and keep your grandfather company – he looks a bit lost without your grandmother on his arm.' Danny turned round to his daughter. He loved her dearly, despite what her mother had said. Rosie appreciated the farm and the world around her, and never said a bad word about anyone. At sixteen, a year younger than her cousin Jane, she was just the opposite: a young woman with a love of nature and a gentleness for the people around her. How could Harriet say that he had no time for her? They were as close as a daughter and father could be.

23

'So, Mother's decided to go home then? She's been worrying all day about our Ben and Georgina. Although Ben seemed well enough this morning; he gave me a load of cheek when I went into his bedroom. He even threw one of his pillows at me as I left.' Rosie smiled at her father – he was everything to her. He was so different from her mother, who always seemed to be fighting the world. He smiled and had time for her, and she loved to be with him, cherishing every moment.

'Aye, well, you know: mothers and sons, there's a special bond.' Danny linked his arm into his daughter's.

'A bit like fathers and daughters?' Rosie smiled as she walked over to her grandfather. She enjoyed having her father to herself.

'Just like that, my dear.' Danny squeezed his daughter's hand tightly before speaking to his father. 'We should be on our way, Father, as the day's doing well to hold the rain back.' He looked up at the grey sky and at his father standing at the grave's edge, looking down upon the coffin of the one he loved.

'Aye, if you say so, lad. Folk have said that they'll see me back at Windfell, so I suppose I'll have to leave her here. You know we have barely ever been apart since the day we married. It is going to be hard to live without her.' Archie leaned on his stick and wiped a tear from his eye, before walking stiffly away from the grave.

'Here, take my arm, Grandpapa.' Rosie left her father's arm and linked her arm through her grandfather's as she smiled with affection at him.

'You are the image of your grandmother – who you

24

were named after, lass. You've just the same looks and ways. You remind me of her every time I look at you. Your father's mother was sweetness itself and I loved her just as much as my Lottie, but somehow Lottie's light shone brighter, and I was attracted to her like a moth caught around a flame. So she was waiting on me when your grandmother died, and that's how it is. I've loved and I've lost two good women in my life. The world can be hard sometimes.' Archie stopped for a minute and caught his breath, thinking back to his first wife, Rosie.

'But you've still got all of us, Gramps. You've Aunt Isabelle and Uncle James and all my cousins – we will all look after you.' Rosie waited patiently as the elderly man climbed into the carriage to take him home.

'Aye, but you forget, they are not my flesh and blood, not like your father. He's my true son.' Archie paused for a minute. 'Danny, I need to speak to you in the morning, in the study on your own – there's something I need to ask.' Archie looked across at his son as the carriage rocked into action.

'Ask me now, Father.' Danny looked worried, wondering what his father wanted with him. 'Nobody can hear us.'

'No, I'll bide my time because I need to speak to Isabelle first; it's only right.' Archie looked out of the window at the overgrown hedges full of cranesbill and meadowsweet passing by. 'Hey up! It's raining; well, my old lass, tha' did get blessed from heaven afore they filled you in, after all.' Archie sat back and smiled at his granddaughter and thought of the coffin that held Charlotte being rained upon, and of the love she had given him. It was a pity his son hadn't quite the same affection from his own wife. Happen he shouldn't have talked Danny into getting wed to Harriet all those years ago and maybe, if they hadn't lost the children, things would have been different. He sighed and leaned on his stick. Nay, but hindsight was a marvellous thing; if you knew what life was to throw at you, you'd never do anything, he thought. Time would tell if they sank or swam; and the news he was to tell Danny the next morning would have a huge bearing on his son's future, but it was something he had to do before he, too, departed God's good earth.

3

Isabelle looked at her husband lying back in the unmade bed, half-asleep but half-awake as he listened to her ranting. She'd tossed and turned all night, thinking about the repercussions of her mother's death. When she'd asked what was to become of Windfell, Archie had completely ignored her.

'What if Mother has not left me Windfell? It's my home. I hope she realized how much I love the place. You do know that my true father bought it? That's why it should belong to me.'

James yawned and rubbed his head, giving up on getting any peace as he pulled the covers back and sat in his nightshirt on the side of the bed. 'I thought your father was broke and beyond help, until your mother stepped in and saved the day.' He relieved himself in the chamber-pot and immediately regretted his response.

'Oh, shut up. You know nothing when it comes to my family.' Isabelle looked at her husband. 'I'm beginning to realize that the family history I was told was perhaps a little bit in favour of my mother, especially if Windfell is not to be mine.'

'All I know is that Archie has always been here for all of us, and your mother loved him,' said James. 'Besides, he didn't say anything. Wait until you've spoken to the solicitor this afternoon. Old Walker will tell you everything.' James pulled his nightshirt off and looked at his brooding wife. 'Do you know how dark you look when you are in such a mood? Be thankful for what you have got, Isabelle, else it looks like you are a money-grabbing bitch. We've got Ingfield, thanks to your aunt, whom nobody had a good word for. It's a grand house, with plenty of bedrooms and all you need in a home. What do you need Windfell Manor for?'

Isabelle stared at her husband and didn't reply as she walked out of the bedroom, slamming the door behind her and leaving James in no doubt that the day ahead was going to be a hard one. She walked along the long adjoining corridor, with its stained-glass window bearing the coat of arms of the Ingfield family upon it, and hesitated at the top of the stairs. Ingfield House, it was true, was a lovely home and she had been lucky to inherit it from her Aunt Dora, although that had only been by default, as Dora had died without making a will, leaving Isabelle – the closest and only traceable heir – to inherit all that was now around her.

She sighed; the shop in Skipton, a property and business in the Queens Arcade in Leeds and a rented shop in Bradford's Foster Square she already knew were hers, as they were in her joint name with her mother. But the place she loved was Windfell, and her heart was yearning to own it. She felt her lip tremble and her eyes started to fill with tears. She broke down as she turned back towards her bedroom, sobbing uncontrollably as she met James on the landing.

'Hey now, enough of this. Your mother was a good woman. She loved you; she will have done right by you. Have patience and wait until you hear what the solicitor has to say.' James knew Isabelle had set her heart on the family home, and he knew how much it was hurting her to realize that possibly it was not going to be hers for the foreseeable future.

'I don't ask for much. But I just wanted Windfell. It's right that Danny and Archie have Crummock, but I had my heart set on Windfell!' She hid her face in James's jacket, crying relentlessly as she remembered the days she had shared with her mother in her old home. How she missed both. Her mother was gone forever, and it had just hit her that she would never hear her voice and feel her kisses again. But she knew she would remember Charlotte every day if she lived at Windfell and spent her life alongside the spirit of her mother, which filled every nook and corner of the manor.

Danny sat across from his father and watched him as he finished his late, leisurely breakfast.

'Are you alright this morning, Father? You looked tired last night, that is why I left you early.' He watched as Archie drew breath between his two rashers of bacon –

the same breakfast he'd eaten for as long as Danny could remember.

'Aye, I'm alright; you have to be, haven't you, lad? Moping about is not going to bring her back, no matter how much I miss her. Lottie was an exceptional woman, and I only hope Isabelle will take a leaf or two out of her book.' Archie sipped his tea and looked across at his son. 'Isabelle can be spiteful sometimes. She's expecting to inherit everything, and I don't like that.' He stirred his tea and noticed the puzzlement on his son's face. 'Lottie has left Windfell to Isabelle, but only after my day – or until I feel I want to leave it. She'll find out this afternoon; Charles Walker will tell her.' Archie grinned. He loved Isabelle, but she had a lot of her true father in her, and he had ignored her prying at the funeral into what was to become of Windfell.

Danny sat back and looked at his father, who was a devil for keeping things to himself when he thought it was for the best.

'Anyway there's something I want you to ask Harriet, and I've something else to tell you – something I think you should know.' Archie's face clouded over.

'Go on then, Father, tell me your worst.' Danny waited.

'Nay, we'll go into the study. Give the servants the chance to clear my breakfast away.' Archie looked at his one place setting on the large mahogany dining table, remembering that there used to be up to six places set most mornings, not that long ago. He rose from his chair and walked across to the study, Danny following behind him. 'Shut the door, lad. I don't want anyone to listen in.'

30

Danny sat down in the chair that Charlotte had loved so much, noticing the tapestry down by the side of the chair that had never been finished by her, and never would be now.

'What's wrong, Father? You're not ill, are you?' Danny looked at his father and noticed how worried he looked.

'Nay, I'm fine. But I can't see the point in rolling around this big house, and I hate them bloody stairs because of my bad knees – and Isabelle will not want me here, if I offer for her to move in with me. Besides, I couldn't keep my thoughts to myself when it comes to how they spoil Luke. Jane is another matter, but they've ruined that lad.' Archie paused. 'Would you and Harriet be able to put up with me at Crummock? It's more where I belong; and Crummock, I know, will be yours after my day.' Archie looked across at his son. He knew he was asking a lot, for Harriet would not welcome the news gladly.

'Aye, heavens, Father. You don't have to ask. I presume it'll be your farm after today, and you know you can stay with us. It'll save you trailing the road up to us, because it's what you will do, if you live here alone or with Isabelle.' Danny sighed and tried to smile in reassurance at his father, wondering how he was going to break the news to Harriet.

'But what about Harriet – she'll not want me under her feet?' Archie knew what his son was thinking, realizing full well that Harriet would complain.

'I'll not have her say a bad word about it. We've two

31

spare bedrooms, and we owe you and Charlotte for everything we have, so she will have to lump it,' Danny blustered.

'Right, if you are alright with that, then that's what I'll do, and then Isabelle can have her Windfell. It's where she belongs; this was Lottie's dream, not mine. I'd rather be sitting at Crummock's kitchen table than at that big dumb thing in the dining room all by myself.'

'Is there something else that's bothering you? ' Danny glanced at the worried-looking man across from him and waited. It seemed it was a morning of confessions.

'Aye, this is why I wanted you to close the door.' Archie hesitated. 'I went to Ragged Hall the other day, as somebody told me Bill Brown wasn't too well. So I went to see him, seeing as we've traded things together over the years. And that was when I saw his grandson. I nearly dropped down dead – he was the spit of you.' Archie stopped in his tracks and looked across at his son. 'The baby that Amy Brown was carrying all those years back was yours, lad, and he's back: grown up and living with his grandfather.'

Danny stared at his father, not knowing what to say.

'He even carries your name – Daniel. His grandfather said nowt, and I didn't either, but I'm sure old Bill knows he's yours. It's up to you to introduce yourself, if that's what you want. I think the lad deserves to know who his true father is, and perhaps you could make up for all the lost years. But I thought it fair that I let you know my thoughts.' Archie looked across at his son; he didn't know what to advise: whether to leave the lad alone, or suggest that Danny go to Ragged Hall and make himself known. The decision had to be Danny's.

Danny rubbed his hand through his hair. 'I've never told Harriet about Amy Brown and me – let alone about the baby that I suspected was mine. We aren't seeing eye-to-eye at the moment, as it is, as she's never satisfied with her lot. Finding out I fathered a baby before we were married would be the final nail in the coffin.'

'Aye, I've heard her moaning at you. She'll not really want me living with you, but she might have to bite her tongue a bit, if she thinks I'm listening in. Wait until I'm there with you and then make up your mind. Daniel's not going anywhere. Part of the reason he's with his grandfather is that he and Amy's husband don't get on, so Bill told me. Her husband probably realizes that he's got a cuckoo in his nest.' Archie rubbed his hand over his knees because they were aching, and thought about the young man who had greeted him and taken him by surprise as he entered the yard of Ragged Hall.

'Is he good-looking, Father? How tall is he? Does he really look like me?' Danny leaned forward; he knew full well that, now he was aware of his son's existence, he was going to have to meet him.

'Aye, if you can remember yourself in the mirror from twenty years back, then he's you. A bit thinner perhaps and doesn't look right happy, but by the sounds of it he hasn't had the best home life. He's the oldest of five, and it'll have been a struggle for your Amy, bringing them all up at Slaidburn.' Archie noticed the look of concern on his son's face.

'And Amy – did Bill mention how she is doing?' Danny remembered the wild young lass with dancing eyes who had captured his heart that long, hot summer. He should have married her, not Harriet, but the family had to come first back then.

'He never mentioned her. Sorry, lad.' Archie looked at the disappointment in his son's eyes. 'Best you think what to do about the lad, and leave Amy alone. Remember, you've responsibilities of your own; you've enough on your plate.'

'I know, but I've never forgotten her.' Danny hung his head.

'No – nor I your mother. But they are both in the past. Anyway, I've told you my news. Think about it, but don't go hurting your own family; they should come first. And today let's go and face the music with Isabelle; she'll be in a slightly better mood if she thinks she can move into Windfell and get rid of me from under its roof.' Archie smiled as he watched his son struggle with the news. He wondered if he shouldn't have told him about Daniel, but if his own son had been living across the other side of the dale, unbeknown to him, he'd have wanted to know. Whatever Danny did, it was up to him now.

Isabelle looked at Archie and wiped her nose and eyes as the family group stood outside the solicitor's, after hearing the will being read. She looked at her family group. 'Well, I didn't know what to think when you ignored me yesterday, Father. As it stands, dear Mama has done right by all of us. I presume you will be staying at Windfell,

34

Father?' Isabelle looked for support from James as he stood next to Danny.

'Nay, lass, you can have Windfell now. It's of no use to me. I've decided to move out. I've asked Danny if I can move in with him and Harriet, then you can have your home back all to yourself. I need nowt with that big posh house. I hate climbing those bloody stairs. With hindsight, I should never have sold my father's home of Butterfield Gap.' Archie looked at Isabelle and watched as her eyes flashed, thinking of Windfell becoming her new home and the consequences of Archie moving into Crummock.

'You are going to live at Crummock? Does Harriet know? She'll not be very happy. She's never happy about anything nowadays.' Isabelle shot a glance at Danny. She was at the end of her tether with her sister-in-law and her surly ways.

'Danny's asking her later in the day. She'll be right with it. After all Crummock will be theirs, after my day, and your mother gave her a sweetener when she left her those few shares in the firm. It'll make Harriet think herself valued at long last.' Archie looked sternly at Isabelle. 'You be right with her, Isabelle – you and Harriet used to be so close. You just made different decisions, but Harriet deserves a bit of the profit from the shops.' Archie had noticed Isabelle's face cloud over when old Walker had disclosed a 10 per cent share in the chain of shops to go to Harriet.

'I am right with her. It's Harriet that's got bitter and twisted over these last few years. I can't help being me.

35

She shouldn't hide herself away so much up at Crummock. I'd welcome her back any day to help run things, if she would only ask.' Isabelle was tired of trying to be all things to all people. She'd put every waking hour into her mother's chain of shops, as well as having her two precious children, and hadn't time for listening to the gripes and moans of Harriet.

'Aye, well, she's different from you. She prefers to be a wife and mother rather than a hard-headed business-woman like you and your mother. Harriet lost two bairns, remember that. A mother never gets over losing a child.' Archie looked at James and Danny, who were also like chalk and cheese but never spoke a bad word between them. If only the women of the family were like them. He watched as the two men shared a joke and laughed out loud as they turned to join in the conversation between Isabelle and Archie.

'So, sir, you are to live with Danny?' James looked with concern at Archie. 'You don't have to leave Windfell because of us; we are quite happy where we are at.' He admired his down-to-earth father-in-law and felt that perhaps Archie was being hasty in his decision to live with his son.

'Nay, lad, Windfell's too big for one person. You will fill it well. Jane and Luke will enjoy living there and, besides, it's where Isabelle belongs. I can help our Danny up at Crummock, and I'm sure Harriet will get used to me being about. I don't take a lot of looking after.' Danny smiled at James. He was not a hard northerner, but was

36

softly spoken and gentle, perhaps too gentle for the hard-headed Isabelle.

'As long as you are sure? You can return and live with us if you wish; there will always be a welcome, I'm sure.' James shot a glance at Isabelle and noticed the dark look she gave him.

'Nay, lad. Windfell can be all yours, once I've moved out. It'll make life easier for all.' Archie patted James on the back. 'Now, I'm off for a gill in the King Billy – something I haven't done for years. You lot get yourselves home and explain to your families what's to happen next. I can do no more.' Archie looked at his pocket watch. It was three o'clock; he'd have a gill and then get a carriage back home, just in time for his supper. He needed the peace, some time away from all the squabbling. He could just imagine the chatter and racket at both houses, once they were on their own and able to discuss their futures. Both siblings caused nothing but worry and were never satisfied with their lot. He'd just been happy with a full belly and a roof over his head, and hadn't expected anything from his parents, when he was their age. Where did it all go wrong?

4

Isabelle stood in the hallway of the manor, looked around her and sighed. She was home. She'd always known Windfell would be hers one day, and although she was sad she had lost her mother, she was overjoyed that at last she could move her family there. The clock that Archie had brought from Butterfield Gap chimed, as if to remind her that Windfell was not quite hers yet – not until Archie signed it over to her, as he had agreed earlier in the week. 'Well, you can be thrown out; you never did fit in with the rest of the house,' she said to the chiming clock, as she stood with her hands on her hips. She remembered her mother putting up with it, after it was placed in the hallway on the death of Archie's father. Nevertheless, it was going to be good to be back in her beloved bedroom, and to be able to walk down the sweeping stairs knowing that now she was the new mistress of Windfell.

She turned as the front door opened, realizing that the summer's day had slipped into a warm sultry evening and that James and her daughter Jane – the new apprentice – had just returned from their first day working together in the shop at Skipton. *Her shop*; the words seemed strange as she mulled them over in her head. The shop that she now owned, along with the one in Leeds and the one rented in Bradford.

'Well, I can see what you've been doing all day, while Jane and I have been working hard to earn you more money.' James hung up his bowler hat on the hatstand by the door and grinned at his wife. 'Playing lady of the manor, by the looks of it.'

'I have not, I've just been remembering how many good times we had here, and looking at what Father is taking with him and what needs doing before we move in next week.' Isabelle linked her arm into James's and smiled at Jane, who was yawning and looked tired, next to her father. 'Tired after your first day at work?'

'I'm exhausted. Am I expected to do that every day of the week? Bert Bannister never shut up about my grandmother, and said I had to learn from the bottom of the firm upwards, just like she had. Can't I be in the office, Mother, or even learn to dressmake, if I have to?'

'It won't do you any harm to know the warehouse, and to deal with the orders coming in and out – Bert's quite right. You've got to know how the firm works, and get to know everyone we deal with. After all, one day it will all be yours, just as my mother has left it to me.'

'But, Mother, I could help Father develop his photographs and help tidy his studio. Anything but be with old

Bert Bannister; he's so slow and everything has to be done so precisely,' said Jane.

'You respect your elders, madam,' said James. 'And it is "Mr Bannister" to you. No matter what position he has or age he is. Manners will get you a long way in this life.'

Jane scowled at her father. What did he know? She was sure he had never been her age. 'I'm going out to look at the foal in the paddock. I could hear her whinnying at the sound of us arriving. She must be lonely, she's been used to having someone looking after her all the time.'

'If you find Luke out there, tell him we are going home shortly. I think he said he was going down to the river,' shouted Isabelle after her daughter, as Jane scurried out across the hallway. Turning to James, she pulled him close to her. 'We are going to be so happy here – I love Windfell.' She kissed him on the lips and smiled, knowing that she had everything a woman could wish for.

'Perhaps we have too much. I have a strange feeling, when things are going this well, that something is bound to go wrong.' James smiled at his wife and held her tightly as she sighed with contentment.

'Don't be such a pessimist. Nothing – and no one – can touch us now. God bless my dear mama. I do realize that I owe her everything.' Isabelle pulled James closer to her.

'You'd do well to remember that, and dear Archie. He's about to give up his home for you.' James hoped Isabelle's feeling of self-importance would pass quickly. He was uneasy that everything in her life had come easily to her and that sometimes she took things for granted.

*

'She's a bonny thing, isn't she?' Ethan leaned over the drystone wall and chewed a grass stalk as he leaned back and admired the foal and the young woman standing before him.

'She is, she's got spirit.' Jane watched the young chestnut foal race up and down the paddock, its short stubby mane and tail blowing in the wind as it played in excitement at being able to enjoy the freedom of the warm summer's day. 'I wish I was her, wild and free. Not be-holden to anyone.' She flashed her eyes at Ethan and smiled at the dark-haired lad, whom she knew her cousin, Rosie, had feelings for.

'You moving in here then, next week? My father says he's going to miss your grandfather and hopes we will all be keeping our positions.' Ethan moved closer to the lass he'd partly grown up with. He was now starting to real-ize just how beautiful the ugly duckling she had once been had become, and that he had to acknowledge Jane as the next heir to Windfell, along with her brother.

'Yes. Mother says we are moving in next Monday, once Grandfather has moved out. I can't see her chan-ging any of the staff, so your father needn't worry.' Jane turned to look at Ethan, who stood just inches from her face. 'Why, would you miss me, Ethan Haygarth? Would it break your heart not to see me each day?' She smiled.

'Aye, I'd miss looking at you every day. We've always been good friends.' Ethan reached for her hand and pulled it towards him. He'd been building up the courage to kiss the girl, who was now nearly a fully grown woman. The flash of eyes and the warm smile had confirmed Jane's true feelings, and now was the time to make his move.

'What do you think you are doing? I don't want to hold your hand. Remember your place, and be thankful that you'll be keeping it, as stable boy,' Jane spat.

Ethan pulled her towards him and held her tightly as he kissed her hard on the lips. She might be the granddaughter of his late mistress, but she'd been flirting with him for months, of that he was sure. He held her against him as she wriggled and protested, finally giving in as she kicked him on the shins.

'How dare you!' Jane slapped Ethan hard across the cheeks as he let go of his grip. 'You dirty gypsy, don't you dare put your hands on me again,' she screamed. 'I'll tell my parents, and you and your family can start packing your bags.'

'No, no, Miss Jane – I thought that was what you wanted. You looked so jealous when Rosie and I were talking together the other day. And just then you smiled and encouraged me. You shouldn't have led me on, with your false feelings.' Ethan stood back from the angered young woman.

'I most certainly did not, and I wasn't jealous of farm girl Rosie – you are decidedly wrong. You and she are welcome to one another.' Jane stomped away from her long-faced would-be suitor, stopping only to shout back at him, 'Your days are numbered, Ethan Haygarth,' while she made her way down to the river at the bottom of the parkland, in order to find her brother, Luke.

Jane walked hastily through the flowering grassland, the stalks catching in her laced boots and long skirts as she looked back and saw Ethan following her. This made her break into a run as she tried to escape from him, although secretly she wanted him to catch her. She shouted down towards the river bank in a bid for Luke to hear her, realizing what Ethan could do to her if he caught her, and wanting Luke to be aware of her presence, as back-up.

'Luke! Luke, where are you?' She held onto an ash tree's trunk as she picked her way over its roots and the slippery white limestone of the river's edge. She lifted up her skirts as her feet crunched over the shingle while she made her way to what she knew to be Luke's favourite fishing pool, just below the mighty roar of one of the many waterfalls along the River Ribble. She was aware that she was moving slower than her pursuer, impeded by her long skirts. 'Luke!' she yelled out, as a hand moved over her mouth and Ethan whispered in her ear to be quiet.

Above the waterfall, Luke suddenly heard his name being yelled, and peered over the moss-covered falls to see Ethan and his sister talking and what appeared to be arguing. He waved with his spare hand as he balanced on a particularly slippery boulder, with his rod in the other hand. He edged nearer the falls and waved his rod at the couple, who seemed to be urging him towards them. Picking his way in bare feet, he balanced on the edge of the falls, trying to find an easy way down, as he looked into the gushing waters and the deep pool below him.

'Luke!' Jane yelled out as Ethan suddenly stopped arguing, after realizing the danger Luke was in. Gone were all his thoughts about trying to amend the misinterpretations of earlier, which were what had led him to follow Jane down to the river's edge. Now he had to make sure no harm came to Luke, who was oblivious to the depth of the pool below him.

'Can he swim?' Ethan asked a frantic Jane, as he untied his boots. They both watched Luke balance his rod and wave at both of them again, not concentrating on his actions and deafened by the roar of the river in flood.

Jane shook her head. She screamed as Luke picked his way on the slime-covered stones, only to lose his footing, his rod flying up into the air as he bounced off the moss-covered rocks through the gushing white falls into the deep, dark pool below.

'Stay there, I'll jump in and get him.' Ethan pulled off his waistcoat and pocket watch and quickly jumped into the pool, leaving Jane at the side, frantically yelling Luke's name and peering into the frothy waters of the river. The cold water caught his breath as he dived below the falls, filling his lungs with icy shards while searching deep down for the white shirt of Luke. Ethan gasped for breath as he surfaced and then dived again, after noticing Luke's body trapped between two boulders at the side of the falls.

Jane watched, counting every second that both were under the water, fearing the worst for her brother.

Ethan appeared spluttering, pulling Luke behind him as he splashed awkwardly out of the side of the pool. 'Go and get your father – he's alive, but he's hit his head and is bleeding badly.' Struggling with Luke, Ethan pulled the boy's body out of the water and laid it on the sand and shingle at the pool's edge. 'Go, Jane, go and get help.'

She froze for a second or two as tears ran down her face while she gazed on the lifeless body of her brother. Blood ran down his forehead, staining his white shirt and trickling into the water's edge.

'For God's sake, go!' Ethan yelled as he pummelled Luke's chest to clear his lungs of water.

Jane fled just as Luke was drawing breath. He coughed and spluttered as Ethan talked gently to him and sat him up, before pulling off his own shirt in order to tear a shred off to bandage Luke's bleeding head. Ethan watched and said a silent prayer as Luke whispered his name. Thank God he'd not drowned; he would have been to blame, that was for sure, and he was certain he would have lost both his own and his family's positions, if Jane had opened her mouth.

'You're alright, mate, you fell down the bloody falls. We are going to have to learn you to swim this summer.' Ethan leaned back and watched Luke gain his breath, looking up at the green foliage of the whispering trees above, as they swayed quietly in the gentle summer breeze. He waited for what felt like an age before Jane appeared, with her father and Ethan's behind her.

'Oh my God, Luke – are you alright?' James Fox bent down and picked his son up in his arms, gasping at the sight of so much blood on the white-shirt bandage and at Ethan catching his breath. 'What were you thinking of? How many times have I told you to steer clear of this deep pool?' He helped a sobbing Luke up from the river bank and then passed him to the stronger arms of Jethro. 'Thank God you were there, Ethan – he'd have drowned for sure if you hadn't have jumped into the river after him.'

'I did nothing, sir; really you should not be thanking me.' Ethan hung his head and felt ashamed at the fact that he was standing bare-chested in front of both his master and Jane, waiting for the chastisement that was certainly going to come. He'd dared to touch the new master's daughter and had nearly caused his son's death. He'd be lucky not to get a thrashing.

'Nonsense! Jane told me how you did not hesitate for a second to save Luke. We will always be in your debt.' James held his hand out and shook Ethan's firmly, before turning and running quickly to catch up with Jethro, who was halfway across the field and making his way to the manor, holding Luke up under his arms.

Ethan looked at Jane, who was standing at the river's edge staring at him. 'You didn't say anything to your father?'

'What was there to say? You saved my brother.' She made her way up from the river bank and stood at the edge of the field, waiting for Ethan as he put his boots and socks back on. 'Besides, I lied. I have been flirting with you on the quiet, and I deserved all that I got. Which I must say was very fine, Ethan,' she giggled. 'However, I was only trying to make my milksop cousin Rosie jealous. She's the one who really likes you, but you are too blind to see it. You are a typical man! I've no intentions of courting anyone yet; indeed, I don't think I ever will.'

Ethan hopped on one leg as he pulled his boot onto his left foot.

'Rosie doesn't like me in that way, does she? I thought she was just showing interest in the horses.' He walked quickly to catch Jane up as she ran her hand through the long grasses.

'You are so gullible, Ethan Haygarth. And I'm sorry I slapped you and called you a gypsy.' Jane grinned. 'But yes, Rosie has confessed to me that she thinks you are handsome.'

'It's no skin off my nose. I deserved it, and I'm quite proud I'm part gypsy.' Ethan smirked, thinking about Rosie. So he *had* taken her eye. That was quite something he could be proud of, and Rosie was the nicer of the two girls.

'Well, let's remain friends, and don't you say a word to Rosie about me telling you that she likes you.' Jane stood and waited for his reply as she watched her mother and father lift Luke into the waiting carriage to take him home to Ingfield.

'Won't say a word, I promise. And thanks for not telling on me.' Ethan blushed and looked down at his feet, knowing that he had pushed his luck.

'Jane, come quickly, we need the doctor to look at your brother,' shouted Isabelle as she climbed into the carriage.

'Coming, Mother,' Jane yelled as she rushed across the pebbled drive to join her parents and brother.

Ethan watched as the carriage made its way out of the gates, before joining his father in the stable.

47

'That was a near do.' Jethro stood by his son and looked at him. 'It could have ended in tragedy. As it is, I think Luke's just knocked the front of his head badly. Better to spoil his beauty than his brains – not that he's got many.'

'Aye, he's going to have to learn to swim. I'll teach him this summer.' Ethan lifted the horse harness that he'd been cleaning earlier, before he'd got distracted by the sight of Jane admiring the foal. He put it back on its peg on the stable wall.

'Now, lad, I'm giving you a bit of advice. There's them – the posh 'uns – and there's us. You can look, but you don't touch. We are not in their class and never will be, and an ill wind will always blow if you dare to do any other. You let his father teach him to swim, if Luke wants to do so. And as for Miss Jane, you leave her be, lad. She's not right for you.' Jethro spat his mouthful of tobacco out and looked at his son.

Ethan dared only glance at his father. Was there nothing he didn't see or know? He'd never noticed him there when he'd tried to kiss Jane.

'Aye, alright, Father.'

Jethro watched as his son sloped off to the barn to fill the horse hay-racks. He leaned against the stable doorway and looked across at the manor house. It didn't seem five minutes since he had had the same feelings for Charlotte, who was at that time the new mistress of Windfell. But he'd known better than to show them. Instead, he'd always been there to support her. Commoners and posh folk should never mix, especially when young Jane had

48

pointed out that they were only gypsies. Her grandmother would never have been so cutting and demeaning. There was a new breed shortly to inhabit Windfell, of that he was sure, and Ethan would be better off away from them. The lad had ideas above his station in life, ideas that were going to get him into trouble.

Back at Ingfield House, Isabelle and James stood over Luke's bed, watching their son sleep.

'Thank God he's alright. The doctor says the wound on his head looks worse than it is. There was so much blood.' James reached for the hand of his fretting wife. 'He'll be fine in the morning.'

'I thought we were going to lose him – he looked so white. I can understand now how Harriet felt when she came home to the news of the twins being dead. Our sons and daughters are the most precious things we will ever have. No wonder she cannot forgive Mama and myself for dragging her in to work that day. Thankfully, in our case Ethan was there to pull him out of the water, otherwise we too would be without our son.' Isabelle ran her hand over Luke's brow and smiled as he turned in his sleep. 'What Ethan was doing down in the river, I don't quite know. Perhaps tickling one of our finest trout, knowing him. Like father, like son. I've seen Jethro down there many a time when I was growing up. Mother and Archie used to turn a blind eye to it. However, I don't see why we should.' She walked to the gas light and turned the flame down, before urging James out of the room.

'The odd fish or two won't hurt, Isabelle. It matters not

that it is not Ethan's right to fish in that part of the river. We need to keep our staff on our side, and if that's what it takes to keep Ethan and Jethro happy, and encourages them to get my horse and carriage ready for me first thing in the morning, then I'm satisfied. Besides, he saved your son's life,' James whispered as he closed the bedroom door silently behind him.

'It starts with one fish, and then we'll find him liming the river for all the fish. I think we should watch that lad. Mazy should never have married into a family like that. She was worth more than becoming a gypsy's wife.' Isabelle strutted along the landing, her skirts rustling as she reached the top of the stairs, and stopped sharply.

'I think you are wrong. Jethro and Ethan have always been good with your family.' James knew that disagreeing with his wife meant harsh words to follow, for she always spoke her mind.

'James, leave the running of Windfell to me. I am the new mistress and I aim to make everyone know that. I appreciate your participation, but the household is my concern. Your help with business is more than enough worry for you, along with your photography studios. After all, you have studios in Leeds and Bradford in our stores – you seem to be always busy with them, the amount of time you spend there.' Jane waited for his reply.

'Yes, my dear. Of course you know best. But I am here, if you ever need—' James was stopped in his tracks.

'I am my mother's daughter. She taught me everything I know. Just like I'm teaching Jane. I was brought up to be strong, and that is what I'll be; and while I know you are more than capable of running the household, it is my job.' She descended the stairs without looking back at her husband.

'Yes, dear,' whispered James. He was married to a stubborn woman.

5

Things had not been easy between Danny and Harriet since he had announced his father's intention of coming to live with them at Crummock. And today was no exception.

'You never once thought of consulting me, did you? You just said, "Of course it will be fine with the wife," because my wants don't even come into it.' Harriet felt stressed. Ben was back on form and had decided to do one of his disappearing tricks, making up for the weeks that he had been confined to his bed with German measles. Plus baby Georgina was still not 100 per cent, crying at the least little upset. On top of that, it was clipping time, and the sheep were in the normally tidy farmyard waiting to be sheared and have their thick woollen coats removed for the hot summer months ahead. The noise of their bleating was driving her mad, and the mess that would have to be swept up after they had been shorn would be unbelievable.

'What would you have me do? Say, "No, Father. We

don't want you"? How ungrateful would that have sounded, after he'd just said that Crummock would be ours, after his day had passed?' said Danny. 'Will you stop your moaning; he'll be no bother, and in fact he will be a blessing. He'll be able to give me advice whenever I want it, and you know how much Ben and Rosie love him. I wish he was as fit as he used to be, because I could really have done with his help this morning, looking at this lot to clip and place our mark on.'

'Well, I'm glad for you, but to me he's just another mouth to feed. I've enough on lately, and it'll mean I'll have to get him a room ready.' Harriet could nearly cry; she'd had enough. Four weeks of sickly children, and the death of Charlotte, had made her spirits low. It was as if nothing was going right, and looking around the yard at more than a hundred and fifty sheep, and all the neighbours who had come to help in the yearly event of clipping, was just about the last straw. She appreciated that everyone was here to help, but they would all want to be fed, and she would be expected to wrap the woollen fleeces up into a ball, ready for the wool merchant from Long Preston to collect later in the year. All of this, with Ben missing, Georgina bawling and Rosie unable to wait a minute longer for her grandfather to arrive, just made Harriet feel like breaking down.

'Get Rosie to make my father's bed up and tidy his room – she's old enough. Ben will turn up when he's hungry; he will be down at the wash-dubs with his mates. It's a good day for having a dip in that pool down there.' Danny looked up at the blue skies and regretted straight away that he'd said Ben might have gone swimming. Harriet would imagine all sorts of calamities.

'A dip in the wash-dubs – he'll be to bury! He's only just got over the measles.' Harriet stood on the steps that led down into the yard and rubbed her face with her hands. She just didn't know where to start.

'Come on, old lass, this isn't like you. You usually take everything in your stride. My father will be no problem and, if he is, we can always send him back to Isabelle to look after, although he is my responsibility really.' Danny put his arm around Harriet and felt her sobbing. He kissed her gently on the neck as she trembled.

'I'm sorry, it's just that I'm not feeling myself at the moment. The children have been a worry, and although I know we owe everything to your father, I don't know if it will work with him living here. Anyway,' Harriet pushed him back, 'take your hands off me. We'll have none of this, Danny Atkinson – you are showing me up. Look at Henry from Sowermire wondering what's up; you'd swear he'd never seen a husband give his wife a hug before.' Harriet pushed him away and wiped back the tear that had trickled down her cheek.

'He probably hasn't, and he definitely won't have hugged his wife for a while. I doubt his arms would reach around her, she's such a size.' Danny tried to brighten Harriet's mood.

'Shush – he'll hear you. Patsy might be big, but she's a good woman; she'll feed you well, when you go there clipping. Which is more than can be said of me, if I don't stir my shanks and get that rhubarb pie in the oven and find a cheese from out of the pantry.' She lifted up her skirts and made for the kitchen doorway. But Danny's shout stopped her in her tracks.

'You've one less worry – here comes our Ben with my father. They are just coming round the end of the wood.' Danny leaned against the garden wall and wiped the sweat off his brow with the back of his cap, as his father opened the farmyard gate with Ben by his side. 'Where do you think you've been trailing? Did you not think to tell your mother where you were off to?' he asked Ben, who was busy chatting to his grandfather.

'I found him on the green lane going over to Wharfe; he was only making his way to play with the Knowles lad. It's a good day for trailing and adventures, isn't it, Ben?' Archie rubbed his small grandson's head of curly brown hair, before whispering that he had to say sorry to his mother for upsetting her.

'Sorry, Mother. I just hadn't seen John for so long, and I didn't think you'd miss me.' Ben bowed his head, knowing he was in a spot of bother as Harriet pulled him into the house by his shoulder.

'Let him stop out with us, lass, we'll keep an eye on him. He can help pick up the loose bits of wool and put them in a sack; it'll keep him out of mischief.' Archie looked at his son, wondering if he had done right.

'Leave her, Father, she'll give Ben a chastising and then he'll be out with us. It'll be like water off a duck's back at the moment, for he tends to do his own thing and have a mind of his own, does our Ben,' sighed Danny.

'Aye, I had one of them, and look what he grew into!

55

A bloody big stubborn bugger, who still tends to do just what he wants.' Archie laughed and patted his son on the shoulders. 'Right, let's get these sheep clipped.' He reached into the bag on his back and pulled out a shining pair of sharp steel sheep-shears. 'The sooner we get started, the sooner we get done. Is that not right, lads?' he shouted to the four neighbouring farmers, who were already handling sheep, turning each animal onto its buttocks and then holding the struggling sheep fast between their legs. The sharp shears started cutting the fleece away from the sheep's stomach, and then up around the back and next to the head, carefully keeping the fleece whole and not nicking the sheep. Once bare of their fleece, the sheep were then marked with a red waterproof mixture, with the letter A, to denote that the sheep belonged to the Atkinsons, before they were let back out of the farmyard to the holding pasture where their spring-born bleating lambs were waiting. The marking would help if a sheep got lost on the open fell and would reveal who its owner was.

'You needn't think you are clipping, Father. Not on those doddery knees. First sheep that struggled, you'd be knocked over.' Danny looked at his father, whose disappointed face said it all. 'Why don't you roll the fleeces up? Harriet was going to help, but she's got enough on, with the baby still under the weather.'

'But it'll be the first time I've missed clipping my sheep for the last fifty years. I can do the odd old one.'

Archie looked at the yard full of grey-faced Rough Fells and Swaledales, all breathing hard and bleating in the warm summer's sun. The flies they were attracting buzzed around them, and as Archie watched them he realized his son was speaking the truth and he would have to face up to the fact that he'd be more bother than he was worth.

'I suppose you are right. It's a bloody sad day when your father is doing a woman's job. But I don't want to be a burden to anyone.' Archie pushed his way through the flock of sheep and made for the first shearer with a fleece ready for wrapping. He shook out the lanolin-filled fleece, folding all the odd pieces of it into the middle, and just leaving the tail-end to be used for tying the fleece up. He rolled the fleece tight like a rolled-up blanket and then pulled the tail-end tightly around the fleece. Then he tucked it into itself, before throwing the fleece into the huge hessian sack that the wool merchant had left to be filled on the back of the cart in the corner of the farm-yard. He then quickly moved on to the next.

Danny watched his father. He was an awkward old devil. Why didn't he just take it easy and sit and watch them all? Clipping was a young man's job, and he wished Archie had stopped down at Windfell, just for today. He picked up his shears and joined the group of men; as his father had said, the sooner they all started the better. It was going to be a long day.

Archie leaned back and stretched. He ached from bending down and rolling fleeces. He sat back on the edge of the garden steps and watched those who, to him, looked like young men, as Harriet poured a drink of tea into enamel mugs and made sure each man was amply fed with warm bacon and hard fried-egg sandwiches, followed by rhubarb pie and cream. She was a good woman really; the death of her two children had made her hard, though, and had spoilt her onetime gentle ways. He had always thought she was right for Danny, a good farmer's wife as well as being a good mother, despite what Harriet thought of herself. It was a pity they weren't getting on so well at present. No doubt he hadn't helped by wanting to move in; and telling Danny that he had a son at Ragged Hall would only have made him think about what he might have had. Perhaps he shouldn't have said anything.

'Thanks, Harriet, that looks grand. You make a good pie, just like my mother did, and that's a true compliment.' Archie smiled up at her as she stood beside him with the enamel jug of tea, after pouring him a cup.

'Thank you, Father, and thank you for rolling the fleeces for me. It's been a good help.' Harriet pulled her skirts around her and sat next to her father-in-law. She did love him, she just hadn't wanted him to live with them. Things were fraught enough, without another body to look after.

'Our Danny thinks I'm not fit for clipping, so it's the least I can do. It seems he's right anyway, because I feel knackered. I'm not as fit as I used to be, and these lads clip fast. A lot faster than I ever did.' Archie put his head back after a long sip of his tea and looked into the vivid cloud-free blue sky, watching the swallows and swifts as they screeched above his head.

'It'll come to us all, so don't worry. Rosie and I have

made your room up. You are welcome to join us any time now. Danny and the children can't wait for you to arrive.' Harriet looked at Archie and saw how tired and aged he seemed since the death of Charlotte.

'I'll try not to be any bother, lass. I'll keep out of your way and will help when I can. I know I'm just another responsibility, but I'll take young Ben fishing and sing to Georgina when she's twisty. Not that it will stop her gurning,' laughed Archie.

'You'll not be any bother, Father. Now go and have a lie-down, I'll finish rolling the fleeces. Georgina is asleep, Rosie is baking a cake and, as you can see, Ben is helping his father mark the sheep.' Harriet put her arm round Archie. He looked shattered, and her heart softened to the old man.

Together, they looked across at Danny and Ben and smiled.

'Look at Ben: the next owner of Crummock, lass. He's a right farmer.' Archie smiled before standing straight. The truth was that the day was telling on him. 'I might just go and have forty winks. Am I in the end bedroom?' He looked up at the long, ancient farmhouse and yawned.

'Aye, I thought you'd be quietest there.' Harriet watched as her father-in-law stiffly climbed the few steps into the garden and walked up the path. He was old and in need of care; no wonder he wanted to come home to Crummock. She'd have to learn to bite her tongue. She owed a lot to Archie Atkinson, and the least he could expect was a bit of comfort in his dotage. He never took sides and had always been kind to her, she should remember that.

Archie lay on his bed and looked up at the cracked whitewashed ceiling of his new bedroom. It was a step down from the beautifully plastered ceilings of Windfell Manor and their ornate cornicing. He listened to the men in the yard talking and laughing to one another, and smelt the fruitcake that Rosie was baking in the fireside oven of the kitchen. This was what he had missed – the simple things in life – not having to announce to the world his intentions for the day, what he wished to eat and where to eat it. He closed his eyes; life had gone full circle and he was back in the world that he'd been born into, albeit without his Lottie. But she would always be waiting for him in his dreams and thoughts.

6

Isabelle stood back and looked around the drawing room of Ingfield House, watching the parlour maid as she scurried around with the dust covers that were being thrown over the furniture they were going to leave in their abandoned home.

'That's right – I'm taking that vase. Be careful, I don't want it breaking,' shouted Isabelle at the hauliers who were moving the possessions that were to join her in the family's new life at Windfell Manor.

'Do we really need to take all these belongings to Windfell? Where are you going to place them? Windfell is full to the rafters already.' James sat down in one of the covered chairs and watched as his wife gave orders to the scurrying young men. They dared not answer back to his domineering wife.

'Really, James, we need to make our mark on Windfell – make it ours. My mother and Archie have always kept the house smart, but some of their furniture and

61

decor are a bit dated. I aim to stamp my own mark on Windfell and make it our home. I'm so glad that we don't have to sell Ingfield. I hope that one day the house, and most of the contents, will make a good wedding present for our Jane, if and when she is to wed.' Isabelle glanced at her husband as she stood and looked around at the emptying room.

'Jane to wed – I hope not! Or at least not for a few years yet, she's only seventeen and it would be a brave man that tackles her. Do you know I caught her reading one of the ridiculous pamphlets those visiting suffragettes to Skipton were handing out the other day? She's definitely got a mind of her own.' James sighed as he watched his wife remonstrating about how her belongings should be handled, instead of listening to him. 'She even had the cheek the other day to quote their saying, "Deeds, not Words", to me when I said I had not spoken to your father about offering help when he moved out.'

'Perhaps she had a point, my dear. After all, all you have done is sit there and moan, and we are trying to get us moved into Windfell before the evening,' Isabelle said curtly. Her thoughts were both on the move and on where she should really be: making her mark as the new owner of Atkinson's. And she hadn't time for her husband's relaxed ways; he might just as well have gone to Skipton and supported Jane, by coping with some of the backlog of orders that had occurred because of her mother's passing.

'I object to you saying that. I did help Archie with his belongings this morning – not that he took a lot with him. He seems to have turned his back on his old life, now that your mother has gone. I only hope he and Harriet see eye-to-eye, as we both know Archie does things his own way and doesn't think of the consequences.' James rose from his seat and looked out of the window of Ingfield's drawing room onto the busy street in Settle. 'I'm going to miss seeing the people going past our window. At Windfell, all I'll be able to do is see that row of beech trees and listen to the gossip of the staff.'

'Well, there will be enough of that, especially at the moment. I don't think I'll be very popular with Jethro and Mazy, as I've told them Ethan's services will be no longer needed. There's just no need for two in the stables, especially now that Archie is going to live at Crummock.' Isabelle joined her husband at the window and looked out onto the bustling street, full of people going about their business.

'You didn't tell me! Do you not think that decision was a bit hard, after he saved our Luke's life? ' James was shocked.

'I didn't tell you because I knew how you'd react. I know he saved Luke, but I've seen the way he looks at Jane; and he's always creeping about the place, poaching the odd fish and catching the occasional rabbit. Believe me, I'm not often wrong: if he stays at Windfell, Ethan will bring trouble. He doesn't seem to know his place in society – unlike his parents.' Isabelle straightened a cover and turned her back on her husband. She knew her decision would not be popular with him, and she had already felt the coolness of Mazy's reaction to it.

'Have you made any other decisions behind my back?' James waited.

'No, not yet, although we are going to have two lady's maids at Windfell, and I think I might have to let Lily go. After all, she's not getting any younger, and my Dorothy looks after my needs so well.'

'But Lily was your mother's favourite!' James looked horrified.

'Exactly – my mother's favourite – and, as such, she always had my mother's ear. She never treats me as the grown woman I am, and never will.' Isabelle remembered the time when Lily had told tales on her and her former lover, John Sidgwick, something for which she had never forgiven her. 'Everyone else can stay. I don't want to be seen as uncaring.' She had known how James would react and had been hesitant to reveal her thoughts.

'I know that you must be prudent, but Lily was dear to your mother's heart. And you have to deal with Mazy and Jethro every day. I don't think you will be helping your reputation. As the doctor told you, your mother's shoes are hard to fill.' James watched as his wife struggled to realize that she would not be liked for her actions.

'Perhaps if I find Lily somewhere to live, it might look like I do care. It was a trick my mother used to employ, whenever she felt her staff had to leave. Although all the Lock Cottages are occupied, I could perhaps speak to my godfather and see if he has any cottages empty. The ones on Jubilee Terrace at Langcliffe would be ideal. I'm sure he will be able to help. As for Ethan, I'm afraid I stand by my decision.' Isabelle walked over to the doorway and watched as the carriers closed the tailgate of their cart after they finished loading the Fox possessions. 'Can you lock the doors and make sure all is secure?' She turned and looked at her scowling husband.

'Why, where are you going?' James walked over to her side.

'I'm going to Grisedale's on Victoria Street. I'd like a new bedroom suite for Jane's bedroom, and I saw just what I wanted in their window.' Isabelle tidied her plaited hair and placed her elaborately decorated hat on her head, glancing in the hallway mirror as she picked up her parasol from the umbrella stand.

'But, Isabelle, there are four perfectly good bedroom suites upstairs that you could take to Windfell, not to mention the ones already there.' James shook his head.

'She needs a new one, something modern that reflects the age we live in. A new broom sweeps clean, James – you should know that.'

He watched as his wife walked down the path of Ingfield House. He knew Isabelle would have whatever she wanted, despite what he had to say about it. He respected her for being a strong woman, but sometimes she was so stubborn. Stubborn to the point of stupidity, especially when she would not back down after realizing her mistakes. He sighed and gazed around Ingfield House, before closing the heavy oak door and locking it securely behind him.

He ran his hand down the mock-Roman pillars on either side of the porch as he stepped down the pristine white, donkey-stoned steps. He would miss living in

Settle, and would have to get accustomed to the quiet evenings at Windfell. He looked around him at the grand house they were putting into storage. Life would never be the same, now that Isabelle was the new mistress of Windfell. He was just thankful that he worked in Skipton and was his own master in his photography studio at Atkinson's. That was a part of his world that Isabelle knew better than to interfere in. He should be grateful for small mercies.

Archie sat next to Jethro as they made their way gently, with the horse and cart filled with the possessions that Archie had decided he wanted for his new life up at Crummock. The horse ambled amicably along the rutted track out of Austwick, and Archie looked across at the scars of white limestone called Norber, feeling content with his lot.

'We'll miss you at Windfell, sir,' said Jethro quietly, as he gently encouraged the horse while they climbed the hill towards the turn-off to Sowermire Farm and then on towards Crummock itself.

'Aye, well, I'll still be about, and you'll be alright with Isabelle and her family. She's her mother's daughter – she'll take care of you all.' Archie leaned back and looked at the rolling hills and fields that stretched out in front of him.

'Nay, sir, I hope I'm not talking out of term, but Mistress Isabelle is not totally like her mother; she's causing a bit of a stir at our house at the moment.' Jethro had thought about biting his tongue to Archie, but then he had reconsidered, knowing that Archie would not be happy that Ethan had been told to look for work elsewhere.

'What do you mean, lad? What's she been up to?' Archie leaned forward and looked at the worry that lined the tanned face of Jethro, a man he respected for his horsemanship and his country ways.

'Perhaps I shouldn't tell you, but she's told our Ethan he's to look for new employment. That he's not needed.' Jethro paused and waited as a silence came between them. He watched as Archie shook his head and licked his lips as he took in the news.

'Nay, she'd no need to do that, there's plenty of work for both of you. Especially as that lad of hers is worth nowt. But you didn't hear me say that.' Archie shook his head again and looked at Jethro. 'She's obviously not thinking straight. But I'll not see your lad out of work. If she won't see sense, I could perhaps have an answer to your problem.' He thought for a moment, before asking Jethro, 'What would you say if Ethan came and worked for me up at Crummock? I can't make our lass keep him on at Windfell, but he could still work for me.'

'I'd appreciate that, sir. Crummock would be the right spot for Ethan. I'd not deny that he's as wild as a mountain hare, but he's a good lad really.' Jethro breathed out in relief. If Archie Atkinson employed Ethan, he'd have a good master and he was better away from that Miss Jane, whom Ethan had shown more than a passing interest in.

'Right, well, leave it with me, I'll speak to both of

mine and make it right with them, and you tell your Mazy, and then it will be sorted.' Archie gazed in front of him, trying to understand why Isabelle had given Ethan his marching orders. After all she was more beholden to him than to anyone else in her service, after he had saved Luke from drowning.

Spirits were low in the kitchen at Windfell, after the realization that they were to lose both Lily and Ethan.

'You know, I thought better of Miss Isabelle.' Ruby sat back and hugged her cup of tea while she looked around at the crestfallen staff.

'That's the trouble – we all still think of her as "Miss Isabelle", but she isn't the young woman we all knew; she's a grown woman with children of her own. And now Mr Atkinson's gone to live at Crummock, and with Mrs Atkinson at rest, she's our mistress.' Lily's eyes filled with tears. 'She can do what she likes with any of us. Besides, she's laid off all the staff at Ingfield except for Dorothy Baines, so you should think yourselves lucky.'

'But what will you do, Lily? Where are you going to go? Windfell's been your life.' Nancy stopped for a minute from peeling potatoes and looked at the sniffling lady's maid.

'Well, I'm not going into one of the Lock Cottages or into one of Lorenzo Christie's cottages. I've got my pride, I've got savings – I'll find my own little cottage. So she needn't worry her head about where she's going to put me, just to ease her conscience. I'll have a look down in Settle this afternoon; find myself something small, just right for one. And then, when I'm settled in, I'll take in a bit of mending, to earn a little money. I'll not go without, don't you worry.' Lily breathed in and looked around at the long faces that surrounded her. 'Aye, I'm not dead yet – just moving out.' She tried to muster a smile.

'What with you and our Ethan, I don't know what she's thinking about. It isn't as if she's skint.' Mazy leaned against the kitchen sink and looked around her. 'She's even talking about putting that new fancy electric all through the house – imagine the mess! We've only just got over the new boiler and the bathroom being put in.'

'It was good news that Mister Atkinson is going to take Ethan up to Crummock, but you'll miss him, Mazy.' Ruby rose from her chair and put her teacup and saucer next to her, before patting Mazy's shoulder lovingly.

'Aye, both Jethro and I are grateful to the master. He's a good soul. We can grin and bear what life throws at us, but you always wish for something better for your children. Ethan says he'll come back down home on a Sunday and he's not that far away, so we will just have to grin and bear it.' Mazy glanced up at the stairs leading to the main hall, hearing the sound of feet approaching, and placed her finger to her lips to stop everyone from gossiping as Dorothy Baines entered the kitchen.

'Is Mistress Isabelle alright this morning?' Ruby looked at the newest pretty maid to arrive at Windfell, trying to divert the conversation and stop the silence that fell when Dorothy was present.

'Yes, thank you, Mrs Pratt.' Dorothy looked around at the group, which she knew was hostile to her new position at Windfell and which she'd never be part of. 'Look, I'm sorry the mistress has decided to replace Lily with me, and I realize that I will always be the odd one out because you have all been here so long. But what would you all have done, if you were in my shoes? I could hardly have said no to keeping my position. I'm just like the rest of you – I need the money to survive.' She slumped down onto the pine chair at the head of the table and put her head in her hands.

Ruby walked over and ran her hand over the young girl's shoulders as she talked to her. 'We know, lass, but we have all been together so long; and if you kick one of us, we all limp. We know it isn't your fault. We'll just have to adjust to the changes that are coming and make the best of things. God bless Mistress Charlotte – she was one of the best. We can only hope Mistress Isabelle is going to follow in her footsteps. And don't worry, lass, you'll get used to us and our ways and will soon forget these first few weeks.'

Dorothy raised her head and smiled across at Lily. 'Sorry, Lily, I'm so sorry that she has sacked you.'

'Don't be sorry. I was Mistress Charlotte's maid, and not really Isabelle's. My work is done here and it's time to move on. All things come to an end. I wish you all the best, Dorothy, and hope you will be as happy here as I have been.' Lily put her arms around the young girl and smiled at her companions. She was going to miss the kitchen of Windfell and its occupants.

7

'So, I've not only acquired your father, but I've also got his stable lad to feed.' Harriet looked at her husband's reflection in the dressing-table mirror as she brushed her hair with fervour, while she took in the news of Ethan coming to work at Crummock. 'I just knew this would happen – you can never say no to your father.' She swivelled round on her stool and watched as Danny pulled his shirt over his head. He sat on the side of the bed, bare-chested and as handsome as the day she met him.

'Oh, Harriet, Ethan will not be any bother. In fact if he takes after his father, he'll be a blessing. And as for feeding him, he will like enough feed himself. He's a dab hand at catching rabbits and tickling trout, and as long as he supplies the house occasionally, I don't mind turning a blind eye. Unlike our Isabelle, who, as far as I can see, has cut off her nose to spite her face by not keeping Ethan in her employment. The rest of the staff will not be happy with her actions.' Danny looked at his wife, whom he still loved. He just wished that for once she'd see the good side in things instead of being so negative.

'Well, it's typical of your Isabelle: someone helps her and then she does them an injustice. Is Luke making a good recovery? It could have been so much worse, if Ethan had not rescued him. Isabelle should be grateful to that lad. Thinking about it, perhaps he is better off with us. At least he will be appreciated.' Harriet yawned and walked over to the edge of the bed.

'You can ask yourself how Luke is. Isabelle sent word with Father that she would like us to join her for Sunday dinner next weekend. She probably wants to show off her new home to us.' Danny laughed and leaned over and played with the ends of Harriet's long brown hair, hoping that for once she'd be in the mood to please him.

'Oh, do we have to go? I really can't abide the way she talks down to me nowadays. She changed completely when your mother put her in charge of all the stores. As for poor James, I don't know how he puts up with her bossing him about; he's just like her toy poodle.' Harriet sighed. She really didn't want to go to Windfell and feel like the poor relation.

'We will all go. We didn't when it was Mama's funeral; and besides, you now hold shares in the stores, so it would do you good to keep your hand in and make sure all's well with the businesses. You've no excuses; all the children are well now, and it's time you and Isabelle made up. As for James, he enjoys being her poodle. He makes his own way in life, lost in his photography and being

72

given orders to obey.' Danny lay back and pulled gently on Harriet's arm, urging her to join him.

'I'm tired, Danny, leave me be. I've been up since five. Unlike Isabelle, I haven't lots of people looking after my needs.' Harriet pulled the sheets back and climbed into bed, turning away from her husband and the passion he was requesting.

'You are always tired. I sometimes think it's just an excuse and that you don't love me any more.' Danny lay down next to her and kissed Harriet's neck gently, trying to get some of the attention and love that he craved.

'I love you more than life itself, Danny Atkinson, so don't you dare say that. I am genuinely tired; there's always something to do, and the youngest two take so much watching. Rosie does as much as she can, but daydreams looking out of the window all day, wanting to be off over fell and dale, or to be with you. Now her grandfather is here, she's even worse, because he's forever telling her tales of when he was a lad. He fills her head with rubbish.' Harriet turned over and kissed Danny on the lips.

'Aye, they are alike them two, thick as thieves.' Danny ran his fingers through Harriet's hair and held her tightly. 'Our children will soon be grown and away, and then we will have time for ourselves and we will look back and wonder where all the years have gone. Just like my father and Charlotte.' Cradling Harriet tightly, he looked up at the ceiling and thought about the lad that he knew to be his at Ragged Hall. How could he ever admit to having a child with anyone other than Harriet? It would break her heart. The lad would just have to stay where he was for now. And he would have to bide his time and hope that over the next few years, as their own children grew, he would get the opportunity to make good his mistake. His heart was owned by the woman at his side, and always would be. He bent down and kissed Harriet's brow, before both of them pulled the covers up to their chins. 'I love you, Harriet Atkinson,' Danny said quietly.

'And I you, Danny Atkinson,' Harriet whispered, half-asleep.

'Goodnight, my love. All will be well in the end.' Danny turned and blew out the bedside candle and gazed into the darkness of the night, hoping that his words rang true and that all would be well in their world. Time would tell, no doubt.

Bill Brown sat across from his young grandson and decided to say what had been on his mind for some time.

'I'm buggered, lad. This old ticker of mine can't go on for much longer.' He looked at his well-built grandson, the lad he knew was the love-child of his daughter Amy and the farmer Danny Atkinson. 'Now, after my day Ragged Hall is yours, do you hear? Don't let that bastard over at Slaidburn take it off you. It should have been your mother's, but I'm leaving it to you.' Bill caught his breath and dropped his head as he thought of the love-less marriage that his daughter was in.

'Nay, Grandfather, it should be my mother's, not mine. Besides, you are not going anywhere yet, so don't talk of suchlike.' Daniel's eyes filled with tears, for his grandfather had been his saviour, rescuing him from a life no better than a servant with his so-called family.

'You know why I'm leaving it to you, lad. Your mother's told you that you were conceived out of wedlock and to a different father from the rest of her brood. You are Danny Atkinson's son – his bloody father was only in our farmyard a week or two back. I thought then that I should have said something to him, to set you up right, after my day. Like a fool, I didn't, but there's nowt stopping you from making yourself known to them at Windfell Manor after my day. They are a good family. Archie and I went to school together – if you could call the few days we did attend, between helping our fathers out on the farm, schooling. Archie looked at you when I was talking to him, and I know he recognized you as one of his own. With that mop on your head, you stick out like a sore thumb – a right Atkinson. No wonder your stepfather at Slaidburn hated you.'

Daniel hung his head. 'Why didn't Mr Atkinson come and say something to me? Am I something to be ashamed of – a dirty secret, best left alone?'

'Nay, lad, Archie is not like that, nor is his lad, Danny. It's the first time he had seen you. As far as they were aware, you were a Bland. After all, your mother wed and disappeared from Danny's life. Danny went on to wed and have a family of his own, and both your mother and he had to make the best of it.'

'My mother has always told me that the Atkinsons are well-to-do. That they are wealthy, and that part of that wealth should one day be mine. But I'm not bothered about the money. I just want to be acknowledged as Danny Atkinson's son.' Daniel lowered his head, remembering his childhood at Slaidburn with the Bland family. A childhood filled with misery, when he was treated like a dog – not a human being with feelings – by his stepfather and step-brothers. His mother was the only one who showed him affection. She talked about better days before she was married, with a twinkle in her eye and a lightness in her voice.

'Aye, well, like I say, get yourself known to them, after my day. They'll do right by you, once they ken who you are.' Bill breathed in deeply and closed his eyes.

'I will, Grandfather. With your blessing, I will.' Daniel sat back in his chair and looked around the kitchen of Ragged Hall. A farm of his own and a family to call his own – that was all he had ever wished for. And now it lay within his grasp.

Rosie lay on her back next to Ethan. It was a dazzling warm day. The air was alive with the buzz of insects and the hot sun shone down on them both, making them feel lazy. It was a day to relax and enjoy.

'Your father will wonder where I've got to. I don't want to upset the apple cart in my first week of work-ing at Crummock.' Ethan rolled over onto his side and looked at the innocent young woman alongside him. The sun shone on her fine blonde hair, making it look like angel's breath. He watched as she closed her eyes to shel-ter them from the sun's rays. Her long, fine lashes threw shadows on her blushing red cheeks as she lay enjoying the summer heat.

'Don't worry, Ethan, he and my grandfather have gone to the market in Settle. They won't be back until before supper, and they'll not even know you've gone,' she whispered, as she stretched out over the bed of wild thyme that omitted its heady herbal perfume around them.

'But your ma! Won't she be missing you?' Ethan lay back down and looked into the sun.

'She'll not miss me, nor you. I often wander, once I've done my chores. As long as I turn up for my supper, she'll not think anything of it.' Rosie opened her eyes and turned onto her side to look at the young dark-skinned, curly-haired lad. Feeling full of mischief, she picked a sprig of purple-flowering thyme and tickled him under the nose with it, teasing him as he lay back with his arms under his head.

'Stop it, you tease.' Ethan wiped under his nose and laughed. 'Where do you wander to? You shouldn't really, not on your own.' He looked concerned.

'Depends how I feel. Sometimes I just walk down into Wharfe.' She pointed down at the hamlet that lay tucked under the limestone outcrops below them. 'Sometimes I walk over to Clapham and wander through the grand garden that the Farrer family owns. And sometimes I walk over the fells, nearly into Horton. Wherever I go, I prefer to be out on my own. You can smell the breeze and feel the sun on your face while listening to the sky-larks singing, without having to be bothered to talk to anybody.' Rosie tucked her skirts under her knees and sat clasping her hands around her legs. 'I need to be outside, not helping my mother wash or bake in the kitchen. Sometimes I wish I had been born a boy. I'd have been able to help my father more then, and be outside all the time.'

'Well, I'm glad you weren't born a lad.' Ethan looked at the lass with her long blonde hair, which was whipping over her face in the slight breeze of the fellside, and felt a flutter within him that he'd not experienced before. 'Could I come with you on your walks?' Unlike Jane, Rosie had the same love of the natural world around her as he felt. She respected nature and the people in her life, and he in turn respected her for that.

Rosie blushed as she realized what Ethan had said. She enjoyed his company too, his easy ways with animals and his knowledge of plants and flowers. She looked across at him. He was handsome in his corduroy breeches, striped shirt and tight-fitting waistcoat. His curly dark hair matched his almost black eyes, which looked at her, waiting with anticipation for her answer.

'I'd like that – I'd like that a lot.' Rosie grinned. 'Father and Grandfather are always away at the market on a Tuesday, so let's make Tuesday afternoon our time together and not tell anyone.'

'That would suit me; we get on so well and I enjoy your company.' Ethan smiled, showing his perfectly white teeth to Rosie.

'Good, that's a deal. Let's meet at the end of the wood, and then no one will see us. I don't think my mother would be happy with me mixing with the new stable lad,' Rosie whispered.

'You mean it would be the gypsy part of me that she wouldn't want you to mix with. But she should know that my mother and father are both respectable, and that my father doesn't wander the lanes and roads like his own father did.' Ethan bowed his head.

'Have you ever met your grandfather?' Rosie asked quietly.

'Nay, never. My father said he left my grandmother expecting him, and only came back once in a while when he was a lad. He must be a good age now. He's probably dead in a ditch somewhere – best spot for him. Although I'm curious to see how his sort live. I've always fancied going to Appleby Fair, but my father won't hear of it; he says he wants nowt with them ways. But whether he likes it or not, he takes after his father, for nobody can handle a horse like my father, or judge a person just by looking at them – he sometimes knows what I'm thinking better than I do myself.' Ethan looked out over the Dales and pulled at a stalk of fell grass, putting the stalk in his mouth to chew on, as he thought about his lost family and the yearly horse fair at Appleby, which all Romany gypsies attended in order to meet up with their families.

'I've noticed the caravans and horses on the roadsides lately. It's Appleby Fair very soon, isn't it?' Rosie put her arm through Ethan's and smiled.

'Aye, second week in June. They hold it on Gallows Hill, just outside Appleby. I'd love to go and just look around. I'm not bothered about my grandfather, he's not worth looking for. Who could walk out on a woman who was having your baby? He should have done right by her and settled down to a life in Settle. But I would like to see something I've heard about all my life and perhaps, just for once, feel as if I fit in.' Ethan hung his head and twiddled the piece of grass between his fingers.

'You should go. As you say, see what goes on there. Your curiosity will be satisfied then.' Rosie looked at the young man who had been the main topic of conversation in Crummock's kitchen. Her grandfather and father did not understand how her Aunt Isabelle could not keep Ethan in employment, after he had saved her son from drowning. 'I could come with you.'

Ethan lifted his head. 'You couldn't come with me – your parents would not allow it. Besides, how do we get there? It isn't as if it's in the next field. It is at least forty miles away.' He shook his head and pulled a tuft of the herb-filled grass from the earth, then threw it for the wind to blow and do with it what it would. He watched it float away, just like his dreams.

'Leave it with me. You *will* go to Appleby Fair. It's important to you.' Rosie pushed herself up from the warm, fragrant land and twirled round in the breeze as she looked down upon her crestfallen companion. 'Come on, let's walk over to Beggar's Stile and then get home for supper; the day is too good to waste.' She smiled as Ethan pushed himself up and joined her.

'Don't promise something you can't fulfil, and stop teasing me, Rosie Atkinson. Else you are no better than your cousin Jane.' Ethan grabbed her hand, stopping her from dancing in the warm summer sun.

'I never promise something I can't fulfil, and don't insult me by likening me to my cousin. She thinks only of herself and plays with your heart. That is why, if truth were told, you will have been banished to us, at Crummock. We can't have our precious Jane mixing with the lower classes, now can we? Stop that sullen look and catch me if you can. And stop feeling sorry for yourself – we will go to your Appleby Fair.' Rosie pulled away from Ethan and started to run over the short dry grass of the fell land. 'And we will go together.'

'Rosie, we are all waiting for you.' Harriet yelled up the stairs, losing her patience with her teenage daughter.

Rosie appeared slowly at the top of the stairs and looked sheepishly at her mother. 'I don't feel well, Mother, I think I ate too many gooseberries when I was picking them for pies yesterday.' She pulled a face and hoped that the white talcum powder she had covered her face with was convincing enough, from a distance, to back up her story.

'Well, I'm not going without you. I'll only worry the whole time I'm there. Besides, I really don't want to go anyway, as your Aunt Isabelle will only gloat about her new abode.' Harriet reached up and undid the ribbon of her hat and was about to take it off, when Danny stopped her.

'It's only a belly ache, Harriet. Rosie is sixteen, not six, and she's got a tongue in her head. If she gets worse, she can always send for you. Besides, Ethan will be visiting his parents later today, and he can bring word to Windfell if Rosie worsens.' Danny let his hand drop from hers, as Harriet stopped untying the ribbons for a moment. 'She's not a baby, my dear, and don't make her the excuse for not visiting Windfell. It's not every day we get invited for our lunch, so let's make the most of it.'

Harriet sighed and told Rosie, 'Go on, get yourself to bed. As your father says, let Ethan know if you get any worse. It's lucky he said that he'd polish the harnesses and saddles this morning, as otherwise he'd be long gone.' She looked up the stairs and watched as her daughter made good her escape from her gaze.

'She will be fine, my love. Now come, my father and the children are waiting in the carriage and it's a beautiful day, so we can dawdle and enjoy the scenery.' Danny put his arm around his wife and guided her to the kitchen doorway. He was determined that Harriet and Isabelle would talk to one another over lunch, and he knew his sister must feel the same way or she would not have invited them – despite Harriet assuming they were invited just to hear Isabelle gloating.

Harriet looked back. 'I just hope that Rosie will be alright; she never says she's ill, as a rule.'

'She will be fine. As she says, she's been greedy eating those green gooseberries she was top-and-tailing yesterday, that's all.' Danny helped his wife up into the carriage. For once, she had listened to sense and had agreed that Rosie was old enough to look after herself. Perhaps her feelings of inadequacy in motherhood were finally ebbing. He certainly hoped so.

Rosie and Ethan watched out of Crummock's kitchen window as the family's carriage disappeared over the hill, down the rough track towards Austwick.

'When they are past the thorn bushes on the hilltop, we can outride them and take the shortcut down by the wash-dubs, through Wharfe and Helwith Bridge. We will just catch the ten-thirty train at Settle.' Rosie wiped her falsely ashen face with a tea towel and urged Ethan out of the house.

'You are sure you want to do this? Your parents will be so angry with both of us, if they ever find out.' Ethan hesitated. Ever since Rosie had suggested that she pay for the train fair to Appleby he had worried, but at the same time he couldn't help but feel a bit excited at the prospect of his first ride on a train, and a visit to Appleby Fair with a girl on his arm.

'Of course I want to do this. I wouldn't be spending my savings on train tickets if I didn't. Besides, my parents are not going to find out. I heard my father say they were to dawdle and, once they are at Windfell, they won't return until suppertime.' Rosie watched as Ethan mounted the horse that he'd saddled for them both, and which waited outside the back door of Crummock.

Ethan held his hand out for Rosie to join him and sat forward in the saddle to make room for her. 'I know travelling this way isn't very ladylike, but neither of us is heavy and the horse will cope with two of us on it. Using one horse saves money at the Lion's livery stable, and they won't suspect anything if I just take one horse to be stabled.' He hauled on Rosie's hand as she pulled up her skirts and sat down tightly behind him. She wrapped her arms around him. Ethan smiled, enjoying the feel of having her body so close to his. 'Right, hold tight, if we are to catch the train, we've not a minute to waste. You are sure you are alright?'

'I'm fine, Ethan. Don't worry about ladylike manners – you forget that I'm not as precious as my cousin. Now go, just in case my parents take the same road as us and not the road via Settle, as I heard my mother request.'

Ethan flicked the reins of the horse and dug his heels in to urge the animal forward. Together they trotted briskly out of the farmyard and down the bridlepath to Wharfe. Rosie sat close to Ethan and felt the sun on her face as she hugged him tightly. She looked at his dark hair as it shone like jet in the morning's sun and breathed in the smell of him. It was a comforting scent of warm hay, with a hint of the carbolic soap that he had obviously washed in that morning. She wasn't worried that he'd seen her ankles and most of her left leg as she mounted the horse. Her mother would be mortified, but how was she to know?

The horse walked carefully across the stream next to the clapper bridge at the wash-dubs and then carried on trotting down the bridlepath to Wharfe. The limestone walls on either side of them made them nearly invisible on the centuries-old path, until they came to the small hamlet of Wharfe. Luckily it was quiet, with most of the inhabitants at church, praying for the Lord to keep their souls. Once out on the road to Helwith Bridge, Rosie thought she was riding with the devil himself, as Ethan urged his horse into a gallop. She held him even tighter and could feel her long blonde hair whipping her face as they passed the limestone boulders and farms spread along either side of the road. The horse galloped faster and faster, making her cling on for her life as they raced down the road. On reaching the entrance to Windfell, both of them looked up the driveway, hoping that nobody would notice the fleeing pair as they galloped the two miles into Settle. Ethan felt guilty at not seeing his parents on the Sabbath, and Rosie felt guilty at deceiving her parents. Still, it was worth it, just to be near the lad she had feelings for. And the day had only just begun.

Once at the outskirts of Settle, Rosie dismounted, out of view of the prim eyes of the ladies of the district, and walked through the town. She waited on the corner of New Street, and watched as Ethan took the horse into the livery stable of the Golden Lion. She looked across at the clock in the post office's window. It showed twenty past ten; ten minutes to go before the train left for Appleby and then carried on to Carlisle. She felt her stomach churn as she saw Ethan running out of the Golden Lion and, at the same time, her parents' carriage passing the town hall a hundred yards behind him. Hiding around the corner of New Street, she waited for Ethan to join her and hoped that he had not been recognized.

'Bloody hell, that was a close one! Your father's just stabling his horse and carriage while the rest of your family has a look around Settle. I was so close I heard him instruct the stable lad as he drew into the yard,' Ethan panted.

'Come on, we've no time to waste – the train will be pulling into the station, if it's not already there. I can see steam rising. The engine will be filling up with water, before going down the line.' Rosie grabbed Ethan's hand and ran the two hundred yards to the station, then gasped as they saw the train waiting on the far platform. 'We need tickets!' They pushed past people dressed in their Sunday best, and opened the crimson-coloured doors of the ticket office to purchase their tickets.

'Two tickets for Appleby, please.' Rosie caught her breath as she looked across at the ticket officer, with his LMS hat upon his head.

'Return, first-, second- or third-class?' the bespectacled man asked.

'Return and second-class, please.' Rosie wished that he'd hurry up.

'Two-and-six, please, next train is at two.' He waited as Rosie counted out her money, before passing the tickets under his grilled window.

'We're not waiting for the two o'clock train – we aim to catch this one.' Ethan pulled on Rosie's arm as they both turned on their heels and dashed out through the crowds, who were wishing family and loved ones farewell from the safety of the platform. They flew up and over the metal bridge traversing the railway line, both of them gasping for breath as they reached the other platform, breathing in the smoke and fumes of the waiting train.

'All aboard!' The stationmaster started closing the carriage doors as the engine built up steam, ready to leave the platform.

Ethan pushed Rosie into the second-class carriage, with its door still ajar. They were just in time, as the door slammed shut behind them and the stationmaster blew his whistle for the train to depart. Both collapsed giggling into their seats, while the other passengers shook their heads in disbelief at such bad behaviour from the young.

'We made it! We are on our way to Appleby.' Ethan's eyes were filled with anticipation as they looked out of the open window as the train pulled away from the station.

'Yes, we've done it.' Rosie smiled and then sighed, looking at the solitary penny she had left in her posy bag, as they left Settle and the station behind. 'I should have said third-class, then I would have had more money to spend at the fair. But we were in such a rush.'

'We'll make our own amusement, Rosie. Besides, I've sixpence, so we'll not go hungry, and at least you had the sense to get return tickets, so we can get home.' Ethan was excited. Unlike Rosie, he had never ridden on a train before and was watching the houses and scenery fly by. 'Look, there goes Windfell.'

Both craned their necks out of the carriage's window and took in a fleeting glimpse of Windfell Manor. A further pang of guilt clouded their faces as they thought of the lies they had told, to enable their day together.

'We will be back before them, won't we?' Rosie looked across for reassurance from Ethan.

'Yes, didn't you say we can have a few hours at Appleby and will be back in Settle for five o'clock? We won't be that long at the fair.' He looked across at a worried Rosie.

'I guess we will be fine. We won't be missed, I'm sure.' She sat down and looked out at the scenery rushing past her. 'Please don't let us be late,' she whispered to herself. Her parents would never forgive her. As for Ethan, he'd never work for anyone ever again.

8

Jane picked up the morning newspaper and read the headlines with horror.

'Have you seen this, Mother, and you, Father? The poor woman, how could the King's horse run her over like that?'

'I don't think the jockey did it deliberately, my dear. The stupid woman ran directly in front of him, and he couldn't stop.' Isabelle looked across at James for support.

'Poor Emily Davison. She was only trying to make a point by pinning a banner for "Votes for Women" on the horse. Perhaps the King and Parliament will listen to us women, after a death at the Epsom Derby.' Jane lifted her hand up to the violet, green and white pendant that she wore as a sign of solidarity with the fight for the newly named Suffragette movement and its causes. 'Surely they've got to, now that women are going on hunger strike and nearly dying. They must realize how strongly the modern-day woman feels about having equal rights to men.' She sat staring defiantly at her father, knowing that he thought her ideals were rubbish.

'I do wish you would stop your fascination with these troublemakers, Jane. This is a man's world, and women should know their place.' James looked at his young daughter, who had a mind of her own, and sighed.

'Where's that, then? Tied to the kitchen sink, doing sewing and needlework and looking pretty on a man's arm? Grandmama never did any of that, nor did you, Mama. Both of you were your own women – and you still are. Yet we don't get a say in the running of the country. Surely that's not fair?' She folded the newspaper and looked at her father, who was about to explode.

'Enough, Jane, we have visitors about to join us. In fact I can hear their carriage coming up the drive this minute. Now no more talk of suffragettes, women's rights or anything else that crosses your mind. And try to be right with Rosie. I know you are not alike, but you can at least show her a little respect. After all, she is your cousin.' Isabelle rose from her chair and made her way to the hallway, giving James a dark look as she went, in the hope that he would say something along the same lines to Jane while she went to meet their guests.

'Your mother's right: you know nothing about suchlike. You should just concentrate on your role in the firm. That's enough for you to think about at present,' James said gruffly.

'Grandmama would understand. She always knew what was right.' Jane crossed her arms in a sulk.

'Well, she isn't here. So just for once, smile and be pleasant.' James rose to his feet and went to join Isabelle, who was busy making their guests welcome, leaving Jane to continue feeling upset about the death of Emily Davison.

'Harriet, how lovely that you can be with us today. And just look at young Ben and Georgina – how quickly they grow!' Isabelle welcomed Danny and his family to Windfell with open arms. She was genuinely glad that Harriet had accepted her invitation to lunch. 'No Rosie? Jane will be disappointed. She was hoping that Rosie would be with you.'

'I'm afraid Rosie was feeling a little unwell this morning, so she could not join us.' Harriet smiled at Isabelle, feeling that her welcome was slightly over the top.

'She ate too many gooseberries yesterday, giving herself a belly ache, that's all.' Danny sat down in a chair and looked at Harriet and hoped she wasn't going to fret about Rosie being left at home.

Jane had moved to sit next to the window. She sniggered but quickly hid her reaction, as her Aunt Harriet gave her a warning glance.

'That is unfortunate! But easily done, and I do hope Rosie soon recovers. Luke, would you and Jane like to show Ben the foal? She is growing so quickly, and you will all be bored while we adults chat before lunch.' Isabelle watched as Georgina, the baby of the family, crawled around the room, leaving fingerprints on the highly polished furniture. 'I'll ask Lily to take charge of Georgina while we enjoy one another's company. If that is alright with you, Harriet. Lily's got a good way with children, and it is a pity she has no family of her own and will be leaving our service soon.'

'I'd prefer that Georgina stayed with me; she does not know who Lily is and doesn't like strangers.' Harriet looked worried and glanced across at Danny for support.

Archie had said nothing up until this point. He looked around at his grandchildren and thought that he'd rather enjoy their company than sit in the newly decorated parlour of Windfell. 'I'll take Georgina out with me, and we will all go and see this young foal. It'll give you four a chance to catch up in peace and say what you want, out of my earshot.' Archie picked up young Georgina, noticing the worried look between Danny and Harriet as he held her tightly in his arms. He laughed as she tried to pinch his pocket watch out of his pocket. 'Come on, li'l 'un, let's go and look around outside while the grown-ups talk. Jane, you open the doors; and you two lads behave yourselves, otherwise you'll have me to answer to.' Archie made his way out of the parlour like the Pied Piper of Hamelin, with his grandchildren around his feet. It had been the excuse that he had needed. He still hurt when he thought of Charlotte sitting in the chair that Isabelle had now claimed as her own.

'Would you like a sherry, Harriet and Danny? Or perhaps a cup of tea?' James looked across at the couple, who rarely visited them, and noticed Harriet's worried gaze once the children had left her side. He wanted to make them both feel at home.

'A cup of tea would be grand, James.' Danny stood up

and looked out of the parlour window, turning round as James rang the bell for Thomson to come running, on command. 'So, you've settled in, I see. I like the new wallpaper, Isabelle, it must have cost a pretty penny.' He looked round at the newly decorated parlour and grinned at James, who was shaking his head in despair.

'I always did want this room to be decorated with this wallpaper, but Mama would never hear of it. The pattern is called "Strawberry Thief" and is by William Morris. It is so pretty and suits this room so well. What do you think, Harriet? You always had a good eye for style.' Isabelle smiled and sat down next to her sister-in-law.

'Yes, it is very you, and it suits the parlour well. Who else would think of bringing nature into a living space, for us all to enjoy.' Harriet looked around at the patterned wallpaper, depicting birds feasting on strawberries, and remembered the wedding dress that Isabelle had designed for her, after meeting the artist William Morris. They had been so close then, enjoying one another's company and sharing their secrets together.

'It's a bit too posh for the walls at Crummock. So don't be getting any ideas, our lass.' Danny looked around him.

'It cost an arm and a leg. I told Isabelle we could do without it, but she would insist. She likes to get her own way, don't you, my dear?' James stood behind his wife and ran his hand along her shoulders.

'Crummock's walls are practical, and are fine just whitewashed each year, so you needn't fret, Danny.' Harriet looked up as Thomson entered with tea for four, and the conversation stopped until he left.

'Harriet, how are you keeping? I sometimes worry about you, for we seem to have drifted apart and I can't ignore that any longer. We were once so close.' Isabelle reached out for her sister-in-law's hand and squeezed it tightly, after sipping her tea. 'You will have heard that we nearly lost our Luke, when he fell into the river? It was then that I realized how hard and uncaring I had been over the loss of your twins. I hope you can forgive me? It's just that until you have children of your own, you don't realize how precious they are to you. You must have been heartbroken, as I know you both were, but I was too wrapped up in the business and was blinkered to your loss.'

Isabelle's eyes filled with tears as she looked at Harriet, whose head was bowed as she remembered the pain Isabelle had caused when she had flippantly remarked that infant death was something nearly every family endured. It was true and it was part of the times they lived in, but to lose two boys cruelly in one afternoon, without their mother by their side, was a pain of Harriet's that Isabelle would have to live with all her life, and something she hoped she would never have to experience herself. Now, all these years later, she realized how callous she had been, and she wanted to sweep any misunderstandings to one side.

Harriet shook as she remembered the day twenty years ago when she could not get home to her children in time, after working in the shop at Skipton in the run-up to Christmas. 'I still feel so guilty. I put my work first and placed the children in the care of their nanny. I thought it was just a cold they both had. If I'd been there with them, and had noticed their suffering and seen them fighting for breath before I set off for the shop, they might still be with us, if I had called the doctor out in time.' She pulled her handkerchief out of her sleeve and sobbed into it.

'Diphtheria took a lot of lives that year, and it moves so fast – it was not your fault, my dear Harriet. You must not constantly blame yourself. It is I who was to blame, if anyone, by insisting that we finished off the orders before we went home. I know I seemed very uncaring. I beg your forgiveness, dear sister-in-law. And I regret I have not had it in my heart to say these words earlier. Mama often chastised me for not being more caring, and told me that one day I would realize how you felt. Well, I do now, after Luke's brush with death.' Isabelle hugged Harriet to her, as Danny and James looked on, thankful that at last the two women had spoken about exactly how they felt.

'I thought you hated me for staying at home and looking after my children. I know the business was everything for Mama and you, but my children are my world, along with Danny.' Harriet sobbed anew, looking into Isabelle's tear-filled eyes.

'I know, and Mama knew that too. I don't hate you; we've just grown apart, which is truly a shame. From this day forward, let us get back to being friends. After all, Mama wished that to happen, and she left you part of the shares in Atkinson's. Both she and I have never forgotten that without you we would never have been so successful.' Isabelle looked up at her husband and urged James to back up her words.

'All these tears. What are we to do, Danny?' James looked over at a worried-looking Danny. 'Put the past behind you, both of you, and let's all look forward to a better future. I think that is what Danny and I hope for, as we love you both dearly.'

'Aye, that we do. I'm getting a bit fed up of walking on eggshells. Especially now we've got my father living with us, for he's a liability in his own right. He forgets that I've been farming Crummock for nearly twenty-four years without his help every day. And I don't know why Archie has decided he wants Ethan to work for us, as I've hardly any work for him. Although he will come in handy, come hay-time,' said Danny.

'I enjoy having your father living with us,' Harriet sniffed. 'He's good with the children. Ben loves him, and Rosie won't have a bad word said about him. And as for bringing Ethan with him, well, he's no trouble. I hardly ever see him.'

'I'm sorry Archie has burdened you with Ethan. That's the trouble with him: you don't ever see Ethan, and he was never to be found when there was work to be done here. My mother was too easy on him, because she had always held his father in great esteem. And Ethan helps himself to trout out of the river and the odd rabbit or two. I just don't know why Father took him up to Crummock.' Isabelle looked over at James.

'Probably because he cares about Ethan and feels liable for his welfare, my dear. Especially as he saved our Luke's life,' James added quickly.

'Well, if I were you, Danny, I'd keep an eye on him. But

let us forget about Ethan for the moment because the family is more important. My dear Harriet, let us put our differences aside and get back to being the friends we were, all those years ago. We don't have dear Mama as our buffer any more, and I would so like us to be there for one another.' Isabelle looked at Harriet with pleading eyes, meaning every word she said. She needed her sister-in-law, and especially her knowledge of the business. Jane would take years of training, but Harriet knew everything about the trade and would be an asset to the firm, if she could get her interested in it again. 'Come and have afternoon tea in Atkinson's next week with the children and see our new designs – they are stunning this year.'

'I'd like that. Rosie would, too.' Harriet smiled and cast her mind back to the fitting and cutting room, which she had enjoyed working in, until the fateful day when her life had stopped.

'Is Wednesday alright with you? James can take the children's photographs while you visit me. Can't you, James?' Isabelle smiled.

'Certainly, my dear. Dress them up in their Sunday finery and I'll do my very best.' James grinned across at Harriet, knowing full well that his wife was sweet-talking Harriet back into the firm.

'Splendid! Now, let's see where Father has gone to with those children. You will be wanting your lunch and to get back to Rosie, if she is not feeling well.'

'Yes, I would appreciate getting back a little earlier than we anticipated, just to make sure she's alright.' Harriet was relieved that Isabelle understood.

'I understand. I'll ask Thomson to hurry Cook along.' Isabelle linked her arm through Harriet's as they walked into the hallway. 'Danny, do you want that old grandfather clock? It really does not fit in this hallway; it was another thing that my mother put up with, but didn't like.'

'It's belonged to my father's family for years – you can't just throw it out. We'll have it up at Crummock, won't we, Harriet?' Danny looked shocked at Isabelle's lack of love for a family heirloom.

'Yes, it will fit well at the bottom of the stairs. Archie will no doubt like to have it back with him.' Harriet smiled.

'Then I'll get Jethro to bring it up to you on the flat cart next week. Now, where are those children?'

The train pulled into Appleby station after making its way through the tunnels and cuttings that spread along the length of the remote railway track. The engine heaved a sigh of relief as it came to rest after the steepest climb on the line, known as 'the long drag'.

'That was a journey! How beautiful did Dentdale and Garsdale look as we passed through them? The houses looked so small, way down in the bottom of the valleys.' Rosie smiled and tried to keep up with Ethan as he made his way through the station gates, following the crowd down into the town of Appleby.

'Mallerstang looks so rugged, even on a beautiful day like this. Just think what it would have been like when they were building the railway line. It's a wonder they didn't freeze to death when they were laying the track down.' Ethan stopped in his tracks and watched in wonder the number of horses and travelling people that lined the streets of Appleby. Flat-bedded wagons and round green-topped caravans painted with bright-green, red and gold decoration crowded through the narrow streets, drawn by horses of every description. Black-and-white pintos, brown-and-white skewbalds, chestnuts and roans were all were being led and ridden by their owners, who were not bashful when it came to showing off their horsemanship. Amongst the horses, droves of sheep and cattle were also being driven in the direction of Gallows Hill, the main field for Appleby Fair.

'White heather for your girl, Mister?' A beautiful, sultry young gypsy girl came and enticed Ethan with a basket full of heather and wooden clothes pegs. 'It'll bring you both luck.'

Ethan shook his head and looked at Rosie, knowing that between them they had very little money.

'Some pegs for your ma, then?' She tugged on his sleeve.

'Sorry, no money.' Ethan hung his head.

'Good luck to ya anyway.' The young girl moved on to her next victim, and both Ethan and Rosie watched her as she wove her way through the crowds. Her long colourful skirt swayed and her bracelets jangled as she cleared a passage away from them, watched by the visitors to Appleby.

'Sorry, Rosie. I would have bought you some heather, but we both need whatever money we've got.'

'It doesn't matter, Ethan – we can pick our own

heather. I've never seen anywhere so busy. There's so many people, and they are all selling something or riding horses. You can't walk safely along the street because of the horses racing up and down.'

'It's called "flashing", and they are riding them to the places I've heard my father talking about, called Flashing Lane and Long Marton Road. It's where all the gypsy men show off their horses by riding them up and down the lane to put them through their paces, and to show their best points before selling them. We can go there, if you want; or down into the village to watch the horses being washed down at a place called "the Sands", which is just under the main bridge that spans the River Eden.' Ethan waited as Rosie made up her mind.

'Can we go and see the horse being washed? I don't want to go near the racing horses. It looks dangerous, and there are so many people. I don't want to offend you, Ethan, but some look like they can't be trusted.' Rosie had never seen such a raggle-taggle collection of people, and she was beginning to regret agreeing to spend the day at Appleby Horse Fair.

'They are only travelling folk, Rosie. They love their horses and country ways. You'd look a bit worse for wear, if you didn't know where you were going to rest your head from one night to the next and were out in all weathers. Besides, somewhere in these people will be my relations, so they can't be that different from me.' Ethan looked at the fear on Rosie's face. 'Here, put your arm through mine, I'll look after you.'

She looked up at Ethan and saw the excitement in

his eyes. He was loving the smell and the mix of what he thought to be his own people, but at the same time he wanted to protect her. She smiled and put her arm through his, and felt safe as they pushed their way past the crowds to stand on the top of the bridge that crossed the mighty River Eden. There they looked down, watching the gypsy men washing their horses in the deep waters. The two of them gasped as they watched the horses swim in the deepest parts of the river with their riders on their backs, and cringed as the riders made the horses climb the banks out of the river with a deft whipping.

'I think it's cruel.' Rosie held Ethan's arm tight.

'It's good horsemanship, that's all.' He watched as a beautiful black-and-white stallion snorted and tossed its head, in defiance of its owner.

'No, I don't like these ways.' Rosie looked around at the crowds and decided that Appleby Fair was not for her. She saw linnets that were being sold in cages so small they could hardly stretch their wings, and women offering to tell fortunes to people who only wanted to hear good things. 'These aren't our people, Ethan, we belong back home.'

'We'll be home soon enough. Give us another hour and we'll catch the train. I'd like to go up onto the main field and just have a look around the horses for sale, and wander through the caravans. I don't know what my grandfather looks like, or if he is even alive, but I'd like to see his lifestyle and his ways, while we have time.' He pulled on Rosie's arm and they made their way back through the crowds towards Gallows Hill.

101

'Alright, I know it's important to you. I know you would really like to find your grandfather, if you were truthful. Just an hour, though, and then we must return.' Rosie tried to smile, worrying that Ethan was getting carried away with the atmosphere of the fair.

'I promise we will only be another an hour, and then we will catch the train.' Ethan flashed his winning smile at the girl on his arm and set off in earnest pursuit of his grandfather. They wandered around the covered wagons and flat carts, with the families that lived in them huddled around camp fires, telling stories and exchanging the year's news together. Dogs barked and sniffed around their feet, with a lurcher showing its teeth at Rosie, as Ethan dragged her away from harm.

'Please let's go home. We'll not find your grandfather here.' She looked at the tanned, weather-worn faces and at the women in their colourful skirts, and wanted the safety of her home. These were not her ways, although they were country folk like her.

'Alright, we'll be away. But I'm going to return because somebody somewhere will know my grandfather.' Ethan looked disappointed, but knew Rosie was right: if they didn't go back now, they would miss their train home. He looked back at the campsites they were leaving behind and vowed to visit them again on his own, for this was a life he could enjoy.

Rosie sat quietly, lost in her own thoughts as she watched the scenery pass by her outside the train carriage. Her hair and clothes smelt of the camp fires they had wandered amongst, in their pursuit of an elusive grandfather whom both of them knew they would never find. Her skirt and boots were covered with mud from the churned-up field at Gallows Hill. She knew she looked a mess, and she only hoped she could change and wash before her parents returned home. With every clatter of the railway line beneath her she wished she was home, safe and sound. She cast her mind back over the day, at the horses being put through their paces, and the beggars selling whatever produce they could; the smell of rabbit stew drifting on the wind, and the brightness of the painted wagons that were home to the wandering gypsies. It was a completely different way of life from hers and a different language. She had not understood a word that some of them had spoken, and had felt as if she was an outsider in her own world.

Ethan sat across from her, half-asleep, content that he'd visited the legendary Appleby Fair and unconcerned that his presence might be missed at home – unlike Rosie. With every mile they were nearer home she felt sick at the thought of having to explain her disappearance, if her parents had already returned to Crummock. She'd not thought of the consequences of her trip; but now, with hindsight, her mother was going to be frantic, whereas Ethan had no one to answer to. He'd not lied to his parents, he just hadn't gone to visit them, and he'd not spent every penny that he had. The sixpence he said he had in his pocket had remained there all day and they were both going home hungry, filthy and tired. Rosie wondered if Ethan had any money on him at all, for they had drunk from a spring that fed the River Eden, rather than Ethan spending his elusive sixpence. How she wished she had not been so easily led. It was her fault; after all, it had been her idea and she had no one else to blame.

'She's not in her room. Where is she, Danny?' Harriet came rushing down the stairs, frantic with worry.

'She'll not be far.' Danny tried to calm his wife. 'I'll go and look outside and ask Ethan if he's seen her.' He reached for the kitchen door, while Archie looked out of the kitchen window and spotted a horse and riders galloping like the wind, up the lane to Crummock.

'Don't bother going to look for either Ethan or Rosie. Come and look here. God only knows where they've been, but they are in a hell of a hurry to get back home.' Archie sat down in the chair next to the unlit fire and looked up at his son's scowling face.

'I'll bloody kill him! What does he think he's doing, taking one of the horses and putting our Rosie up behind him? You should never have brought him here, Father. Isabelle said he was more bother than he was worth.' Danny made it to the back door and opened it wide.

'Now just think on. Rosie was the one who said she was too ill to join us today. They've obviously planned their day out together. Besides, they might not have been far.' Archie tried to talk some sense into his son. It was no good that he was just blaming Ethan.

'The fire's not been stoked since the minute we left this house, nothing has been touched – she's been out with him all day. By God, they are both going to tell me what they've been up to,' Danny swore as he closed the door behind him.

Sensing the tension within the house, baby Georgina started wailing, and Harriet sent Ben to his room as her eyes filled up with tears at the thought that her daughter had lied to her.

'She's at that age, Harriet. She's not your little lass any more, she's nearly a grown woman,' Archie said, as he crumpled newspaper into the dead hearth and added a few dry kindling sticks, before lighting the fire with a match. 'She'll have been alright, don't you worry. Ethan is not the devil that Isabelle makes him out to be. There will be an explanation.' Archie watched as the kindling sticks took hold, and then gently added pieces of coal until a good blaze roared.

'She's still our little girl, she's only sixteen. Danny will kill Ethan.' Harriet consoled Georgina with a biscuit from the tin above the fire, and sat her down on the pegged rug next to her grandfather.

'Nay, he won't. Not if he remembers that he was young himself.' Archie smiled down at his youngest grandchild. 'They are no bother when they are your age, but they are nowt but worry when they grow up, eh, li'l 'un?' He listened as he heard his son raising his voice at the pair, who had just entered the farmyard on the hard-driven horse. He knew that perhaps he was to blame, after introducing Ethan to Crummock; lately he had noticed the smile on Rosie's face whenever he was mentioned. It was worth it, just for that. Besides, Ethan was a good lad; a bit wild maybe, but he hadn't a bad bone in his body. The back door was flung open and Rosie walked in, tears streaming down her face and her clothes splattered with mud.

'They've been on the bloody train, up to Appleby. Just look at her, coming back looking and smelling like a bloody gyppo!' Danny pushed Rosie into the kitchen. 'That bloody lad – he trailed her up there, to be with his own. They'll be running away together before you know it.' He was fuming.

Rosie pulled her arm away from her father and looked at her mother and grandfather. 'It's my fault, not Ethan's. He didn't make me go. I suggested it – it was my idea. He really wanted to see if we could find his grand-father. I'm sorry I lied, but I knew you'd not let us go, even if we asked,' she cried.

'Too bloody right, lass. Now get yourself up the stairs, and don't let me see your face until the morning. Just be glad you are not going to get the braying I'm going to give Ethan, before I send him on his way,' Danny growled.

'No, Father, please don't send him away. It wasn't his fault; please, it was mine. I'd rather you took your belt to me,' sobbed Rosie.

'Just get yourself to bed, Rosie.' Harriet watched as her daughter, still sobbing, made her way down the pas-sage and up the stairs to bed. 'You can't belt Ethan. And, like you said, you'll need him in the next month or two for hay-time. Have a word with his father – he'll sort Ethan out. Rosie's come to no harm, and it's as clear as the nose on your face that she's sweet on him, otherwise she wouldn't have lied to us.' Harriet glanced quickly at Archie as she put the kettle on the now-blazing fire.

'It's all your bloody fault, Father. I should have said no to Ethan coming here.' Danny spat into the fire.

106

'Nay, lad, you can't blame me for his curiosity about where he comes from. Everybody wants to know that. Rosie was only being kind.' Archie looked up at his son and then poked the fire, knowing he shouldn't say another word on the subject.

'Aye, well, she's back now, I suppose that's all that matters,' said Danny. 'But I will have a word with his father; happen he can square Ethan up a bit.'

Harriet went quietly to the pantry and cut a slice of bread and cheese, then took it up to her heartbroken daughter without Danny noticing. 'Don't cry, Rosie, your father's not going to do anything to Ethan. He's never hit anybody yet, and he knows he needs him this summer-time.' She ran her fingers through her daughter's long hair as she sobbed in her arms. 'You know, you may think a lot of Ethan, but he's just the first boy in your life, and there will be a lot more yet. And he isn't worth lying for.' Harriet kissed her daughter on her brow and hugged her tightly. 'He didn't do anything to you, did he, Rosie?'

'What do you mean, Mother?' Rosie looked up at Isabelle.

'You didn't lift your skirts for him, did you, dear?' Harriet hated asking, but it was one of the first things that had entered her head when Rosie came into the kitchen.

'Only to climb onto the horse. He did see my ankles, Mama.' Rosie blushed.

'That's alright, dear, we'll let him get away with that. Remember, though, that Ethan's nearly a man – a man with urges. Don't get too close to him. Now you eat your bread and cheese and tidy yourself up. Your father will have calmed down by the morning and will soon forgive you both.' She stood up and looked down at her distraught daughter.

'I'm sorry, Mama,' Rosie sniffed.

'Just don't let your heart rule your head, Rosie. You are almost a woman, and you can't act like a child any more. Perhaps more time with your cousin Jane would help. She's quite the young lady, and you could do worse than follow her lead.'

'Please, Mama, I think I'd rather be belted by my father than spend time with Jane.'

'We will be visiting Skipton and the store next week. You are having your photograph taken by Uncle James. You can see Jane then, while I spend time with your Aunt Isabelle. Thank heavens she can't see you in this state. Now, get yourself washed and to bed, for tomorrow is another day.' Harriet closed the bedroom door behind her, listening to the sobs of her daughter. Archie was right: she was growing up, but she was still a little girl really, and always would be, in her mother's eyes.

Jethro pulled the ropes tight, securing the old grandfather clock from Windfell's hallway tightly onto the cart.

'You'll not be too hard on him, Jethro? Ethan's only young and curious.' Mazy looked at her husband, who had been in a mood since Danny Atkinson had told him of their son's trip to Appleby with his daughter.

'I'll tell you what, woman: he's got to learn his place in the world, instead of looking at what he can't have. Bloody running away with Miss Rosie in search of his grandfather.

I'll give him something to remember his grandfather by. This isn't the first time he's messed about with the lasses of the big house. I saw him trying to kiss Miss Jane, and told him to leave well alone. What's wrong with the lad?'

'Nowt's wrong with him – he's just young.' Mazy watched as Jethro climbed up onto the cart and whipped the horses into action, making the bell on the grandfather clock chime with the jolting vehicle. It was rare that Jethro lost his temper, but he'd had time to brood on his son's wild ways and that was always a bad thing.

'I'm glad you could find time to bring the clock from Windfell, Jethro,' said Archie as he watched the strong man lifting the oak-cased clock down from the cart, before hauling it on his shoulder into the farmhouse at Crummock. Jethro returned to the cart for the clock face's case, then helped Archie carry the weight that pulled on the clock's chains to make it work.

'Aye, well, I need to square up that lad of mine while I'm here. I'm sorry he's caused you and your family bother. He should have known better than to do that. You don't bite the hand that feeds you.' Jethro stood in front of Archie and wiped his brow with his neckerchief.

'Nay, it was our Rosie just as much to blame. She'd paid for the tickets and put the idea in his head; they are a lot alike, those two.' Archie looked at the brooding man and knew that Ethan was going to get the rough side of Jethro's tongue.

'Nay, they are not alike, if you don't mind me saying, sir. Your Rosie is a lady, and my lad needs to know his place.' Jethro spat out a mouthful of saliva and grabbed the horses' reins. 'Is he in the stable, our lad?'

'No, he's in the calf shed, mucking it out. Danny kept him near home today, knowing you were coming. Don't be too hard on him, Jethro. Nobody was hurt, and they both came home none the worse for their day out.' Archie was trying to calm him down, but knew Ethan was going to be in for a belting, even though he was old enough to take on his father.

'He'll not be doing the same again, sir. And thank you for keeping Ethan on here. I wouldn't have blamed either you or Master Danny if you had sent him packing. It's what he deserves.' Jethro grabbed the reins of his horses, unable to talk to his former master any more without showing his true feelings. He led the horses around the back of the farmhouse to the stables, stopping for a moment as he watched his lad busy with a pitchfork, mucking out the calf shed into a wheelbarrow.

Ethan looked up from his work, after hearing the horses and cart come into the yard. 'Father, I knew you would come. Before you do anything, I'm sorry if I've upset you.'

'Too bloody right, lad. And aye, well, you know why I'm here.' Jethro dropped his horses' reins and strode over to his son, undoing his thick leather belt from around his waist and wrapping the buckle end around his fist.

Ethan cringed and cowered back into the calf shed. He knew all too well what his father's temper was like, when pushed. He stood with his back against the wall.

'I'm too old for that now, Father, you can't belt me any more. I didn't do any harm. Rosie and I just had a day away together, that's all.'

'Rosie, is it? It's "Miss Atkinson" to you, lad.' Jethro raised his left hand and slapped Ethan across the face and then, with the belt buckle round his right hand, belted Ethan again and again over his back, as his son begged for him to stop. 'You'll show the Atkinson family some respect. You owe your very existence to them. Know your place, lad, and leave their young women alone.' The belt cracked repeatedly on Ethan's back, cutting through his shirt and raising blood across his back.

Jethro stood over his son, who lay sprawled in the manure of the calf shed, shaking with fear at his father's wrath, not daring to fight back.

'Miss Rosie is not for you, lad, and the sooner you realize that the better. And as for finding that grandfather of yours, get the idea out of your head because I hope he's dancing with the devil. He did nowt for my mother and nowt for me.'

'Jethro! Stop at once. There was no need to go that far,' shouted Danny across the farmyard, after hearing Ethan's screams from within the house. 'He only needed a word, not flaying to within an inch of his life.'

'Nay, words are wasted on him; he's been told once before. This time he knew what was coming.' Jethro picked up his cap from where it had fallen after his attack on his son. 'He'll not be giving you any more bother. Will you, lad?' Jethro scowled at his son and didn't show an ounce of pity.

111

Ethan looked up at Danny Atkinson, with his bloodied back against the whitewashed walls of the calf shed and tears in his eyes, and mumbled, 'No, sir, I know my place.' But within him still flashed defiance. He dared to look at Jethro, who was grovelling next to his master, instead of being proud of his son. No wonder his father was still just a groom; he had no ambition and didn't dare to dream. Ethan vowed that would be the last beating he would ever take from his father, or any man.

'Get yourself home, Jethro. Ethan, go up to your room above the stables and take care of yourself for the rest of the day. Mrs Atkinson will bring you a bite to eat.' Danny watched as Jethro mounted the steps to the cart and moved the horses out of the yard. It was a side to Jethro he had never seen before and didn't want to see again. The lad hadn't deserved such a belting. As his father had pointed out, neither of the youngsters were the worse for their trip away together. So why be so harsh?

Ethan pulled himself up and made his way slowly to the stables, climbing up the ladder to the warm, safe hayloft where his mattress lay in one corner. Lying down on it, he ran his finger over the welts that he could reach and looked at the blood on his fingers. He'd not let his father do that again. In fact he'd make a point of never seeing his father again, if he could help it. Nobody would tell him what to do from now on, unless it was worth his while. As for Rosie, well, she was still his girl. Belting or no belting.

*

'Ethan? Are you there, Ethan?' Rosie whispered into the darkness.

'Aye, I'm up here.' He crawled to the edge of the loft and looked down at Rosie in the dim light of the candle. She was in her nightshift, and her golden hair hung loose around her angelic face.

'I've brought some of my mother's best salve for your cuts. But they don't know I'm here. I've sneaked out while they are all asleep.' Rosie climbed up the wooden ladder in her bare feet, placing the candle and the pot of salve next to Ethan.

'They'll hang us, if they find us both together,' Ethan whispered as she sat down beside him.

'They'll not find out, if you are quiet. Now, take off your shirt and let me put this on your cuts.' Rosie unscrewed the lid of the pot and looked at the face of Ethan, who she knew had taken a beating for her. She ran her fingers gently over the welts and heard him gasp with pain as the salve seeped into his wounds. 'I'm sorry, Ethan, this is all my fault. It was me who bought the tickets, and me who thought it was a good idea.' She sat back into the darkness of the hay-loft as she watched him replace his tattered shirt.

'I'd do it all again, just for you to visit me like you are tonight.' Ethan leaned over to Rosie and pulled her towards him. 'My father was wrong: we are not that dissimilar. Kiss me, Rosie. Let them not part us, no matter what our differences.'

Rosie looked across at the lad she knew she had feelings for. She knew she shouldn't have, but she closed her eyes and waited for the kiss she had been dreaming of.

She held Ethan tightly and kissed his lips, before drawing back from his arms as she caught her breath.

'I'll have to go,' she whispered. 'They might miss me.' She liked the feel of Ethan's warm, firm hands on her body, and knew that if she stayed any longer it would be asking for trouble. She picked up the candle and climbed down the ladder, looking up at the face she knew she loved, before disappearing into the night.

Ethan watched the small flame blend into the darkness. Now that was a dream worth chasing, and one that merited the thrashing of his life.

9

Isabelle sat back in her office chair and gazed out of the window. Papers and invoices were strewn over her desk, along with cloth samples and designs. She was snowed under with work, but still she could not concentrate on the tasks in hand. Something was wrong with James, but she didn't quite know what. Ever since they had moved to Windfell, he had been more distant towards her. Perhaps he missed the busy streets of Settle, as he did seem to be going out walking on his own more of late.

She picked up the latest pattern books from Viyella and looked at them, barely giving the latest fashion of hobble skirts a second look before throwing the books back on the desk; she just couldn't settle. She decided to take a walk through the store, which usually made her feel more relaxed and ready to take on her duties. She'd go and see how Bert was getting on with Jane, down in the warehouse, after visiting each department.

'Morning, Mrs Fox.' The waitress quickly curtsied

and then went about her business as she served the demanding visitors in the upstairs tea-room.

'Morning, Grace.' Isabelle prided herself that she knew every one of her staff and always made a point of remembering their names. Heads turned as she walked around her welcoming tea-room. She spoke to the people she knew, and watched as they ate delicately cut sandwiches or fancies and cream cakes while chatting to their friends and neighbours. Atkinson's was the place to be seen, and the clientele reflected this, with only the best-dressed people and the highly reputable eating there.

'Isabelle, my dear, how lovely to see you. I trust you are keeping well?' Lady Crofts caught her by the wrist.

'Yes, thank you, extremely well. And you?' Isabelle smiled at the round-figured elderly woman, who was known by everyone and was a terrible gossip.

'Yes, I'm fine, dear. Just enjoying some of your delicious cakes with my friends. We were all hoping to catch a glimpse of that husband of yours – he's a dashing fellow and such a charmer.' Lady Crofts smiled and looked round at the group of ladies, who hung on her every word.

'I'm afraid he is in Leeds today, at our shop in the Queens Arcade, along with my new seamstress. They won't be back until much later.' Isabelle smiled and looked around at the wealthily dressed group, most of whom were clad in her designs.

'That's such a pity, my dear, but still we have enjoyed spending a moment with you. And we just needed an excuse to visit your store and catch up with any news over a nice cup of tea.' Lady Crofts picked up her teacup and took a long sip, before turning her back on Isabelle, putting an end to their conversation.

Isabelle walked away and made for the doorway before looking back at the group, who were intent on gossiping. She noticed that they were all looking at her as she left the busy tea-room, and she smiled. If they were talking about her, then at least they were leaving someone else alone. And what they didn't know they made up, she thought, as she made her way down to the warehouse.

'Now, you are in bother, lass – your mother's come to check up on you.' Bert Bannister looked across at his new ward, Jane, who was busy unpacking the latest consignment of Devon Violets perfume and moaning about how much she hated the smell.

'How's Jane doing, Bert?' Isabelle leaned over the packing table and looked at the old man and her daughter, who seemed bored.

'She's alright; could perhaps do with working upstairs for a while, in the perfume department, seeing as she loves the scent she is unpacking at the moment.' Bert grinned at Jane. If her mother had not been there, she would have pulled a face at her instructor, knowing that she could get away with it, as Bert was more a family friend than an employee.

'I just don't know why anyone would wish to smell so sickly. It's so sweet.' Jane blew the packing straw off yet another bottle and straightened the green ribbon around its neck.

'Violets were your grandmother's favourite flowers,

along with primroses. She always had to have a bunch on her desk, once spring was upon us.' Bert looked across at Jane and smiled.

'You miss her, don't you, Bert? We all do. In fact, since her death I can't seem to turn my hand to anything with vigour,' Isabelle confessed.

'It's only to be expected; she held everyone together and was always there for them. A good woman, that's what she was.' Bert shook his head as he thought about days past.

'I've some good news anyway, Bert. Harriet and her family are visiting us on Wednesday. James is to take a family photograph, and then I hope to try and persuade Harriet that the firm still needs her.' Isabelle looked around her and watched as a carter dropped off his load for Bert and his small team to unload and unpack. Bert just had to look at the two warehouse men for them to know what was expected of them.

'It will be good to see Miss Harriet back with us. It's what your mother would have wanted. How old is her youngest now? I lose track of time.' He looked across at Isabelle, remembering when the two sisters-in-law used to work together.

'She's one next week. That's why I thought a photograph of the children was apt.' Isabelle smiled.

'Aye, that'll mean a lot to Miss Harriet. Especially since the two twins died. It broke her heart and she's never been the same since, despite going on to have more family. You never get over the loss of a child. My old lass and me have lost two – one at birth and one who was just not born right. They were always sickly, but we still remember them.' Bert looked across at young Jane and smiled. 'Is Mr Fox at Leeds today with Madge Burton? They were saying upstairs that she's quite a good seamstress.'

'Yes, James has a full day of bookings, and Madge is meeting the manager at the shop in Queens Arcade. I thought it was time she made herself known to him. They went on the seven o'clock train together this morning.' Isabelle twiddled with the string that sat on the packing bench and thought about James and his visit to Leeds with Madge. He hadn't wanted to go with her, and had made such a fuss when he left her that morning.

'She's a bonny woman, is Madge; she could do with finding herself a good single man.' Bert's face clouded over.

'You don't always have to be dependent on a man,' young Jane spouted up. 'Women should be independent. I don't think I will ever marry.'

Both looked across at the young lass with a mind of her own.

'Jane, will you stop reading the rubbish that the stupid women of the Women's Social and Political Union keep feeding you? Of course you will marry; it is what is expected of you, when the right man comes along.' Isabelle sighed.

'The times are changing, Mistress Isabelle, even I know that. Better to be single than unhappily married.' Bert looked at his mistress, who was oblivious to all the gossip within the store, which he had tried to ignore.

'Well, I never thought I'd hear that, Bert Bannister:

you telling me, at your age, to move with the times. It must be working with our Jane; you must have heard too many of her radical ideas.' Isabelle stood back and looked at the pair who were trying to tell her the way of the world.

'Aye, well, sometimes we can't see what's going on under our own noses, and I'm as guilty as the next man of that.' Bert walked over to the consignment of goods that had just arrived and thought better of saying anything about his concerns. After all, it was only idle gossip that he'd heard and there was always plenty of that in Atkinson's department store.

10

James Fox sat across from the new love in his life and did not feel one bit guilty for his thoughts about the sweet-faced young woman who had captured his heart.

'I can't believe we are travelling to Leeds together, James, and that your wife knows and doesn't suspect a thing.' Madge giggled and looked at her employer, and the man she had made it her business to fall in love with.

'Ssshh! Keep your voice down. Nearly everyone knows me on this train, as I make this journey regularly. Anyway you've to meet the manager at Queens Arcade, and I have a full morning of photography. The afternoon, however, will be ours to spend as we please, and I can think of lots of ways to pass an hour or two.' James winked at the young blonde-haired woman with cupid-bow lips and come-to-bed eyes, and couldn't believe that someone her age would possibly look at a middle-aged man with greying hair. A slight pang of guilt caught him by surprise when he thought of Isabelle, hard at work in the main store at Skipton; but he shook it off as Madge smiled at him in such a seductive way that all thoughts of guilt were banished. If only Isabelle would look at him that way and have time for him, instead of being hard-headed and caught up in her work. It was always the children, Atkinson's or Windfell; there was no time in Isabelle's life for him. Or at least that was how it felt.

This afternoon he would enjoy his time with Madge, who showed him quite openly the love he craved. He'd booked a room at the new Queens Hotel at the station, which wasn't out of the ordinary, as he had stayed there in the recent past when he was needed for more than one day in the studio at Leeds. He was going to make the most of his day with the alluring Madge, and no one need be any the wiser. He smiled as his new flame looked out of the window at the passing countryside. The after-noon could not come soon enough – a bottle of cham-pagne and a nice double bed were already calling him away from his work.

Nearly a week had passed since James and Madge had shared an afternoon of illicit passion together, and Madge was beginning to wonder about the true reason for Isabelle's invitation for Harriet and her family to visit Atkinson's.

'What's Harriet like? Is she like your wife?' Madge looked out of the window of the photographic studio down onto the busy High Street of Skipton, while quiz-zing James about the impending visit of his sister-in-law and her family.

'Oh Lord, no! She's anything but. Harriet is very

maternal – her family is everything to her. She's not material in the least.' He looked across at the woman he was besotted with, as he made ready for the Atkinson family photograph. 'Why do you ask?'

'I just wondered. Everyone seems to be talking about Harriet with a wistful fondness and, as I've never met her, I am curious. And, if I'm truthful, a little worried, as everyone says she is an expert seamstress. Your wife won't be replacing me with her, will she?' Madge turned to face James and looked at him with a worried expression.

'Madge, my dear, whatever gave you that idea? Isabelle would not replace you – I'd not let her.' James walked over to her and ran his hand down her back and kissed her on the cheek. 'My wife is just hoping that now her mother has died, Harriet will come back to the fold, as it were. She needs Harriet's support when it comes to running the firm, until Jane shows more interest.' James let go of Madge and looked out of the window. 'There's Harriet, over on the other side of the street, with baby Georgina in her arms and her daughter Rosie and son Ben. They are making their way here, so you'd better make yourself scarce.' James held her at arm's length and quickly glanced around the studio to make sure everything was in place for the photo he was about to take. 'Go on, get back to your dressmaking before you are missed.' He patted Madge fondly on her bottom.

'It's just that I know some of the workers in Atkinson's don't like me. I hear them whispering about me, and have done ever since I arrived here.' Madge turned into James's arms and looked up into his face.

'You imagine it, my dear. Besides, they are always gossiping about somebody on the shop floor. It's the nature of shop girls; too busy living somebody else's lives, when they should be living their own.' James pushed her away. 'Go on, get gone.'

'But—' Madge stopped quickly as the door opened.

'There you are! Mrs Middleton is waiting in the fitting room. Had you forgotten your eleven o'clock appointment? And what are you doing here?' Isabelle looked angrily at Madge. She'd had to pacify Mrs Middleton with a free cup of tea, as she and Jane had scoured the building for Madge.

'It's my fault, dear. I asked Madge to give me hand putting up the backdrop for Harriet's photograph. That will be all, Madge, you had better go quickly and see to Mrs Middleton.' James dismissed her without blinking and smiled tenderly at his wife.

'Yes, sir.' Madge curtsied and quickly gave him a loving smile behind Isabelle's back.

'Really, James, you have Jane to help you with little jobs like that. Don't drag Madge away from her duties again. She is already a bad timekeeper and doesn't need any further encouragement to get behind with her work,' Isabelle said haughtily, glancing around the studio.

'Harriet is on her way. I've just seen her and the family cross the road. It will be good to see them here. There was a time when I didn't think she would ever step into Atkinson's again.' James quickly changed the subject and walked to line up the camera with the backdrop, ready for the family shot.

'I'm glad we have made up and that I decided to show Harriet some sympathy. Madge has such an air of superiority about her, as if she has no respect for me. Even though she is excellent with a needle, I often think I'd prefer to work with Harriet, if I could persuade her to return to the fold. After all, she is part owner, and Mother would have approved. I only hope she has forgotten now the words that we both said in anger. I personally regret every word I said.' Isabelle stood with her hands on her hips and watched as James played with the lens, getting the focus right.

'Don't even consider it, Isabelle! All the times I have heard you cursing Harriet and her family for letting you down. Besides, Harriet wouldn't leave her youngest. Georgina's not quite one yet.' James turned and looked sternly at his wife. Madge had read the situation correctly and Isabelle was plotting her downfall.

'We'll see. I'm going to try and tempt Harriet back, despite what you say. Perhaps with a little sweetener at first. Now, if you'll excuse me, I'll go downstairs and greet them.' Isabelle looked at her husband, whose face was set sternly.

'I'll be late home tonight. I thought I might go and look at the new motorcycles that Pratt's are displaying. I've had my eye on one for a while, and now I think I may treat myself,' James shouted after her.

'What on earth do you want one of those for? They are noisy, dirty things; they will never catch on.' Isabelle stood in the doorway and sighed. 'I suppose you will suit yourself, despite what I have to say about it.' She lingered there and then decided not to wait for a reply, as she heard her guests coming up the stairs. James would do as he chose, and at the moment seemed to be his own master. She was getting tired and a little worried about him and his changing ways.

Rosie stood alongside her mother. She'd been told to put on her best clothes and had protested while Harriet put a ribbon in her hair. She hated the ribbon, it made her look like a child. The big pink satin bow hung down at the side of her head and irritated her, as she stood in front of the camera with her mother and siblings. She tried to smile, as her Uncle James made silly comments so that they all laughed, but it didn't help that Jane was standing at the back of the room looking every inch the young lady, while in her own eyes Rosie looked stupid. But she tried her best. The sooner it was over, the sooner she could go home, so she forced a smile as the shot was taken.

'There, that wasn't too bad now, was it, children?' Harriet looked round at her family and ushered them off the make-believe set of a grand house, and smiled as Isabelle took baby Georgina from her arms. 'Rosie, are you going to go with Jane? I think she wants to show you around the firm. I'm going to have tea with Aunt Isabelle and will take Ben and Georgina with me; you can both join us when you've seen enough.'

Jane looked almost as excited about taking Rosie under her wing as Rosie herself did. In truth, neither girl particularly liked the other, but both knew they had to be polite in their parents' company.

'Yes, Mama.' Rosie walked over to Jane, who scowled

at her as she opened the door, leaving the adults talking and Ben seeing how the camera worked with his Uncle James.

'Don't you think you are a bit too old for wearing ribbons?' Jane looked at her cousin and smirked. 'I haven't worn ribbons since I left school.'

Rosie reached her hand up to her hair and pulled the offending satin bow out of her blonde locks. 'Mama made me wear it. I hate the thing.' She shoved the ribbon into her pocket and walked down the stairs onto the shop floor, trying to walk as elegantly as her cousin. 'Is Luke not here today?' Rosie enquired.

'All Luke thinks about at the moment is the Officers' Training Corps that he's volunteered for. He's always down at Giggleswick School, even in his holidays. And if he's not there, he's over at the outdoor range they've got at Attermire Scar. He's even got his own rifle. Mother hates seeing him cleaning it; she's frightened he will fire the thing, even though he's told her that he is allowed only blank cartridges.' Jane stopped at the bottom of the stairs and waited for her cousin. 'Luke's not fit to look after himself, let alone be in possession of a gun, if you ask me.'

'I think I can hear them firing when I'm at the top of Moughton Scar – at least, that's what Ethan says it is. You can hear the guns distantly above the skylarks singing, they disturb the peace up there,' Rosie said innocently.

'You walk up Moughton Scar with Ethan! He's only a stable boy, you know, you shouldn't even talk to him.' Jane looked with disdain as she weaved in and out of the customers, making her way to the warehouse and delivery bay.

'Grandfather says we all come from the same maker, and no one's better than anyone else. Besides, Ethan and I are good friends, he likes the same things as I do.' Rosie blushed.

'He's a dirty gypsy. One you should keep your eye on. I certainly would not want him near me.' Jane opened the warehouse doors for Rosie to pass by her and, as she did so, Rosie looked her snobbish cousin up and down.

Jane might be better dressed than her, in a pin-tucked, high-collared white blouse adorned by a silver brooch and a tight beige skirt, with her hair piled high upon her head, but she was not a nice person. In fact she could be downright vicious. From now on, Rosie would not mention Ethan's name to her ever again.

'Miss Rosie, I meant to talk to you at your grandmother's funeral, but I never got the chance.' Bert Bannister looked across from his bench and smiled at the young woman he'd known all her life. 'I heard that you and your family were coming to visit, so a good thing may have come out of your grandmother's passing. It will be good to see your mother taking an interest in the firm again.'

'Thank you, Mr Bannister. We are only here for a few hours, but it is nice to be able to look around at where my mother once worked alongside Aunt Isabelle.' Rosie smiled at the old man whom her grandmother had revered.

'She did more than work here, lass. She was the one who built it, along with Miss Isabelle. They worked well together

128

back then; it was a shame bad things got in the way of their happiness.' Bert breathed in deeply and thought of all the years and bad feelings that had built up since the opening of Atkinson's department store.

'It was Grandmama's store – she was the one with the money. Atkinson's is nothing to do with Rosie or her side of the family,' Jane said curtly.

'Nay, that's where you are wrong, lass. Archie, your grandfather, pulled his weight alongside his Lottie. They worked together, and he was her prop. She might have had the brass, but Archie was the rudder that steered your grandmother's ship, keeping her straight. Rosie has as much right to be here than any one of us – she's a true Atkinson.' Bert grinned and patted Rosie on the shoulder. 'Here, I've something for you: a bottle of your grandmother's favourite perfume, "Devon Violets". We couldn't put it out on the shelf because the label is torn, and Jane here doesn't like it, so I kept it to one side, thinking I'd give it to my old woman. But it's more right for you, as violets were what your grandfather always picked his Lottie in the spring.' Bert smiled and looked at the delight on Rosie's face as she glanced at the little green bottle with a violet ribbon attached.

'It stinks, I don't know how anyone can wear it,' growled Jane as she watched Rosie place the precious bottle in her pocket.

'It can't smell that badly – it's one of our leading sellers, Miss Jane. Perhaps it is a matter of differing tastes.' Bert grinned. 'Now, I'd better get on with my work, but do mention me to your mother, Rosie, and tell her that I'm glad to see her back within these walls.'

'I will, Mr Bannister, and thank you for the perfume.' Rosie smiled.

'No problem, lass. I know it's gone to a good home, someone who will appreciate it.' He threw a knowing look at Jane as he made his way down to the bottom of the warehouse.

'I think old Bert is losing it a bit; all he talks about is the good old days. He never talks about the here and now, and it is always about Grandmama and when he first worked for her. I swear he doesn't like me, although he seems to like you well enough, giving you some of Mother's products to take home with you.' Jane looked at Rosie, who was handling her precious gift.

'I can give it back to you, if Bert shouldn't have given me it. I don't want to get him into trouble.' Rosie touched the bottle and hoped that she could keep it.

'No, Mama won't mind. It's only cheap stuff and, as I say, it stinks, despite what Bert says. I wouldn't be seen dead wearing it.' Jane put her nose in the air and walked through the shop floor, strutting like a prize peacock, ignoring the shop girls and smiling a sickly grin at the customers she knew. 'We only attract the best customers at Atkinson's; they deserve the best, and that is what I will definitely give them, once the store is mine.'

Rosie listened and watched as her cousin showed her all the way round the store. She was amazed at all that was on offer and at the number of customers the goods attracted, but what also amazed her was Jane's arrogance.

She only worked in the warehouse with Bert and was still learning the job, with fewer responsibilities than she herself had back at Crummock Farm. Jane's mother might own most of the firm, but Rosie's mother owned a part of it, too – a fact that Jane was definitely overlooking. Rosie breathed out with relief when they finally climbed the stairs to join their parents in the tea-room. She'd had enough of the precious Jane and her forthright views, and was ready for home.

'So, I can't entice you back for a day or two each week? Just to take fittings and help Madge Burton, while I look over the accounts and do the other things that I now find myself doing.' Isabelle lifted her teacup to her lips, curling her little finger elegantly as she sipped.

'I'm sorry, but no, those days have gone. I've got the children and the farm and, now that Archie is living with us, he takes looking after as well. He's not as good on his legs as he used to be.' Harriet shook her head. She had been tempted as she looked through the design books and at work in progress in the busy cutting room. It had reminded her of the love she had once felt for her work. But she knew her place was at Crummock, helping Danny with the farm and bringing up her children.

'You could bring baby Georgina with you, and you need only work when Ben is at school. Surely Rosie is old enough to take on some more responsibilities, like my Jane? After all, she's not far off seventeen.' Isabelle smiled at her sister-in-law. She'd noticed the glint in Harriet's eye as she looked around the cutting and fitting room; there

131

was still a love of fashion running through her veins. A love that she aimed to rekindle.

'Rosie has enough on. Besides, she helps her father more than me, as she loves the farm more than housework.' Harriet smiled at her daughter and caught a smirk on Jane's face; a smirk that she would have liked to wipe off it, if Jane's mother had not been there.

'Well, think about it. You don't have to decide here and now. I'm just glad we are back on better terms with one another, and that I had the chance to tell you how much I have missed you.' Isabelle looked across at Rosie. 'You know, your mother is a wonderful seamstress – a hundred times better than the one I've got at present. I do wish that you'd try to persuade her, my dear.'

Rosie glanced at her mother and then smiled at her aunt. She knew why her mother didn't want to return to work at Atkinson's. It was true, Harriet did live for her children and the farm, but Rosie also knew that deep down Harriet did not want to become involved in family politics again. That was what had torn the family apart previously, and it was likely to continue to put strain on the situation for some time, if Jane was ever put in charge of the firm.

'It's up to Mother, Aunt Isabelle, but I will try and persuade her, if you wish,' said Rosie. She glanced at her dark-faced uncle, who definitely did not look amused at her aunt's suggestion.

'Thank you, my dear. I hope Jane looked after you this afternoon? She's such a well-mannered young lady that I'm sure she did. I think I've taught her well.' Isabelle glanced at her daughter.

'She was the perfect host, Aunt Isabelle, thank you,' said Rosie. Although she didn't enjoy it, she could play the game as well as anyone else.

11

'Well, how did you go on today with Isabelle?' Danny looked across the table at Harriet.

'Alright. I think she wants me to come back and join her again.' Harriet looked at her father-in-law as he grunted.

'Missing her mother's work already, is she? She never was one for hard work.' Archie looked up from his supper plate and thought of the hours that his darling Lottie had given to Atkinson's. The hours that his stepdaughter was now beginning to appreciate.

'I might be wrong, but I don't think she likes her new seamstress, although even I found her a bit demanding. She's only young, but she has this air of complete confidence about her.' Harriet had not been impressed by her first meeting with Madge. It had only been brief, but she could see why Madge perhaps did not fit into the ethics of Atkinson's.

'It's called being young, my dear. Can't you remember

when you and Isabelle had your first shop in Settle? You would have taken on the world, back then. Besides, our Isabelle can be a funny one, and you of all people should know that.' Danny sat back in his chair and smiled at Harriet. 'Would you like to go back and do a few hours? It would probably do you good. Rosie can do a bit more around the house, and we could always get somebody else in for a few days. I can tell that you've missed it – you look full of life this evening.' Danny was pleased that Harriet had enjoyed her day with his stepsister. It had been a long time in coming, but the wounds were gradually healing.

'I don't know, I'll think about it. Georgina is still so young. Perhaps in another few years; then it gives Rosie more time to enjoy her life before settling down in her own marriage and home.' Harriet drank her tea and smiled.

'Where is Rosie anyway? I know Ben and Georgina are in bed, but Rosie is usually around the table with us.' Danny breathed in and watched as his father finished his supper.

'She asked if she could take some bread and cheese and a piece of bannock for her supper. She's been cooped up with Jane all day today, and you know she hates not being outside, so she said she was going for a wander before it gets dark. She'll not have gone far, she'll be back before nightfall.' Harriet stood up and collected the dirty plates.

'I'd want to be out and all, if I'd been with Jane all day,' said Archie. 'I used to think she took after my

Lottie, but lately she's got an edge to her. One I don't like. I think I might have to bring her up sharply soon. She should be a kinder soul. Not everyone is as privileged as her, she should remember that,' he commented as he made his way from the kitchen table to his usual resting place next to the kitchen fire. He sat down in his trusted Windsor chair and reached for his pipe from above the fireplace. 'She does right, does Rosie. She needs a bit of fresh mountain air to clear her head of all the sarcastic remarks she will have had to have put up with today. I don't blame her.' He lit his pipe with a spill and leaned back and looked at his son. 'She's like you, is your Rosie. Happy with the land, and doesn't want owt else.'

'She's growing up, Father. Soon lads will be coming a-calling.' Danny joined his father, sitting across from him next to the fire.

'Time enough for that yet, lad. Let her enjoy trailing the fells first. Then she can find herself a fella.' Archie puffed on his pipe, content with his lot. He loved Rosie; she was a grand lass and he hoped she would stay young and innocent for as long as possible, God willing.

'I thought you were never coming!' Ethan propped himself up on one elbow and looked across at Rosie as she ran across the clapper bridge to the grassy bank where he lay.

'I couldn't make it too obvious. Besides, I'd the dogs to feed and the eggs to collect, as I'd missed doing that this morning, with going to Skipton.' Rosie sat down beside him and kissed him quickly on the cheek. 'Don't complain anyway, I've brought us both our suppers. Mother said I'd to help myself to cheese and bread and a bannock, so I made sure there was enough for both of us.' She untied the napkin that held their supper and laid the contents out amongst the grass and flowers that grew on the banks of the river at the wash-dubs.

'That looks bloody good. Here, let me supply the pudding.' Ethan leaned over to the side of the dry lime-stone wall that stood behind him and pulled some small wild bilberries from the stumpy, wiry bush that grew below it. 'And this is for my girl, to match her eyes.' He leaned over again and picked a sky-blue scabious, then placed it behind Rosie's ear, kissing her as he did so and touching her cheeks lovingly with his hand.

'We shouldn't, Ethan, we vowed we would just be good friends.' Rosie blushed and looked coyly at him.

'I can't help it – you know I can't. I feel different when I'm with you. I couldn't stop thinking about you all day. This evening couldn't come quick enough.' Ethan kissed her again and held her in his arms.

'Me, too. I hated my time with Jane. She is such a clever devil, but, in all honesty, knows nothing.' Rosie lay back in Ethan's arms. His breath was slow and sure next to her and she let her fingers trace the opening of his shirt, which revealed the dark hairs of his chest.

'Don't! Now you are teasing and I don't think I can control myself.' Ethan sighed. 'You know, I do think a lot of you. But you also know that what we are doing is wrong – your father and grandfather would kill me, as

137

would my father. Well, you saw last time what my own father would do to me.'

'Well, they are not about to find out. I'm not going to say anything, and who else is there to witness our meetings? I think I love you, Ethan, I really do.' Rosie rolled onto her side and looked into his eyes as she opened his shirt more and ran her hands over his chest as she kissed him.

'Rosie, my Rosie, we shouldn't, you know we shouldn't.' He breathed in deeply and kissed her hard on the mouth, before rolling her onto her back and lying upon her. 'I'll be gentle, I promise. This is our secret,' he whispered as he pulled her skirts up and undid his buttons. He'd been waiting for this moment all summer and could resist no longer.

'You do love me, don't you, Ethan?' Rosie whispered, her heart pounding as he could hold back no longer. But Ethan didn't reply, he just kissed her and carried on undoing his trousers, before entering her and taking over her body with every thrust that he made. She winced with both the pain and the thrill of having sex with her wild lover. 'You do love me. Don't you?' she whispered again. But Ethan still didn't reply, as he put his finger to her mouth and smiled down at her. She'd given herself willingly to him and now he was making sure he enjoyed his innocent farm girl.

The bread and cheese had gone stale in the dying summer's sun, untouched and unwanted, as they lay back in one another's arms and thought about what they had just done.

Rosie pulled her skirts down and didn't know if she wanted to cry or laugh. She'd taken part in something that, up until now, she had only seen animals do, but she knew what the consequences might be. She lay back and worried. It had been her fault, as she had teased Ethan; she should have known what she was leading him towards, and that a decent woman would have waited until they were married.

'What if I'm . . .?' She turned and looked at Ethan.

'You won't be, I pulled out in time. You'll be fine – stop worrying. That's the last thing we both need. I'm not that daft.' Ethan sat up and looked across the trickling stream as a dragonfly darted and skimmed over the waters in the dying light. In truth, he didn't know for certain, but he hoped nothing would come of the dalliance. 'The sun's going down, you'd better be off, or else you'll have to answer to your father.' He got up onto his feet and offered Rosie his hand. She took it and pulled herself up next to him. 'Stop worrying, you'll be fine.' He kissed her on her cheek.

'I'm sure I will, but I can't help worrying. I shouldn't have egged you on; it was my fault.' Rosie smoothed her skirts and threw the wasted bread and cheese into the river, before picking up the napkin.

'It was both our faults,' Ethan said, as he kissed her once more. 'Now, get yourself home. I'll walk up by the Wharfe track, just in case someone comes looking for you. You go up the home track, it's not as far.' He held her at arm's length and noticed she was near crying. 'Don't cry, you'll be fine.'

'I know, but if I'm not . . . you'll stand by me?' Rosie whispered.

'Of course. But it hasn't come to that yet. Now, go.' Ethan watched as Rosie balanced over the clapper bridge and made her way home along the lane. He stood and looked over to the rocky outcrop of Norber and watched the sun slowly sink, filling the sky with oranges and pinks as it disappeared from sight.

What had he done? He didn't even know if he did love her, in truth. Rosie was just a young girl, and he had known she would be an easy first conquest. Tomorrow he would tell her not to visit him in the loft. After all, the Irishmen were coming to help with hay-time and he didn't want them knowing their secret. It would give them both time to come to their senses.

12

'Doesn't Luke look smart? Just look at him in his uniform, like a true soldier.' Isabelle gazed proudly at her young son, dressed in his latest cadet's uniform, with his Lee Enfield rifle strapped over his shoulder. He stood in front of both of his parents in his khaki breeches and tunic, peaked cap, knee-length puttees and brown leather boots, loaded down with belts and ammunition pouches. The brass badges on his shoulders and cap, stamped with 'Giggleswick OTC School', shone in the sun.

'I'm lucky to have got this rifle.' Luke grinned. 'My mate Palmer still has to use his old Martini–Henri carbine, which is really heavy to carry when you have the full kit on, and it only fires blanks.' He touched and stroked his rifle lovingly and smiled at his father as he did so.

'Just mind what you are doing with the thing. I never have liked guns. I still can't believe that Giggleswick School has been given a sub-target machine. I don't think they should really be offering military training. I really don't believe in this wave of militarism that is sweeping through the school.' James looked up from his paper and scowled at his young son. 'Besides, that uniform has cost all of thirty shillings, and that is on top of the subscription of seven-and-six, and the use of that damn rifle at two-and-six per term. You'd think we were made of money. And for what – for our son to learn to kill someone or perhaps be killed, if a war comes?'

'James, we are not at war, nor likely to be. This makes our Luke happy and he's good at it. Captain Pierce said Luke was one of this year's leading cadets. He's already put his name down to go to Hagley Park next year, to train with cadets from Eton and Harrow and elsewhere in the country. You should be proud of him.' Isabelle smiled at Luke, who looked a little crestfallen. 'Luke, sing your father the song that I heard you and the other cadets singing about Giggleswick forming a military band – you know, the one that is sung along to the tune of "The British Grenadiers".'

'Do I have to, Mother? Father is obviously not impressed.' Luke stood uncomfortably and ran his finger around his high-collared tunic.

'Yes, go on, and then he will understand the pride that you boys have in being an officer-in-training at Giggleswick.'

James sighed as his son stood awkwardly in front of him and started to sing:

142

'Our numbers have increased this term; our
Recruitment Sergeant's grand.
To make us quite complete, we lack but a stirring
military band;
And if our CO speaks the truth, next term
there'll surely be
An ear-splitting Rat-a-plan, Toot, Toot, Toot,
from the Giggleswick OTC.'

Luke breathed in deeply as he finished and looked across at his father, waiting for any praise that might come his way.

'Perhaps you would be better joining that band, instead of being so handy with that gun of yours. But, as per usual, your mother will decide, and I will not be listened to.' James rose from his seat and walked away from his wife and son, who was intent on going down the military path even though there was unrest in the world. Neither of them knew what they were doing; to Luke, it was just a game, and in Isabelle's eyes he was doing something she could be proud of.

'Don't listen to your father, he's just in one of his moods. You concentrate on doing as well as you can in all your subjects, and with the OTC. I can see you making an officer, if what Captain Pierce says is correct.' Isabelle smiled at her son.

'Yes, Mother, I enjoy my role in the cadets. I feel that I'm doing something special for my country. And Father is right that we are training in case war ever comes, but

I'm not even seventeen yet, so I'd be too young to go anyway.'

'Don't talk of such things. War will never happen, despite the war in the Balkans, and Germany building up its naval fleet. Prime Minister Asquith is anti-war, and he'll not let Britain get drawn into anything. You enjoy the training. I'll settle your father down, and he'll come round to the idea.' Isabelle watched as her son left the room. Perhaps James was right, and perhaps Luke should not be training as a soldier; but as Archie had said, it was giving her boy discipline and a purpose in life, and Luke was good at it.

James walked out of Windfell, slamming the door behind him as he put on his jerkin and new motorcycle goggles. He needed to get away from his family, and his new acqui-sition was calling him – as well as his mistress – as he strode across the pebbled driveway to where it stood.

'Going for a ride out, sir?' Jethro looked at his master, dressed in his new attire, and watched as he lovingly rubbed his hands along the handlebars of his motorcycle.

'I am, Jethro. I thought I'd have a ride down the road and happen up to Ingleton. I'm still getting used to what my machine can do. Isn't it beautiful?' James stood back and looked at the Scott motorcycle that he had acquired through the new motorcycle company based in Saltaire. 'She's a twin-stroke, you know? I've got her to go as fast as thirty miles an hour – it feels like you are flying.' James smiled at Jethro, who was shaking his head.

'You'd not get me on the back of one of them. Give

me a horse any day. They are a lot less noisy, for a start, and probably more reliable. And I haven't got a clue what a twin-stroke is, so you're wasting your breath telling me that.' Jethro thought nowt of the new machine that was his master's pride and joy. 'What do you want to go that fast for, anyway?' He watched as James put his leg over the motorcycle and beamed as he pulled his goggles down, before kick-starting it into action.

'Until you've done it, Jethro, you don't know what it feels like. Otherwise, you'd want to do it,' James shouted above the roar of the engine, urging it into action as Jethro looked on.

Jethro shook his head again as the smell of fumes filled the yard, and he listened as James and the motorcycle made their way out of the drive of Windfell Manor and down the road towards Settle. Give him a horse any day, not a noisy heap of metal. These young folk, with their new ideas, had no respect of the old ways. He shook his head again and made for his beloved horses; at least they showed him respect.

James sat back on the bike's seat. He could feel the purr of the engine beneath his legs. He felt he was completely in control of the machine. It made him feel like the man he had longed to be for some time, especially now that he had Madge hanging on his every word and giving him her complete attention, unlike Isabelle. His life was beginning to be more bearable.

He smiled to himself as he let out the bike's throttle to climb the steep hill – called Buckhaw Brow – outside the village of Giggleswick and then cut off along the rutted road to the small hamlet of Feizor. He couldn't wait to hear what Madge had to say, once she saw him on his motorcycle. He knew her reaction would be different from that of Isabelle, who had moaned about what it had cost and the fact that she had no intention of ever being seen on the thing. He made his way across the small ford that ran through the hamlet of Feizor and hoped that the motorcycle wouldn't splutter and fail as he came out the other side and drove it over the limestone roadway to the cottage where Madge lived.

'Oh, my Lord! you've gone and got one of those contraptions,' Madge squealed as she opened the door, wondering what the noise was outside her quiet home. 'You've come to see me on it. Everyone will be talking!' She giggled and screamed as she looked at her lover, whilst he took his goggles off and brushed back his greying hair. She gasped as she gazed at the bike in amazement, and then kissed James on the cheek. 'I've got to have a go on it, you've got to give me a ride!' she shouted as she walked around the bike, looking at every inch of it.

'I don't know, Madge. I'm only just learning to handle it myself. Besides, it's not very ladylike. You'd have to pull your skirts up and sit in tight next to me. What if someone sees you?' James looked shocked.

'I don't care, I've got to have a go.' Madge hoisted her skirts up and sat sharply on the small leather seat, holding James close to her on the back of the bike.

'Mind your legs – the exhaust is hot, it will burn them. Tuck your skirts in tight, I don't want them catching in the chain. I don't think we should do this, Madge.'

146

James breathed in deeply – he didn't want her to think he was not man enough to be seen with her behind him – and decided to kick-start his bike with her still on it. The closeness of her body to his made him forget his fears and he shouted above the roar of the engine, 'Hold on tight and remember, mind your skirts.'

They made their way unsteadily down the rough road from Feizor and then onto the better road that led back down Buckhaw Brow into Giggleswick and Settle. Madge laughed and screamed at every corner, as James tried to counterbalance the weight behind him, stopping at the top of the brow of the hill and looking down upon the slate roofs of the houses of Settle in the valley below.

'Go on – what have we stopped for? Take me down, I dare you!' Madge laughed and urged him on as she pulled her long, knotted scarf around her neck and checked her hair. 'Are you frightened that we might be seen? Or is it that the bike's too big for you?' She giggled, squeezing him tight.

'No, it's just that I shouldn't be on it with you. The bike's new to me. And I worry what people will think of you, if they see us together.' James put both of his feet on the ground and steadied the two of them.

'There's no one about. Look, you can see the road is clear almost until Settle. People are eventually going to know about us anyway, if your promise to leave Isabelle for me is true,' she cried. 'Go on, keep driving, then turn around and take me back home. I'll have had my thrills for the day by then.' Madge kissed him on the ear and hugged him close. 'Please,' she whispered. 'You know I love you.'

James breathed in deeply. Despite his better judgement, he fired the engine up and started down the hill. Madge screamed with delight and her scarf flew like a pennant behind her. The road dipped and the wind lessened, making the scarf fly low and limp, until it dragged downwards near the back-wheel sprocket and chain. She paid it no heed as the bike built up speed and she screamed with excitement. But all too quickly her screams of joy turned to screams of panic, as the scarf became entwined in the motorcycle's chain and back wheel, pulling at Madge's neck and making her unable to breathe. The scarf became more and more entwined as the motorbike picked up speed and dragged her from behind James. She tried to yell and scream and she clawed at James to save her, as she and the bike flew across the road, unseating James and leaving Madge, still and unbreathing, on the stony road of Buckhaw Brow. Battered and bleeding and with a broken neck, her body was lifeless. The scarf was still entwined in the gears of the motorbike, while its wheels continued to turn.

James lifted his head. His leg hurt and he could see that blood was beginning to pour and seep into his moleskin trousers, leaving a dark-red pool on the white of the stony road. 'Madge, Madge!' he yelled as he dragged himself across to her, every inch of road being more painful than the first. His face and arms became peppered with grit and stones as he pulled himself over to where Madge lay, and he realized that he must have broken his leg, as he pulled at the body of his love. He looked at the twisted scarf and the once-beautiful face of the carefree woman who had been so full of life until a few minutes before. Now she was covered with blood, bashed and torn as the bike pulled her underneath it.

'What have I done? I knew you shouldn't have got on it – you knew I was worried about your skirts. Why didn't you think to secure your scarf?' He sobbed and then winced in pain. The two loves of his life lay broken and exposed on the wild fellside, with the sun glistening on Madge's blonde hair and on the gleaming metal bike frame. James lay back and looked up at the sky. His head felt faint and his stomach was nauseous. God, what had he done? How was he ever going to live with himself? And how would he explain Madge's death to Isabelle? She'd never understand, and he knew she would never, ever forgive him.

13

'Dr Burrows has gone. He's happy with your progress.' Isabelle pulled the morning room's door to and sat down next to James. She glanced at him, sitting upright in his invalid chair, and breathed in deeply. She couldn't bear the sight of him at the moment; he'd bought shame on her family and, most of all, to her. They were the talk of the community.

James looked at Isabelle. She had hardly spoken to him since the afternoon the Bradley brothers had carried him into Windfell, after finding him unconscious and Madge dead and broken on the road at Buckhaw Brow.

'Isabelle, I'm sorry. How many times have I to tell you that I'm sorry?' James held out his hand for her to hold.

'Sorry – you're sorry. Sorry that you were found out, and that Madge Burton is dead because of your unfaithfulness. That's all you are sorry about. I should throw you out, along with that awful machine, but I've to think of our family. So just be grateful that you still have a roof over your head and that I'm even talking to you.' She glared at him.

'Madge meant nothing to me. I keep telling you: she just saw me riding my motorcycle on the road to Ingleton and begged for a ride. How could I refuse her? You know what she was like. I just wish both of us had not been so foolish.' James looked out of the window, unable to keep eye contact with her. He knew she knew that he was lying.

'So that's why all the locals are talking about you calling at Madge's door at all hours of the day and night. And I suppose there is a valid reason for all the staff at Atkinson's to be smirking and talking about your little tête-à-têtes with Madge behind my back. I must have been blind and stupid!' Isabelle pulled her handkerchief from her pocket and dabbed her eyes. 'This isn't the first time a man thinks that I'm too stupid to realize what's going on under my nose. But this time it's not going to get the better of me.'

'I don't think you are stupid. Honestly, there was nothing going on. People gossip, you know that. They put two and two together and make six. I just wish poor Madge was still alive to back me up. I'd do anything for her to be here, standing now in front of us both.' James sighed and tried to get comfortable in his invalid chair as he gingerly moved his splintered leg.

'I bet you do. I suppose you'd rather it was me they were burying on Tuesday, and not Madge. That would have been more convenient for you.' Isabelle breathed in deeply, waiting for the next round of attack.

151

'The funeral's set for Tuesday then. I must try and go.' James looked down at his broken leg.

'You will not even think of it. You've brought enough disgrace to this house, without showing up at her funeral. I personally hope she's rotting in hell, the little hussy. I gave her a good job, paid her well and gave her responsibilities. But no, Madge was not happy with that; she wanted my husband and, like a fool, he fell for her charms. To think that I even let you go to Leeds together. I bet, if I checked, there would be a room for that date at the Queens booked in your name. I'll go to the funeral. I'll hold my head up high and suffer the indignant looks that people will give me. We owe her parents that much at least.'

Isabelle turned round in her seat and opened the roll-top desk that her mother had sat at when she was alive; she couldn't help but think of how her mother must have felt when she discovered that Joseph Dawson, her husband and Isabelle's father, had another woman in his life. It had been the making of Charlotte Atkinson in the long run. She herself would just have to ensure that James had not endangered her family and all their futures.

'Aye, Isabelle, I've heard your news.' Danny looked across at his sister and felt for her.

Archie looked up from lighting his pipe and also looked at Isabelle. 'I'd never have thought James was capable of that. I always thought he'd eyes for nobody but you. Folk are awful gossips, and sometimes they get it wrong. It's a sad do that the lass died, like, but happen best that she's out of the picture, as it is.' Archie noticed

152

how crestfallen Isabelle appeared. Usually she was as hard as nails, but today she looked vulnerable.

'Father, I meant that we'd heard about Madge dying and that James broke his leg. Not the other rubbish that folk are gossiping and saying.' Danny quickly corrected his father and gave a pleading look for help to Harriet, as she placed a cup of tea down beside her sister-in-law.

'You don't have to pussyfoot around me. I know the stories and I can tell you now that they are probably true, although at the moment James denies it all. But I can tell when he's lying, and he has not been acting himself these last few months, so I knew something was wrong, but didn't know what.' Isabelle pulled off her crocheted gloves and took a sip of her tea. 'I just hope the children don't hear. People can be so cruel, and I have made a few enemies of late. It's not easy following in Mother's footsteps.'

'Oh, Isabelle, I'm so sorry. You must be hurting. I would really like to say what I think to James and give him a piece of my mind. I knew I didn't like that Madge as soon as I saw her at Atkinson's. There was just something about her, as if she had one-up over everybody else. I shouldn't talk ill of the dead, but that is how I felt, as if she was superior to us.' Harriet put her hand on Isabelle's arm and squeezed it lovingly.

'I've been blind, but life goes on. We will have to try and make the best of it. I think, looking back, that Bert Bannister tried to tell me a few weeks ago, but I didn't take the hint. I wish he'd come straight out with it. At 'least then Madge would still be alive.' Isabelle dropped her head and stared into her teacup.

'Bert always did know everything. That's why your mother thought a lot of him. He always looked out for my Lottie. He's a good man, but getting a bit long in the tooth, like us all.' Archie stared out of the kitchen window and looked wistfully across the valley below to his first home of Eldroth.

'Are you off to the funeral? And what are you going to do at Atkinson's? James won't be able to open the studio up for a while, and you'll need a new seamstress.' Danny sat back in his chair and looked at his sister. He was certain she hadn't come to Crummock on a social visit. She was here for a reason, and it would probably involve Atkinson's.

'I'm closing the studio for a few months, until James gets back on his feet. As for a new seamstress, I don't know what to do. I'm at a loss and my order books are full.' Isabelle paused and then looked up at Harriet. 'I don't suppose I could ask for your help, Harriet? Just for a few weeks, until I find a replacement? I'd arrange transport there and back for you, and pay you a wage. I'd even employ a first-class nanny to look after Georgina. It would be such a help and I'd be so grateful.'

Harriet looked across at Isabelle. She knew that what Isabelle was saying was genuine, but she hesitated in answering.

'I really am in a mess and I need those that I trust and love around me. Just as you helped once before, when you gave me the strength to pick myself up and move on

154

when I was hurt by that awful man, John Sidgwick. Help me again, Harriet, please.'

'I don't know. Georgina is still young and there's the house and the farm. We've only just finished hay-time, and it will be winter before we know it. I'd like to, but I already have enough on my plate.' Harriet saw all eyes watching her make her decision.

'Rosie will look after the house; it's time she was more of a lady than a tomboy,' said Danny. 'And if you get a nanny, Georgina and Ben will be fine. Just start with two days a week and take it from there. See how it pans out. You've talked of nothing else since your visit to Skipton.' He looked across at Harriet. He knew that she secretly yearned to be back working again, despite her life as a mother and housewife at Crummock. She could also give Isabelle a run for her money – something he knew Harriet had been wanting to do since their disagreement all those years ago.

'I'll see – give me some time to think about it. I don't want to be hurried into something I might regret.' Harriet breathed in deeply and looked at Isabelle. 'You'd get me a nanny and transport, and I could come and go as I please?'

'Yes, I said so, and I'd be so grateful. It would be like old times, except that we are both much wiser.' Isabelle smiled and knew that she'd got what she'd come for.

'Aye, old times. Remember the bad as well as the good, and then hopefully neither of you will fall out again.' Archie spat his mouthful of tobacco into the fire, making it hiss.

'We'll not fall out, we've both learned a lot since those days.' Harriet smiled wistfully, remembering the better days with her sister-in-law. 'I'll come and help. Only a few days, mind, and we will see how it goes.'

'Thank you, I just need somebody to be there for me. And I knew I could count on you.' Isabelle rose from the table and hugged Harriet and then looked around her. 'Crummock looks lovely. Mind, it always did at this time of year.'

'Aye, you've got to learn to take the sunshine with the rain, otherwise you'll not survive long up here, or in life. Get home to your man now, you've done your business; and make sure you look after him first. Happen then he won't wander off again,' said Archie.

'Father, be quiet.' Danny stood up and tried to stop his father from saying any more.

'It's alright, Danny. Father always says what he thinks, we both know that. And perhaps I don't always put James first, but he doesn't with me, either, so on that score I think we are even.' Isabelle made her way to the doorway. 'Harriet, I'll let you meet all the nannies that I think are suitable, and Jethro will pick you up for the station in the mornings.' Isabelle smiled as she made her way out into the late summer's day. 'I'm so grateful, believe me,' she said as she made for her carriage.

'She's just like her bloody father. Crafty and cunning, but you can never say no to her. That James will have to pay for his hour or two of pleasure, if I know Isabelle. He'll rue the day he went behind her back – although I think he'll be doing that already.' Archie looked at

Danny and Harriet. 'Make sure she's right with you this time, lass; take no rubbish from her.'

'I won't, Father. This time I know she needs me more than I need her.' Harriet smiled.

Isabelle stood at Madge's graveside. It had begun to rain and she looked up towards the falling raindrops pattering onto the spreading leaves of the sycamore trees that surrounded the churchyard. The weather matched her mood. She could have cried, too, shedding tears of hurt as she watched the coffin being lowered into the ground. How could her husband have deceived her so, with her own seamstress, whom she had trusted? Looking back, she should have known something was wrong: all the times James had returned home late, and the occasions when she had found them both together, looking coy and secretive. She should have known. Instead she had been oblivious to the people sniggering behind her back. All of them had known more than she did about what was going on under her own nose.

She looked up at Madge's parents, who were heartbroken and at a loss to make sense of their daughter's death and the scandal that had enveloped them. Their daughter found lying dead, next to James Fox on his new contraption of a motorcycle. The whole district was talking about it. Isabelle breathed in deeply; she wouldn't give her condolences to the family, she would just walk away and leave them in their grief. Besides, if Madge wasn't dead, she would have wished her so; nobody took anything off her, especially not her husband. She looked around her at the whispering mourners and made herself scarce, leaving them to gossip for as long as they liked. No doubt the rumours would give birth to more rumours, and this would just be the start, for the gossips. She must protect the good name of Atkinson's above all else. James would have to learn who was really in charge of his life.

14

'Are you there, Ethan?' Rosie whispered quietly as she climbed the ladder up to Ethan's sleeping quarters above the stable. The smell of newly harvested hay filled her nostrils. It was a reminder that summer was nearly over and that soon it would be autumn. She heard Ethan move as she peered into the darkness and rubbed her eyes to adjust to the light of the hay-loft.

'Aye, I'm here. What are you doing, creeping up here at this time of night? I thought I told you to keep away until the two Paddies had gone home.' Ethan turned on his side and looked towards where Rosie's voice came from.

'I had to come and see you. It couldn't wait any longer,' she whispered as she hoisted herself up on the wooden floorboards and made out the form of Ethan, who reached his hand out to light the stub of a candle in its candlestick.

'What couldn't wait?' Even by the light of the candle, Ethan looked concerned and his voice whispered shakily.

'I . . . I'm worried Ethan. I think I might be having

your baby.' Rosie felt her eyes filling with tears and she started to sob. She'd practised saying the words over and over again in her head as she tossed and turned in her bed, wondering what to do and how to tell Ethan of her predicament.

'Stop it! Stop blubbing and keep your voice down. Else those Irishmen will hear and tell your father, and you don't want him to know. Besides, you can't be – we've only done it once and I was careful. That is, unless you've been with someone else.' Ethan looked at Rosie in the flickering yellow candlelight and saw how upset she was. He knew she wouldn't have been with anyone else, but didn't want to admit it.

'How could you say that? I'd never lift my skirts to someone else. Didn't I tell you that I loved you? But I've hardly seen anything of you these last few weeks; it's as if you have kept out of my way.' Rosie sobbed. She'd thought Ethan would tell her that he loved her and that everything would be alright. Instead he was lying there, accusing her of being unfaithful, and his dark eyes looked straight through her.

'I've been busy helping your father with the hay, and I thought it couldn't be mine. Anyway, you might be wrong. It's only a few weeks since we were down at the wash-dubs. How do you know already?'

'Do I have to say? I don't like talking about suchlike. But you should know – you are not daft. We both know what goes on.' Rosie caught her breath and trembled as she tried to control her sobs.

'Give it another week. You may be wrong. And it'll

give me time to think. We can't do owt yet. But I know one thing: we are both going to get the hidings of our lives, if you are having a baby.' Ethan ran his fingers through his hair and looked at Rosie in the candlelight. He wished he'd behaved himself that warm afternoon; he'd no intention of being cornered by the farmer's daughter, not yet. There was too much of the world to see before he did that.

'I won't be wrong. I'm never late, if you know what I mean,' mumbled Rosie as she wrung her hands, not daring to look into Ethan's face. She sobbed and wished Ethan would show more concern.

'Well, there's always a first time, and this might be it. It's no good worrying yet. Now get yourself back home, before you are missed and before those two over the yard hear you. We'll sort things out, no matter what. I'm not going anywhere and you aren't, so we will just have to take the consequences.' Ethan smiled and finally hugged Rosie.

'You do love me, though, don't you, Ethan? You will stand by me?' she said as she turned to make her way back down the ladder.

'Aye, I'm upset that you even feel you need to ask me that. You should know what my answer is to both. Now get yourself to bed and stop worrying, it'll be alright.' Ethan kissed her on the cheek and watched as she climbed down the ladder and made her way quietly out of the stable, leaving him to blow out the candle and look into the dark of the night. It was a darkness that was nearly suffocating him with the news that he was about to be a father.

'Have any of you seen Ethan? I've had to take the two Irishmen down into Settle myself, as there was no sight nor sound of him first thing this morning.' Danny threw his cap down onto his chair and stood looking at Harriet and his father.

'He'll be bloody wandering off somewhere, making the most of the day.' Archie looked up at his scowling son.

'He'd better not be – not while I'm paying him. He can just get his backside home, wherever he is,' said Danny.

'I haven't seen him at all this morning. Give Rosie a shout – she might have finished, she's upstairs making the beds.' Harriet raised her head from concentrating on kneading the bread, and wiped her hair with the back of her hand as she looked at her annoyed husband.

'If anyone knows where he is, Rosie will. They are, I think, still as thick as thieves, regardless of his father giving Ethan a hiding earlier on in the year. Although, saying that, I haven't seen him loitering about her of late. I suppose we should be thankful for that, and at least she's not with him this time.' Danny walked down the passageway and stood at the bottom of the stairs and yelled up to Rosie in the bedrooms above. 'Rosie, have you seen Ethan today? He's not about, and he was supposed to do a job for me this morning.'

Rosie stopped shaking the bolster into its slip as she

heard her father shouting at her. Her stomach churned as she heard him say that Ethan was missing. Ethan might wander, but only after he had finished his jobs, and he would never have missed doing something that was expected of him. She knew instantly something was wrong. She breathed in deeply; she didn't want her father to see the worry on her face as she walked to the top of the stairs.

'No, I've not seen him, Father. I've been helping Mother all morning.' She leaned over the banister and looked at the anger on her father's face.

'That bloody lad, he's more bother than he's worth,' Danny muttered as he made his way back into the kitchen.

Rosie's legs shook as she made her way back to her parents' bedroom and the task in hand. She felt sick as she sat on the edge of the bed and looked out of the window at the world outside. Where was Ethan? Was it just a coincidence that he was not to be found this morning, after she had spoken to him the previous day, or had he left knowing that she was carrying his child? He was leaving her, just like his grandfather had left his grandmother all those years ago. She didn't know what to do, as she sat and shed a tear, thinking of the plight she might be in. Her father would surely not take kindly to the fact that she was pregnant, let alone that it was with the farm boy and that he had abandoned her, alone with her guilt. And then she thought of her mother's plans being spoilt by her stupidity. Harriet had never stopped talking about reviving her seamstress skills, back in Atkinson's fold, since Isabelle had visited; and Rosie had seen her mother filled with new life as she counted the days until she re-joined the family firm.

She sighed; her minute of weakness on the grassy bank that sultry evening was going to be her undoing. If Ethan had left her, she would have to face the consequences on her own, but until she was sure, she would say nothing to anybody. She breathed in deeply and controlled her sobs; her mother must not find her like this. She'd check Ethan's home above the stable and then decide what to do. However, if he had gone, she'd keep her predicament to herself for as long as possible, for it would be for the best.

'The ungrateful sod!' Danny swore at the supper table and banged his cutlery down. 'Buggering off without a "by your leave". By, I should have listened to Isabelle.' He scowled across at his father. 'It was you who brought Ethan here, and now he's buggered off to God knows where. I'll go down to Windfell tomorrow and see if he's trailed himself home.'

'He'll happen turn up. You know what he's like.' Archie seemed unperturbed by Ethan's absence and carried on eating his supper.

'Nay, he'll not; he's taken all his belongings with him, even the old straw mattress, and it is as if he was never with us. Are you sure he said nothing to you, our Rosie? You are looking a bit sheepish. You two have always been close.' Danny shot a questioning glance at his rather quiet daughter, who looked white and upset.

'No, he said nothing to me. I'm as shocked as you

164

are.' Rosie held back the tears as her father questioned her.

'At least we've got hay-time over and done with. Plus, he couldn't have slept above the stable this winter. I'd have had to find room for him here, or where the Irishmen have slept in the storeroom. I didn't fancy having him sleeping under our roof. He's such a wild one.' Harriet rose from the table and looked at Rosie. 'You'll miss him no doubt – you look upset. He's best gone, for perhaps you were both getting too close.' She looked at her crestfallen daughter and then smiled. 'I'll have to make you a dress for the dances this coming winter, once I'm back at work. One to attract some lad from out of the village, seeing as you will be seventeen soon.'

'Aye, one with brass. Not a black-haired gyppo, like Ethan. Make your father proud.' Danny grinned at his daughter, teasing her.

'I'm sorry, I have remembered that I need to feed Jip. I forgot earlier on.' Rosie got up from the table; she had to hold back the tears until she got outside, for nobody must know her plight. She pushed her chair back and made her way quickly to the door.

'Look what you've done now! Can't you see she's broken-hearted over Ethan not saying goodbye to her?' Harriet shook her head over Danny's lack of empathy.

'It's good riddance to bad rubbish.' Danny said. 'He's best gone, if she was that fond of him.'

'He'll not be far. He'll land back when he's ready.' Archie moved next to the fire. 'He's making the most of the last days of summer, if you ask me. And, as you say,

165

he'd have said his farewells to Rosie, if nobody else, and you can tell she knew nowt.'

'Aye, well, we will see. If he does turn up, I may not want him back, the trailing little bugger.' Danny wished his father had never brought Ethan to Crummock in the first place.

Rosie sat up high on the hillock called the Knot and looked down on the farmhouse. Swallows and house martins were diving and swooping, catching the last flies and midges of the summer's evening as the sun began to sink lower and lower in the sky. They too were going to take flight to warmer shores for the onset of winter. She hugged her knees close to her and rocked to console herself. Please let Ethan return, she thought to herself. Don't let him be the gypsy that everyone has branded him to be. She loved him and thought he loved her. At least it had felt like that. How could she have been so wrong? Her heart would always be his, of that she was sure. As for their secret, well, that was what it would be kept as, for the next few months at least, until his return.

15

Danny rode up the path to Windfell, straight to the stables, and dismounted at once when he saw Jethro came out to meet him.

'Mister Danny, it's good to see you.' Jethro took the horse's reins and patted its neck. 'Mistress Isabelle is at Skipton, if you were looking for her, but Mister James is at home.'

'It's you I've come to see really, Jethro.' Danny looked at the well-built man and searched his face for any inkling that he knew why he was here. 'It's Ethan; he's left us, and I wondered if perhaps he'd come home.'

'Nay, he's not here, we hardly see him nowadays. He breaks my Mazy's heart many a day, never showing his face. He used to come regular, but he seems to be a law unto himself since he went to live at Crummock. I'll make sure I send him straight back to you, if I see anything of him. He's got wandering feet, has our Ethan, never knows when he's well off. The silly bugger.' Jethro sighed and looked at Danny. 'He's not done owt he shouldn't, has he?'

'Not that I know of, Jethro. But he has taken everything with him and it looks like he's left for good.' Danny looked as the old man's face as it clouded over with worry.

'I'll have to tell our Mazy. She'll be sick with anxiety. It's a good job he's our only one, because he hasn't half given us some trouble over the years. I'm sorry that he's not been decent enough to hand his notice in, and that he's caused you this bother, Mister Danny.' Jethro pulled on the horse's reins as it raised its head, impatient to be off again or stabled with something to eat.

'Well, I just hope he turns up. If he were my son, I'd be worried. Even though Ethan is big enough to look after himself, I'm sure you'd still like to know where he is.' Danny patted the stableman's back and looked at the worry on his face. 'Can you stable my horse for an hour, Jethro? I'll just have a catch-up with James, keep him company for a while.'

'That I can, sir. Mister James will be glad of the company. I think his days are long, since the accident.' Jethro led the horse to the stables. He hadn't wanted to show how much the news of Ethan's disappearance had upset him. But deep down he knew that his son would not have left the safety of a good job for no reason, so something had gone wrong.

'Danny, it's good to see you. You've dared to visit the black sheep of the family then? I thought everyone had washed their hands of me.' James patted his brother-in-law on the back while trying to balance on his crutches.

'Aye, well, I can't say I'm suited with your escapade, but I've only heard part of the story, no doubt. It's up to you to tell me the rest, if you want to.' Danny made himself comfortable in the morning room of Windfell and looked out at the immaculate lawns, remembering the days when he strolled around them with Harriet on his arm.

'I don't know what to say, Danny. I've been a fool, and my head was turned by Madge's beauty and attention. And now look where it has got us: her six foot under, and my marriage in tatters. I'm only telling you this because at this moment I need a friend, and a fellow man to talk to. Isabelle is making my life hell, which she has every right to do. Even though I tell her we were just good friends, she has guessed the truth about Madge and me.' James sat down cautiously in a chair next to his brother-in-law and put his head in his hands.

'Well, mate, you've only yourself to blame – what else can I say?' Danny felt for his distraught brother-in-law; he'd guessed that Isabelle would be making James's life hell. He knew she could never live with infidelity in her marriage. 'Our Isabelle has a hell of a tongue on her, and I'm glad I'm not in your shoes. But look on the bright side: at least she hasn't thrown you out.'

'Don't think she hasn't threatened it. But she couldn't live with the scandal, of that I'm sure. The servants are very cold towards me, and as for our Jane, she either goes to work with her mother or hides in her room reading her

169

precious *Votes for Women* newspaper, which is filling her head with nonsense. Thank God Luke is at school at Giggleswick. Even if I do worry about him, now that he's joined the OTC. He'd be first in line if ever there was a war. But I'm wasting my time with my opinions at the moment.'

'You are in a bad way, my old mate. But like I said, you do only have yourself to blame. Although I'd be a hypocrite if I didn't say most of us have been swayed by a bonny face from time to time. It's just that we don't get caught.' Danny sat back in his chair and looked sympathetically at his usually laid-back brother-in-law.

'Why do you say that? You've never been unfaithful to Harriet. I know you've had your ups and downs, but you always seem to love one another, regardless of how tough it gets.' James peered at Danny, interested that he was confessing to having an eye for a good-looking woman.

'No, I've never been tempted since I was wed, but I nearly didn't get married because of a lass who was very similar to your Madge. She took my eye and my heart, if truth be told. She was everything that Harriet wasn't. There was no talk of marriage and family; she just lived for the day.' Danny sat back in his chair and recollected the time he had spent with Amy Brown.

'That's different – you weren't married. You can't be blamed. Did Harriet ever suspect?' James looked at Danny and saw the wistful look come over him of a man once in love.

'I don't think so. But occasionally she says that I should never have married her, that she doesn't make me

170

happy. She was worst just after after our two boys died, because she blamed herself – and the world – for the loss of them.' Danny hesitated. 'She's come round a lot lately, and I think she will improve even more when she goes back to working with Isabelle. They can plan our downfall together, it will be like old times.' Danny laughed.

'Aye, she's back with Isabelle next week, isn't she? I heard Isabelle arranging a nanny for Georgina, I think. Will Harriet be alright with that?' James leaned forward and looked hard at Danny.

'She seems to be taking it in her stride. Isabelle sent details of some girls who had responded to her advert, and Harriet chose from them. As it is, there was a young woman from down in Austwick that she knew and trusted who had applied, so she was happy with her. We will have to see how she does next Tuesday, and how our Rosie copes with a few more tasks to do around the house. She's got a long face on her at the moment and I don't know why. Perhaps she's not going to have the time she used to have to wander and be with me. And I think Ethan disappearing hasn't helped.'

'Ethan's gone? Jethro hasn't said anything.' James leaned forward, trying to make his broken leg comfortable.

'Aye, packed up and gone. God knows why. His father swears he knows nothing about it. At least we'd finished hay-time. I could have done with Ethan's help for another month, just until I'd sorted out the lambs for sale. Rosie will have to help me with them next week. It'll take her mind off housework, because my father's not up to much these days, and my other farm man is beginning to show his age.'

'Well, I've not seen hide nor hair of the lad around here, and Mazy hasn't mentioned him. I'll let you know if he shows up.' James yawned.

'I'd be grateful for that. Now, I'll be away. And you behave yourself! Don't get yourself any more fancy contraptions and even faster women. Look what they've done to you. I'd have thought our Isabelle was more than you could handle anyway, you silly fool.' Danny looked at James, who was a broken man: responsible for the death of his lover and probably broken-hearted, if he did but tell the truth. Still, it could be worse, for they both could have died.

'Don't worry. I've learned my lesson and I won't be able to forget it, not in this house. It's good to see you. I'm thankful for your company, I've been feeling like a leper of late.' James closed his eyes. He'd not been sleeping. Instead he'd been remembering the broken body of Madge, as the night and the darkness fell around him.

'Take care; things will get better with time.' Danny closed the door to the morning room and let himself out of Windfell. His thoughts returned to his fling with the lovely Amy. He couldn't blame poor James, for sometimes the temptation was just too much. At least James wasn't the father to a child he had never seen; a child Danny was sure would come back and haunt him eventually.

16

'Now, can you think of anything that I've not told you?' Harriet looked at her new employee and at baby Georgina, who had taken instantly to her new carer.

'No, Mrs Atkinson, I think you've covered everything. Besides, as you say, I'm sure Rosie will help me out if I can't find anything.' Mary Harrison smiled. She had been shown around Crummock and told the needs of the two youngest Atkinson children more times than she'd had hot dinners. But she understood their mother's concerns and would have felt the same, if they were her own children.

'The main thing is that Georgina does not get out of her routine, otherwise she becomes so bad-tempered that she doesn't know what to do with herself. And don't let Ben twist you around his little finger. His bedtime is seven, although I hope to be back by then. He's usually home about four o'clock after school; he walks up home with the lad from Sowermire, so he only has the last half-mile to walk home on his own. If he's any later than that you'd better go and look for him, as he's known for dawdling.' Harriet looked around her. She was looking forward to her new life starting in the morning, but at the same time she was dreading leaving her family behind. 'Otherwise, I think you know where everything is. Rosie will see to the meals and cleaning. Not that she wants to, for she's a love of the outside more than home-making, and she's with her father now. She'd much rather be handling sheep than dusting and polishing.' Harriet sighed.

'I'll help her, Mrs Atkinson, don't worry. I can turn my hand to most things – us country lasses have to.' Mary smiled; she was being generously paid by the well-to-do Fox family and knew when she was on to a good thing, despite the recent scandal and the awful death linked to James Fox. 'And I'll make sure Mr Atkinson senior is looked after, although he seems to be quite sprightly for his age.'

'Mr Atkinson will look after himself. As long as he's fed, he'll potter around the house and farm. He's learning to take it easy after all these years, giving my husband guidance on occasion. Although sometimes my husband does not appreciate his advice or help, as he is a bit set in his ways. He forgets that it is now 1913, and things have progressed from when he was a lad. Well, I think that is it. I look forward to seeing you in the morning. The breakfast table will be laid. You can eat with my family or on your own, whichever you prefer. Rosie knows what everyone has to eat, so don't worry about that.'

Harriet held her arms out for Georgina, who was playing with Mary's pendant around her neck. Georgina complained about being removed from her new plaything as her mother prised her away.

'You can play with it again tomorrow.' Mary smiled at Georgina. 'Now, you behave for your mother.' She passed the crying Georgina to Harriet and then pacified her by reaching for a spoon from the table to play with. 'You are easy to suit.' She smiled as Georgina waved the spoon in the air and then grinned as Mary kissed her on the cheek to say farewell. 'Don't worry, Mrs Atkinson. Georgina and Ben will be well looked after, and I'll see that Rosie gets my support too.' She picked up her gloves and put them on, before being shown the door.

Harriet walked back into the kitchen and put Georgina down on the pegged rug. She watched as the baby pulled herself up to her full height and ventured on wobbly steps over to the doorway. 'I only hope I'm doing the right thing,' she whispered to herself. 'I do love my children, but I need my own time, or is that terribly selfish of me? Besides, Isabelle needs me, especially after James and his public fling.' Time would tell, no doubt, she thought as she set about her work.

'Rosie, hold this gate open for me, to let this old ewe through. She can't be sent to market, she won't make the drive down the valley.' Danny yelled at his daughter as he walked amongst his flock, sorting out which sheep he needed to sell before winter and which ones he wanted to keep.

'That's what you want to be selling.' Archie lifted his

175

stick and pointed at the old grey-faced ewe as she bleated her way out onto the open fellside.

'She's on her last legs, Father. It's better that she dies where she knows, rather than being slaughtered at the knacker's yard, because that's all she's worth.' Danny pulled another of his flock to one side and felt how fit it was, as he replied to his father.

'It would save you digging a hole for her in another week or two and you'd get a bit of something for her. Those down in t'mill towns of Lancashire don't know she's not fit to eat. Because that's where she'd end up, on their dinner tables.' Archie shook his head. His lad was too soft, he'd never make a millionaire.

'Grandfather, I really do not like to eat lamb and mutton, as it is, without you reminding me where a lot of these are going. I'm helping to send them to their deaths.' Rosie quickly shut the fell gate, letting another sheep get a reprieve from the butcher's knife.

'That's what farming's about, lass. I don't see you complaining on a Sunday lunchtime when you are tucking into your mother's best roast beef. That's just the same. We butchered that beef, and you saw that calf growing up, but you were still licking your lips after your meal.' Archie grinned.

'No, but it's different with sheep. Some of these I've fed with a bottle of milk when they were first born. Like that big tup lamb over there, with the black-striped face and horns, just coming through. I couldn't eat him,' shouted Rosie to her grandfather over the bleating.

'Well, I can tell you now, he's one to go,' Danny

shouted. 'He's become a bloody nuisance; you've fed him so well he expects something from you every time you go near him. He's getting to be dangerous now because he's such a size. Plus, he nearly stabbed me the other day with them horns, tore a bit out of my trousers with his bullying tactics.' Danny looked at his daughter. He hadn't wanted to tell her, but there was no other way – the tup lamb was beginning to make a pest of himself and was one that had to go to market.

'No, you can't sell my Billy, I won't let you.' Rosie climbed the fence of the enclosure and made her way through the rest of the sheep to her favourite lamb of the last spring. 'Look at him, Father, he's such a grand, big ram. He'll breed well next year, you've got to keep him.' She folded her arms round the ram's neck and hugged him, burying her face in his fleece, smelling the lanolin in his coat.

'He's a bloody nuisance; he's off to market, so leave him be, and you mind what you are doing.' Danny looked at Archie as he sorted another sheep from being sold, and his father opened the gate to give it its freedom.

Rosie clung to the tup's neck, but he wasn't having any of it. If there were no tasty sheep nuts or a mouthful of hay, he didn't want to know. He lifted his head in defiance of her grip. He was too strong for Rosie to control. Then he turned round and butted her in the stomach, before stamping his foot in defiance, as he looked at her with contempt.

Rosie fell over amongst the sheep and her skirts became covered with sheep droppings. She was near to tears. Her ribs and stomach hurt as she swore at her favoured lamb.

'I told you – he's turned into a right bastard. Are you alright?' Danny looked at his daughter as she sat up. 'Another month and he'll be even more of a nuisance. He's come and butted me a time or two, it's time he was off.'

'Aye, let him go, lass, he'll fetch a good price at market. As you say, he's a good one for breeding from; he'll not go for meat.' Archie looked across at Danny and gave Rosie his hand as she climbed back over the fence to regain her place opening the gate. 'Tha's a bit fragrant. You'd better find time to fill the tin bath before supper, or your mother will have something to say.'

Rosie looked down at her long dress. It was stained with sheep droppings and urine, from where she had fallen on the cobbles of the pen. 'Bloody ungrateful thing. And he's hurt my ribs.'

'Now then, lass, no need to swear. Its nobbut a bit of muck, it'll wash off. I think it's your pride that's been hurt, more than yourself. You looked to climb that fence alright.' Archie grinned. 'Go and get washed, I can manage the ones we have left.'

'No, I'll stay. This is my job and I'm not letting him get the better of me.' Rosie leaned over the gate and looked at the wild-eyed tup lamb that had been so ungrateful for her affections. 'I don't care if he is butchered now, the stupid animal.'

Rosie stepped into the warmth of the water in the tin bath, which she had filled from the nearby boiler. The waters were soothing. Her ribs and stomach ached with a dull, nagging pain where the tup had butted her, and she lay back in the quietness of the scullery. Her mother had scowled at her and told her to get changed and washed while she put Georgina to bed. Rosie washed herself with the flannel. She knew that the rest of the house was awaiting the stew that had been cooking in the oven next to the fire that afternoon, so she couldn't be long. Mutton stew, it was all they ever seemed to eat, along with home cured bacon and rabbits that were caught on the land. But that was part of being self-sufficient and Rosie knew that, even though she had protested about the marketing of her favourite spring lamb.

She leaned back in the bath and sighed. She felt tired and sickly of a morning. She rubbed her hands over her stomach and thought about the baby she was nearly certain she was carrying, and the fact that Ethan had deserted her in her hour of need. How could he? She was on her own and frightened, trying hard to block out any thoughts about having to tell both her parents the news that she thought she was with child by Ethan. A tear trickled down her cheek and she breathed in deeply, trying to control herself. She knew all too well that her mother could walk into the scullery at any moment and she would have to explain her misery. She quickly washed herself down with the carbolic soap and then pulled herself out of the bath, realizing just how hard she had fallen when the tup had butted her. She ached all over and winced as she dried herself, pulling on her garments, before emptying the water down the main drain of the scullery and hanging the tin bath back on the wall and then rejoining her family in the kitchen.

'You smell a bit fresher, but you look a bit pale. Are you alright, lass?' Her grandfather reached out for Rosie's hand as she walked past him. 'That tup didn't half give you a belt. It's best that he's off – you've spoilt him too much.'

'I'm fine, Grandfather. Just a bit bruised, but I feel better for a hot bath.' Rosie looked at the half-laid table and decided to help her mother out by finishing the job and getting the bread from the pantry. She didn't like the attention her grandfather was giving her, so she deliberately made herself busy.

'You'll have to get used to this, after this evening; it'll be your job three nights a week. That'll put an end to your trailing.' Danny looked at his daughter, who had been quiet of late, and he suspected that she was sulking about her mother's new role in life.

'I'm looking forward to it. Mother has shown me all that I should be doing, and I know what food I've to make you all for the next few meals. It isn't as if I've never turned my hand to being in the kitchen before. I just prefer to be outside.' Rosie smiled at her father as she went to stir the stew. A pain in the bottom of her stomach made her stop for a minute, and she caught her breath in front of her grandfather. He looked concerned.

'Are you alright, lass?' Archie put his hand on her arm.

'Yes, yes, I'm fine. It's just my ribs, where Billy butted me. They are sore.' Rosie was lying. She knew something was amiss, and it was not just the bruising from her tussle with the tup lamb. 'Can you tell Mama that I'm going to

180

take my supper up to bed with me – it's been a long day and the fall has shaken me up slightly?' Rosie ladled a portion of stew into a bowl and picked up a slice of bread and a spoon from the table.

'Your mother would like you to stay with us tonight, for she's feeling guilty about leaving us all, as it is.' Danny looked up at his daughter, who was acting a little out of character.

'I'm sorry. I'll see her in the morning before she goes, but now I'm going to have to go to my bed. My ribs hurt.' Rosie quickly made for the bottom of the stairs, hoping that she did not meet her mother on the way down from putting Georgina to bed, as the pain in her stomach worsened.

'She doesn't look well, Danny.' Archie looked across at his son, who was looking out of the window, watching Ben teasing the dog.

'She's alright. She never complained when she was helping us finish with the last of the sheep. She's sulking, Father; she doesn't want to take responsibility for the home. Don't let her pull the wool over your eyes. Remember her play-acting when her and Ethan buggered off to Appleby Fair. Well, she's doing it again.' Danny sat back and breathed in deeply. 'There's nowt up with her, she's just got to realize that she's got to grow up – and grow up quickly.'

'Well, I hope you are right, lad.' Archie looked into the fire. It wasn't his place to say any more, but he was worried about Rosie.

*

Rosie lay in her bed. She'd been feeling under the weather before the tup lamb had butted her, but now she was worse, much worse. She'd managed to eat her supper by sharing it with the farmhouse cat, and had put on a brave face when her mother had come to check on her, withholding just how ill she was, but now all she wanted to do was cry. The pain had been so intense and she could feel that the bedclothes beneath her were soiled with blood. If there had been a baby, there wasn't now; it was dead, and her nightdress and bedding were stained with its remains.

She hugged her pillow to her and didn't dare look underneath the sheet at the extent of the blood she had lost, and whether there was anything that resembled a baby. She daren't tell anyone, although she longed to confide in her mother. She wished her mother could be there to comfort her in her arms. Instead, in the morning before anyone else awoke, she'd put her sheets and nightclothes in the boiler to wash and would hope that nobody suspected her plight. At least then neither she nor Ethan would be chastised, and nobody would know any different or suspect that she had been with child. It was the best thing she could do, and perhaps her accident had been a blessing.

She looked up at the ceiling and sobbed. She no longer had a baby to worry about, but there was still no sign of Ethan. He had shown his true colours and she was without anyone. How stupid she had been to fall in love with the stable boy, a gypsy. Her love for him must never be known by anyone and now, with the baby gone, it would be her secret.

17

'What are you doing?' It was only just breaking light when Harriet opened the scullery door to find Rosie swilling her bed linen in the brown earthenware sink and stoking up the boiler.

'Mother, I didn't hear you!' Rosie blushed and looked across at her mother; she'd hoped to get the sheets swilled and into the boiler to soak in the mixture of water and soda crystals before her mother had arisen. 'I didn't want Mary to see my accident. I wanted to wash my sheets before she arrived. I feel so ashamed that I have marked my sheets with my monthly.' Rosie bowed her head and bit her lip. She could have cried quite openly as she looked at her mother.

'Oh, Rosie, is that why you were feeling so ill last night? I lay awake and worried about you into the early hours, but now I know it was that, I feel better. It's a woman's curse, for sure, and something that we have all to bear. Mary would have understood; and besides, there is no reason for her to come into your room. You need not have rushed to wash them. Are you feeling better this morning?' Harriet put her arm around Rosie and kissed her on the brow.

Rosie held her tightly. She wanted to confess all, but didn't say a word about her ordeal. She put her head on her mother's shoulder and smelled the perfume that Harriet wore, the perfume she only wore on special occasions. Today it had been put on for her first day back at Atkinson's. 'I love you, Mother.' She held back a tear.

'Hey, what's all this about? I'll be back later this evening – all is sorted for you. There's a pie in the pantry for you to put in the oven; you only need to peel the potatoes, and all the cleaning has been done. I bottomed everything last week and Mary, I'm sure, will fit in fine. She'll look after Georgina and Ben, once he's back from school.' Harriet held her daughter tightly. If Isabelle hadn't been in such a fix, she wouldn't even be thinking of going back to work at Atkinson's. But now that the chance had occurred, she had to admit she was looking forward to it. She hadn't banked on Rosie being this upset; it was Rosie who had acted strangely, from the moment she had agreed to step into Madge's shoes, albeit just temporarily.

'I know, Mother. I can manage all that. I'll just miss you.' Rosie stood back and wiped her tears. 'You've never been away from home before for so long.'

'It's not forever, my love. And you've got Grandfather and your father at home. Just let me help your Aunty Isabelle for a while; she needs her family at the moment, what with your Uncle James having no more sense than that scrubbing brush of yours.' Harriet looked across at the white sheets in the sink and the red smears that were still on them. 'Finish doing your washing and then come in and have a cup of tea with me, before Jethro picks me up and Mary shows her face. Just you and me, like we used to be. I used to nurse you for hours in front of the kitchen fire, unable to believe that I'd been given such a beautiful baby girl, after the death of my two sons. I didn't think I deserved you. You are more precious to me than life itself and, if you don't want me to go today, then I will tell Jethro to return without me.' Harriet held Rosie tightly.

'No, Mother, go. I know it will be good for you, and we will all manage.' Rosie stood back and wiped her eyes. 'I bet Ben won't argue with Mary; he wouldn't dare. And Georgina already loves her – anyone can see that. We will be fine.'

'I know you will, or at least I hope so. I'm finding it hard to leave you all, as it takes lot to entrust my family to another person's care. Now, let me get that kettle on and let me stir your father. Mary won't want to see him in his nightshirt, like he sometimes wanders down in. I don't know who would be more shocked: your father or her!' Harriet sighed as she left Rosie to her washing. Her little girl was growing up into a fine woman, although she was learning the hard way, as all young women did.

'Back full circle, Mistress Harriet.' Jethro pulled up the gig just outside the gates of Settle railway station and helped Harriet alight.

'Indeed, Jethro. I didn't think I'd be doing this ever

again. Strange how life works out. I just wish it was in better circumstances and that Madge was still alive to be doing her job, despite the rumours.' Harriet looked at the man who was part of the backbone of the workings of Windfell and wondered just how much gossip had reached his ears.

'Aye, well, I never listen to gossip – no good ever comes of it. I know that, because there's been plenty spread over the years about my family.' Jethro held his horse's bridle and looked concerned.

'Speaking of family, have you heard anything of your son, Ethan? I still don't know why he left us. He'd not been reprimanded or done anything wrong, to my knowledge.' Harriet knew that Jethro must be worried, as indeed she was. After all, Ethan was only a few months older than Rosie, and she would have been worried sick if Rosie had upped and left without a 'by your leave'.

'No, not heard a thing. He'll turn up, though; he never could be nailed down, always liked to trail somewhere. Mind you, Mazy is worried. I keep telling her he'll be back in his own time. I'm just sorry that he's caused you some worries up at Crummock. He should have been grateful that Master Archie gave him that job in the first place.'

'Don't you worry, Jethro. And keep me informed if Ethan does return home. I must go now. The train's due, and I can see steam rising down the track.' Harriet picked up her skirts and her bag and made her way to the platform's edge to join the other passengers who were awaiting the seven-thirty to Leeds. She looked around her.

186

They were mainly business people, mostly men dressed in their suits, waiting anxiously for the train to draw onto the platform and take them to their positions of importance. Women – especially those of her age and station – were expected to stay at home and take care of their families, leaving the man to be the breadwinner. Harriet felt very self-conscious while she waited her turn to board the train as it pulled into the station.

Once seated in a carriage with her fellow passengers, she looked out of the window and waited for the stationmaster and porter to clear the platform and blow the whistle. She watched as the steam from the engine blew down next to her window and wisps of white fluff drifted into the early-morning sky. She looked around her. A man in a bowler hat sat across from her, engrossed in his morning's newspaper, while an older gentleman sat with his briefcase on his knee, guarding it with his life.

Harriet rearranged her long grey skirt and breathed in deeply. Closing her eyes, she thought back to her home. Hopefully Mary would nearly have finished getting Ben ready for school, and Georgina would be sitting up at the table in her highchair, eating her chopped-up egg with a toasted bread soldier, if she had not thrown it onto the floor by now. It was a game that she liked to play and one that tested her mother's patience. Harriet knew Rosie would be coping, but she had looked pale this morning; the poor girl was still getting used to her more adult body. Would they all manage without her? What if Georgina took ill? Perhaps she should get off the train and put an end to the stupid idea of helping out at Atkinson's again.

It was too late. The whistle blew and the train jolted into action. The wheels turned slowly at first, and then picked up speed as the carriages swayed backwards and forwards over the tracks, chattering as they went over the points. She was on her way to join Isabelle, for her first day back in work for nearly nineteen years. She only hoped she had not lost her touch, and that Isabelle would hold her tongue if she made any mistakes. That day would tell, and she need not return in the morning if things went badly. But most of all Harriet hoped that her children would not miss her too much and that they would be safe until her return.

'Harriet, I'm so glad you didn't change your mind. I know it must be strange to have to leave your children behind and, honestly, I can't find the words to say how grateful I am.' Isabelle rushed over to Harriet's side as she opened the door and made her way into the cutting and sample room in Atkinson's. She kissed her lovingly on the cheek and held out her hand for Harriet to join her in a morning coffee before they both started work. 'Please do sit down, I had Nancy make enough for us both. Have you eaten? I can always order you some break-fast. Cook is already preparing for our luncheon rush in the restaurant. He wouldn't mind.' Isabelle smiled as Harriet took off her coat and sat down beside her.

'No, I'm fine, thank you, just a little nervous and worried about leaving my family.' Harriet fidgeted in her chair as Isabelle poured her a coffee from the silver pot that had just been delivered to her. Strict instructions had been given to all staff to make Harriet feel most welcome.

'They'll be fine, I'm sure. You made a good choice with Mary, she seemed very sensible and reliable. And of course Rosie is growing up so fast now. I keep forgetting that she's nearly seventeen. She and Jane are so dissimilar, don't you think?' Isabelle sat back and sipped her coffee, watching Harriet worrying.

'Yes, you are quite right. Jane and Rosie have nothing in common, both of them are quite different.' Harriet looked nervous and suddenly came out with what she was thinking. 'I don't know if I should be here. What if somebody takes ill? What if Ben doesn't return from school?' She was beginning to fret.

'Look, it's not like when we were first starting out. We are not under as much pressure as we were the last time you worked here. Atkinson's has grown beyond all recognition. Plus the transport is better, you'd get home quicker; and Archie will keep an eye on everybody for you. God, I never thought I'd say this, but it's a good job we have him. He's a blessing in disguise and he loves his grandchildren – he'll look after everyone. Now let me show you the workbook. It will take your mind off home and get you into the swing of things. The first fittings are in an hour. Mrs Tattersall is wanting a blouse-coat making in crêpe de Chine. She's going to watch her son rowing on the river at Cambridge, and someone has told her that is what all the fashionable ladies are wearing over their hobble skirts.'

Isabelle looked at Harriet. 'It's just a simple, long

189

open coat, Harriet. I've got a pattern out for you to look at, and the rolls of crêpe de Chine are over there. Try and persuade her to go for a natural colour. She's a tendency to choose such garish colours, and it doesn't look good on a woman her age – she should know better.'

'I think I know Mrs Tattersall. Her family farms down near Gisburn, they have horses.' Harriet looked up from her cup.

'Yes, that's her. The youngest son won a scholarship to Cambridge, and she's so proud of him. That's why we have to make her feel, and look, special. Remember that feeling you used to get, when we knew the women in front of us could not be dressed any finer, not even if they had gone to the finest dress shops in Paris?' Isabelle smiled at her sister-in-law.

'Yes, I remember. I enjoyed those days, we worked well together.' Harriet stopped sipping her coffee. 'I've missed them, really.'

'I know, and it was all my fault that you didn't return after that terrible day. But Atkinson's was everything to me then, and I didn't know or realize the deep unconditional love between a mother and her child. I should have listened to you when you said the boys were ill, and sent you back home, regardless of the amount of work we had.' Isabelle put her arms around her sister-in-law.

'You weren't to know what was going to happen. Even I didn't realize they were so ill. Let's not talk about it again – it's in the past. Now, show me the pattern books. What colour do you suggest for Mrs Tattersall? She's got auburn hair. Perhaps a green, quite plain, but well cut, to show her still-decent figure?' Harriet breathed in; she had to move on, for things had changed. Her mother-in-law was no longer in charge, and she and Isabelle had to bury past differences. Today was a fresh start for both of them.

18

Jane sat in her chair, looking out at the rain coming down outside her bedroom window. If the evening had been fine, she would have gone for a short stroll, to get away from the atmosphere that had filled the house since her father's more-than-public accident. But as it was, she had nowhere to hide from the poisonous talk of her parents. They tried to act as if everything was alright, never exchanging words while she was around them, but she knew differently. Her father was now sleeping in the spare room and her mother was acting strangely, as if nothing was wrong, and yet everything was wrong. Raised voices could frequently be heard, especially after her father had reached for his glass of port of an evening. She longed to yell at them, 'I'm no longer a child', but daren't. To make matters worse, the staff at Atkinson's tittered and laughed behind her back and she'd come close to losing her temper, when overhearing their comments on several occasions.

And the staff at Windfell didn't seem to be as jovial as usual and hardly bothered with her. They didn't know exactly what to say to her. It was if she had no feelings, and nobody cared. She couldn't even discuss it with Luke, as now that the new term had started he was back boarding at Giggleswick School, conveniently out of the way, but looked after while her mother and father went about their business. The only refuge was her room, and there Jane lost herself in a good book or reading the latest suffragette news in her *Votes for Women*, which was delivered weekly to Windfell. Her mother abhorred her reading it, and hated even more the friendships that she had built through it, especially with the bobbin girls at Dewhurst's. Isabelle especially abhorred Nellie Taylor, whom she thought to be common and mouthy, and she often reprimanded Jane for becoming friends with a mill girl. But Nellie was different: she stood up for women's rights, often talking about demanding equal pay with the menfolk at the mills, and the need for women to have a vote and a say on how the country was run. And even Jane realized that women were not equal with men, and was not happy to accept her lot in life. After all, she was Charlotte Atkinson's granddaughter, and her grandmother had always striven to be as good as – or even better than – any businessman in the area. She always had to work that little bit harder than most men, but was unable to have a say in the local elections. Surely that wasn't right; everyone should be equal, regardless of their gender.

Jane picked up her latest edition of *Votes for Women*

and read the dedication, to remind herself of the cause she believed in:

> *To the brave women who today are fighting for freedom: to the noble women who all down the ages kept the flag flying and looked forward to this day without seeing it: to all women all over the world of whatever race or creed or calling, whether they be with us or against us in this fight, we dedicate this paper.*

She put the paper to one side. It wasn't just her mother and father falling out that she felt upset about. It was the fact that her mother had put her Aunt Harriet in Madge's place. Why hadn't she asked Jane herself to come and learn alongside her? She knew how to sew and could follow a pattern. Instead, she was treating Harriet as if she was someone special. To make matters worse, the whole of Atkinson's was singing Harriet's praises, saying how nice it was to see the pair working back together. If Bert Bannister had said it once to Jane, he'd said it a hundred times, and she was a little tired of hearing about the glorious Harriet and her skills. Bloody Harriet! All Jane needed now was for the simple Rosie to follow her mother into work at Atkinson's, and that would never do. Rosie didn't even dress well.

Jane looked at herself in her bedroom mirror. Her long auburn hair and pale skin made her stand out from the crowd, but how she hated her hair colour; she had always been teased as a child for the redness of it. Even

194

now, even though people commented on her good looks, she still hated it. Everything was wrong in her life, and nobody cared.

'Jane, Harriet has run out of this red-coloured Sylko. Can you go down to Dewhurst's and pick up six reels, please?' Isabelle entered the warehouse at Atkinson's and gave Jane her latest instructions, showing her a near-empty bobbin reel with a hint of the colour she needed.

'Why me, Mother? Can't one of the warehouse lads go for you? It isn't really my job, fetching and carrying.' Jane looked at her mother and pulled a sulky face. She wasn't a gofer – she would be the heiress one day of Atkinson's.

'You are to go because you were the first one I set eyes on who was doing nothing. Besides, I thought you'd appreciate the walk. But don't think I'll not be timing you. There will be no dilly-dallying with those mill girls, especially that Nellie Taylor. She's nothing but trouble. Now get gone. Tell them to put it on my account – and look lively, as Harriet is waiting for it.' Isabelle looked at her surly daughter. She knew Jane wasn't happy and realized that things were not that pleasant at home for her, but 'there were worse things happening at sea', as her mother used to say to her, when she thought she was having a bad time. She watched as Jane grabbed her shawl and made her way out of the warehouse doors.

'I don't know, Bert, she's nothing but a worry at the moment. I can't do right for doing wrong. What with her and her father, no wonder I'm showing signs of ageing.'

Isabelle sighed and looked at the old man across the warehouse table.

'Tha's nobbut a spring chicken yet, ma'am. Wait until you get to my age. It'll not be long before I'm pushing up the daisies. Or so it would be, if I didn't have this place to keep me going. Isn't it grand having Miss Harriet back with us? It's just like old times. How are you both getting on?' Bert leaned on the table and looked across at Isabelle. His body ached, but he wasn't going to let her know of his pain.

'It's lovely, Bert. I don't have to explain anything to Harriet, as she knows exactly what to do, and the customers love her. She's no problem. It's Miss Clever-clogs I'm worried about; she seems so angry about everything. What with her and her father, I'm beside myself.' Isabelle pushed a loose strand of her greying hair behind her ear.

'It'll settle down in a bit. Give it time, and folk will find something else to talk about other than your husband. As for Miss Jane, well, she hears and sees everything down here. Perhaps you could find her a job on the shop floor, or upstairs with you. I think she's feeling a bit lost and neglected.' Bert had watched the young lass becoming more and more discontented over the weeks, and knew Jane was eager to learn elsewhere in the shop.

'I'll see, Bert, but she should have the patience to learn from the bottom up. Perhaps in another week or two, once her father is back, she could help him, because he will need some assistance for a while.' Isabelle turned to go.

'She's like her grandmother, that 'un. She will never

be satisfied – a bit like yourself at the same age. But she'll enjoy being with her father. And besides, I've learned her all I can, so let her be with him.' Bert leaned over and winked. 'She'll keep an eye on him and all.'

'Thank you, Bert, I hear what you are saying.' Isabelle looked haughty as she walked out of the warehouse. Sometimes Bert did not know his place. Unfortunately, he was nearly always right in what he said.

'Six reels of this cotton, please, and book it to Atkinson's.' Jane handed the cotton bobbin over to the young lad in the warehouse of Dewhurst's and waited. The large, five-storeyed mill was made out of local stone and stood down Broughton Road, on the edge of the Leeds-to-Liverpool canal. The towering red-brick chimney dominated the Skipton skyline. The mill kept more than two hundred people in work, and prior to that had been the place of employment of more than four hundred people – all of them families that relied on King Cotton and the cotton-weaving Belle Vue Mill. But now, along with its original name being almost forgotten, and Dewhurst's making it into a mill spinning cotton silk known as Sylko, its weaving rooms were not as busy. But still the clatter of the spinning machines filled the air, along with the dust from the fibres.

'Jane! Jane, I thought it was you. I was just making my way up to the top office.' Nellie Taylor grinned at her comrade-in-arms, who also defied the non-believers in the Suffragette movement.

'Hello, Nellie. I'm just collecting some Sylko for my

mother. I wondered if you'd be about.' Jane looked at her working-class friend. They made an odd partnership, and sometimes Jane was ashamed of the way Nellie dressed, in her work clogs, grey stockings and drab dresses. But when she listened to Nellie talking, she realized there was more to her than just an ordinary mill lass. Nellie was a firebrand for the Suffragette movement.

'I can't talk long, for old Dewhurst is on my back. He says he's fed up of me whipping up the work lasses with my dangerous talk. It's only dangerous if you are an ignorant man. But then again, he is.' Nellie grinned, her face lit up with wickedness as she beamed from under her mob cap.

'Yes, and my mother's timing me, so I can't be long, either.' Jane shook her head.

'The more money they have, the tighter the bastards get! No disrespect to your mother, Jane. But you know what I mean. Here, are you joining us on our march next Saturday? We aim to walk through Skipton, demanding our rights from the government. I think there's about ten of us so far.' Nellie looked at her posh friend and waited for an answer.

'I don't know. My mother wouldn't want me to be involved. I don't know if I could get away.' Jane saw the warehouse boy coming back with her reels of cotton and was thankful for an excuse to leave. She supported the movement, but it would only give her mother more worry if she joined the protest.

'Go on, lass, we won't get into any trouble. The local bobbies know us all too well – you know what it's like around here. You can't fart unless somebody hears you.' Nellie laughed out loud.

'I'll see. I can't promise.' Jane took the bobbins from the warehouse boy and started to walk away from her friend.

'Twelve-thirty, top of the High Street next to the churchyard. Wear your sash, you can help me carry the banner,' shouted Nellie after her, before walking in the opposite direction. 'I'll see you there. We need you to help organize.'

Jane walked down the cobbled mill yard and made her way over Belmont Bridge, stopping on the top to look at the barges on the canal make their way underneath and unload their cargo along the quayside. She watched as an elderly man kept lowering a bucket full of holes down into the dirty waters of the canal. His body was nearly bent double with age, and she watched as he dragged the bucket along the bottom of the canal until the weight told him it was full of what he was dredging for: black gold, coal from the barges that had supplied Dewhurst's powerful engines and had fallen into the canal. She saw him sort the rubbish from the coal, throwing it back into the canal. He put the lumps of coal into the old wooden cart that she'd seen him trundling around Skipton with, to hawk his stolen gains to those who'd buy it.

What a way to make a living, she thought, as she started her walk back home. But then again, there were many who earned a living from nothing – she knew that. Then there were the likes of her mother's customers, some of whom had more money than sense. Jane realized that she was privileged, but she also knew it was as a result of her grandmother's hard work. How she missed her grandmama, who'd always been there for her; she'd have sorted out the mess at home and would have been there for Jane to talk to. Instead, she had been shoved down into the warehouse and told to collect the bobbins that she now held in her hand, like a common errand girl. Her mother thought nothing of her; all she thought of was her precious business. That's why her father's head had been turned – Isabelle had no time for him, just as she hadn't for her.

Damn it, she would go on Saturday's march just to defy her mother, if nothing else.

19

'Hey up! I didn't think you were going to show.' Nellie Taylor stood with her folded banner at the top of Skipton High Street, grinning, as Jane joined the small group. 'We've not got a very good show today. There's only five of us. Nevertheless, we might be small in number, but we are determined in our beliefs. Let's show Skipton that we mean business, that women can no longer be treated like second-class human beings.' She lifted her banner and looked at all her comrades-in-arms, waiting hopefully for any more followers of the cause. 'What's up with you, Lady Jane? You look as if you are in a mood. All not well in your world?' Nellie didn't believe anything could be wrong in a world filled with the amount of money the Atkinsons and Foxes had.

'It's Mama. She tried to stop me joining you, she just doesn't understand. I hate her at the moment. All she thinks about is the business, nothing else.' Jane scowled and pulled her sash of green, cream and violet straight, as she made ready for the march down the High Street.

'It's people like your mother who are keeping the women of this town chained to their homes and husbands. She pampers to their needs as ignorant kept women – prizes for their men, dressed in their hobble skirts and smelling of perfume. They don't have time to think for themselves. That's why she's so against you being with us.' Nellie was in full voice. 'I've been thinking; we should do what Kitty Marion's done: break a few windows, make folk sit up and take note. Her and Clara Giveen even set fire to the grandstand at Hurst Park to show how strongly they feel. It's no good us feebly walking down the High Street and doing nothing. Nobody's going to give us a second glance,' Nellie yelled.

'I don't know, Nellie. Sergeant Monks is watching us, I saw him when I walked out of the store. He's got his eye on us.' Jane looked worried.

'Nah, he'll be more bothered about his pork pie from the butcher's; he just thinks we are a lot of silly girls and women. Right, come on, ladies: best foot forward. Let's show the good people of Skipton what we want.' Nellie thrust the banner to two girls behind her and linked arms with Jane, stepping out in her black lace-up boots and long full skirt, ready to take on the world.

'Votes for women. Votes for women!'

Nellie yelled as she pushed her way down the bustling High Street, ignoring the jeers from men and the disgusted looks from women of higher society. Jane was pulled along beside her.

'What do we want? We want justice, we want equality,' she yelled, and her followers took up the chant.

The small group made itself known, but it wasn't enough in Nellie's eyes. She wanted everybody's head to be turned and to acknowledge that the Suffragette movement was now amongst them. As they passed Atkinson's beautiful display windows, Nellie stopped. She noticed a loose stone among the market setts and bent down to pick it up.

'This'll make your mother take note. She'll know just how serious you are with this.' Nellie stopped and looked at Jane as she held back her arm, stone in hand ready to be flung.

'What are you doing? Stop it, you'll get us arrested,' Jane yelled, as Nellie lobbed the stone straight through the largest window of Atkinson's. The crash of glass made everyone stop in their tracks. They all stared at a mannequin as its head came off and rolled down the street. The glass shattered everywhere, and women screamed. Such a disturbance had never been seen before on Skipton High Street.

Sergeant Monks blew his whistle loud and clear, calling for backup from the station on Swadford Street. He made a beeline for Nellie and Jane.

'That bloody showed them, they'll know we mean business now, girl! Now, let's bugger off. How fast can you run?' Nellie grinned at the group behind her and took to her heels, leaving Jane wondering why she had become involved in such a fracas and having to turn and run herself, along with the other demonstrating women.

'Votes for women,' Nellie shouted once more, as she ran down to the turn-off for Broughton Road.

'Votes for women, my arse!' a constable shouted after her, knowing Nellie and where she lived. He'd soon catch up with her.

Jane was frantic. She bobbed and tried to hide in the crowd that had now gathered around the scene of Nellie's crime. She daren't go into her mother's firm, but instead watched as her mother came out of the doorway to look at the damage done. Jane quickly took off her sash, which she been wearing had so proudly, and thrust it into her pocket, out of the sight of the gossiping crowds.

'Now, Miss Fox, I think you may have been party to the crime just committed. You should be more careful who your friends are, or at least hide that auburn hair of yours, if you don't want to be caught.' Sergeant Monks put a gentle hand on her shoulder. 'Now let's do this quietly, without making a further scene. I'm sure both you and your mother would appreciate it that way. You just go to the station with Constable Stavely here, and I'll go and talk to your mother.' Sergeant Monks looked at the young lass he'd know all her life and shook his head. 'Take her away, Mike. I'll follow up shortly with her mother. She'll not give you any bother, will you, Miss Fox?'

'No, I didn't know Nellie was going to do that. I couldn't stop her. Mother will kill me for being involved.' Jane hung her head as the constable took her arm and walked her through the crowd. She watched as they muttered her name and shook their heads. 'It's the Fox lass.

204

Her mother will have something to say about this,' she heard one of her mother's customers exclaim.

'All I did was walk with Nellie, I didn't do anything,' Jane protested. 'You don't have to take me to the station. I'll not do it again.' She pulled on the constable's arm.

'Now, Miss, Sergeant Monks says I've to take you there, so just you be quiet and give me no bother.' Constable Stavely held her arm in a vicelike grip and walked Jane up Swadford Street and into the station.

'Got one of these mad women, Bill. Or should I say "girl". A bloody suffragette – she's just broken Atkinson's window, along with her mate. She'll soon be joining us as well.' Constable Stavely leaned over the station's desk and laughed with his fellow officer as they looked Jane up and down. 'Sarge says she'll give us no bother, for he knows the family.'

Jane was near tears. She'd never been in trouble before. She was secretly in fear of the police and, together with the thought of her mother's anger once she came to save her, felt scared stiff.

'Put her in one of the cells – that'll calm her down. Bloody stupid women!' Constable Stavely's colleague passed him the keys to one of the two cells in the station and looked Jane up and down again. 'I'll wait to see what Sarge says, before I take her details and book her.'

'Come on then, you.' Constable Stavely pulled on Jane's arm and led her to the cells at the back of the station, showing her into a small, stark room, with just a wooden bench with a cover on it acting as a bed, and a bucket for a toilet. He then left, closing the door behind him and turning the key in the lock.

Jane looked around her. She'd never been in such a place, and she couldn't even see out of the small window, it was so high above her. The key turning in the lock might have incarcerated her in her cell, but it also unlocked the flood of tears that had been welling up inside her since her capture. She sat on the edge of the hard bed and sobbed. Oh God, what would her mother say? She loved her Atkinson's store. Indeed, Jane did, just as much. She'd known how hard her grandmother had worked for the string of shops to become a success. It was her inheritance and it meant everything to her. How could Nellie Taylor have been so stupid, and how could she herself have let her be?

'You are telling me that my Jane was responsible for this!' Isabelle looked at Sergeant Monks in disbelief. 'She told me she was going to the library, and that she would have no part in the stupid protest we had argued over this morning. The stupid girl!' Isabelle watched as Bert Bannister swept the broken glass up from the High Street and made safe the window.

'Aye, well, she wasn't the ringleader and it wasn't her that threw the stone, you'll be glad to hear. But she did cause an affray, so one of my constables has taken her to the station. That will cool her down, along with the knowledge that you'll have plenty to say, no doubt.' Sergeant Monks looked at Isabelle. She didn't deserve any further scandal in her life. That was why he'd tried to whisk Jane away as quietly as he could.

'Oh, yes, Officer, I'll have plenty to say alright. I bet it was that terrible little Nellie Taylor who was the ring-leader. She drip-feeds her suffragette propaganda into our Jane's ear whenever she can. And I was stupid enough to send Jane to Dewhurst's for some cotton last week.' Isabelle could have cursed. 'Will you be pressing charges? I suppose you'll have to.'

'Aye, you are right – it was Nellie who threw the stone. As for Jane, I'll see how she's behaved, once we get back to the station. She's not as headstrong as her partner-in-crime, so I'm hoping that a few hours in the cells will give her something to think about. I could do without the paperwork, and the last thing I want is a lot of screaming women in my station. Once I've brought Nellie Taylor in, I'll more than likely have that.' Sergeant Monks looked at Isabelle. 'A strict talking-to from both of us should be sufficient. Let Jane stew until you've closed up the shop; it'll not do her any harm.'

'Thank you, Officer, I'd be grateful if that is what we could do between us.' Isabelle hesitated. 'It isn't that I don't believe in the suffragette cause. After all, my mother was a firebrand in her own right, and I believe any woman is equal to any man and should therefore have the same rights. But causing chaos and violence is not the right way to go about it. I will emphasize that most carefully to Jane when I pick her up this evening. I also think that matters at home have perhaps not encouraged her to see things in a better light. I will make it my responsibility that she doesn't give you any more trouble, Sergeant Monks.'

'Aye, things have not been good for you. Perhaps it is Jane's way of letting of a little steam, while protesting for her ideals. Don't worry, Mrs Fox, I do understand. Now, if you don't mind, I'll go and arrest the true culprit. Will you be wanting your day in court with her, ma'am?' Sergeant Monks waited as Isabelle turned to look at him in the doorway.

'I think not, Sergeant Monks. It would play right into Nellie Taylor's hands because it would be a day of hearing her own voice in a packed courtroom, telling everyone the virtues of the Suffragette movement. My mother and myself – and hopefully, one day, my headstrong daughter – have been standing up to men for generations. The world will change, and women will be equal one day, but not through violence. I will be at your station around six, Sergeant Monks. Do with Nellie Taylor what you want, but keep her away from my daughter.'

Isabelle lifted her skirts and stepped back through the revolving doors of Atkinson's. As she did so she sighed; her silly daughter; she applauded Jane's beliefs, but not to the extent of getting arrested. She would talk to her tonight and get to the bottom of what had been upsetting her of late. Although, deep down, she knew that it was because of her father's actions; their home life was not good just now, and it was time to forgive and forget and try to make life return to normal at Windfell. She and James must stop shouting at one another and think of their family, before it was too late and irrefutable damage was done.

20

'This is all your fault. She's upset and rebelling because of the shame you have brought upon the family.' Isabelle was taking her frustration with Jane out on James, as she paced backwards and forwards in the parlour of Wind-fell Manor.

'It's more than that. She must be missing her grand-mother, and I know that she must be upset with us arguing constantly,' said James. 'I am upset about it myself. Isn't it time we put an end to it? What's done is done. I can't amend the past, and I admit that I have been a fool.' He looked at his wife. He'd found it hard to believe that his daughter had as good as been arrested for being involved in smashing her own mother's window. Yes, it was for a cause that was worthy, in Jane's eyes, but it was not like her to be so demonstrative. She'd say what she thought, yes, but she wouldn't normally have caused criminal damage.

'I was going to suggest that, once you return to work,

Jane could be your assistant, as she's not enjoying working in the warehouse. And you will need someone to help you, once you return, in the next week or two. That might give her more purpose in life, and she always has been closer to you than to me. You know what daughters are like with their fathers – in their eyes, fathers can do no wrong. Even if he is the biggest cad in the district.' Isabelle's eyes flashed at James. She would never forgive him for doing her wrong, no matter how hard he tried.

'There you go again – you cannot let it lie. But yes, I'd welcome Jane into the studio to help me. She knows the basics already, and it would save me having to train someone else. I hope to be back next week, once I regain a little more strength in my leg. It would get Jane into a position that makes her feel more important. I don't think she has appreciated having to learn the workings of the firm from the bottom up. I also think she may be a little jealous of Harriet helping you out. Perhaps Jane thought she would be given a better position in the firm, given that she is our daughter, despite not showing one bit of interest in using a needle.' James hoisted himself up and looked out of the window. 'Autumn is here, the beech leaves have turned already. It'll soon be winter and then we will have problems getting ourselves into work, let alone Harriet getting there from up at Crummock.'

'We've always managed, and if Harriet can't make her way from Crummock, then I will have to do without her. I'm going to have to find somebody anyway, I think. We have so many orders and, to be honest, at the moment Harriet is a godsend, but all she talks about is her children and the farm. It's a bit never-ending, and I switch off after a while.' Isabelle walked over to James and stood beside him.

He turned to look at her. 'I'm sorry, Isabelle, I didn't mean to cause you all this worry. I've been stupid. I love you, and our family. It was a few moments of self-indulgence that ended in disaster. A disaster that none of us will ever forget. But maybe it can make our marriage stronger, if we can overcome it.' He leaned on his walking stick and looked at Isabelle. How could he have been such a fool and have allowed his head to be turned by Madge, when the woman he truly loved had always been by his side?

'I can never forget what you have put us through, James. It will never be the same, but we must make the best of it. For all our sakes.' Isabelle's eyes filled with tears; she had missed her soulmate, the man she had always loved. But now, hopefully, he was hers once more. Perhaps some good had come out of Jane's rash actions. She only hoped so.

'That's good to see.' Jane entered the room quietly just as her father kissed her mother tenderly on the brow. 'At least you are not shouting at one another.' She walked past her parents, her eyes still red from crying, after the lecture and strong talking-to that both parents had given her, following the terrible few hours she had endured, locked up in the police cell. She'd been made to feel so unsure of herself, and as if the world was conspiring against her. She had, however, realized just how fervent her friend Nellie Taylor was in defence of the suffragettes, and had listened to Nellie shouting from the next cell, as she too was caught and detained. Poor Nellie, would she still be there?

Even though her mother had told the police to do what they wished with Nellie, Isabelle did not want to press charges. Jane knew the reason behind this was to protect herself and the family, as she would have been called as a witness, and it would be another scandal that her family was involved in. What a fool she had been to get so involved. Nellie, on the other hand, would stand her corner and probably do something more serious next time, following the call of the Pankhurst sisters and their like. That was not for her; she had learned her lesson.

'We were just talking about you, my dear. Your father and I have decided that perhaps it would be a good idea, on his return to work shortly, for you to help him in his studio, instead of being downstairs with Bert.' Isabelle went and stood behind her daughter and put her hand on her shoulder. She hated to see Jane so upset. 'Then perhaps, when he is not so busy, you could come and learn some sewing skills with Aunt Harriet and myself, if you wish.' She glanced over to James for reassurance.

'Yes, we'd work well together. You've always liked arranging the props and you'd get to deal with the customers, and that is what Atkinson's is all about.' James smiled at his daughter and made his way back to his chair.

'That's just it: you always think about what's good for Atkinson's. You never ask me what I'd like, or what I think!' Jane hung her head and started sobbing again.

'Jane, you are always first in our thoughts, along with Luke. We always do what is best for you both. Atkinson's is yours as much as it is mine. I thought you loved the place; you've been a part of it since you could barely walk, and Grandmama used to take you around the shop with so much pride, knowing that some day you would step into her shoes and mine.' Isabelle bent down and took her daughter's hands. 'You miss your grandmama, don't you? We all do. And I threw myself into my work, wanting to prove myself, and forgot that you need attention, too. I'm sorry, my love. These have been terrible times for us all. I still miss my mama; she was such a strong woman to follow, and I know I'll never have the respect she had.' Isabelle held Jane tightly to her.

Jane sobbed even louder.

James looked at mother and daughter. 'We will listen more to you, Jane. We forget that you are nearly a grown woman, and you should have more say in your life. But perhaps not to the extent of hurling stones at businesses down Skipton High Street. No matter how good the cause! Now dry your eyes and stop sobbing. Your mother and I have decided to make amends and, as she says, I would dearly like to have you as my assistant, if you wish. At least then you won't have to put up with the gossip and the looks that the shop floor and warehouse staff will be giving you.' James patted his daughter; he hated to see her upset. 'Have a day or two off and let the dust settle, so to speak, then start back at work with me. We can be two outcasts together, if you are worried about the gossip. I'm sure your mother will agree.'

'I'm not bothered what folk say, as I did nothing wrong. It was Nellie. But yes, Father, I would like to do that. If that's alright with you, Mother? I do feel so ashamed that I let Nellie do it, and I'm sorry. It is because everyone's been so wrapped up in themselves, and I have no one except old Bert Bannister to talk to. I miss Grandmama so much.' Jane raised her head and looked into her mother's dark eyes. 'I love you, Mama, and I'm so sorry for all the worry I've given you.'

'Don't worry, my dear. I was just as headstrong at your age. You always hurt the ones you love, because they are the ones who love you the most and you know you can get away with it. We all have to vent our wrath occasionally.' Isabelle looked up at her husband; he would never know just how much he had hurt her. It was true, she'd hurt those she loved around her too, with words of anger and her actions, most of which she regretted, with hindsight. The trouble was that time was a slow healer, and it would take a long time to amend the last six month's happenings. Jane wasn't the only one who felt unloved.

'What's the matter, Isabelle? Are you still worrying about the smashed window? It's been replaced, and folk will soon forget about it.' Harriet looked up from her sewing and waited for a reply from her sister-in-law, who had been in a mood with her all day. 'It wasn't as if Jane was responsible; it was her friend.'

'It isn't just that, Harriet. My life's in such a mess. I just feel like crying. I didn't think James would ever hurt

214

me the way he has done. I'm trying to put on a strong face and hold the family together, but it is so hard. I've even let him back into my bed at night, but to be honest, I don't want him near me, because all I think of is her and what they got up to.' Isabelle stopped pinning the clothes on her mannequin and sat down next to her sister-in-law. 'The business takes all my time, and my children feel neglected. And in all honesty, I didn't realize just how much my mother did for our families. Since her death everything's gone wrong, and even Archie never comes near me.' Isabelle wiped away a tear that was falling.

'Well, you don't have to worry about Archie; he's just content up at Crummock. You know he was never one for finery, and he'd be the first one to come to your aid if he thought you needed him. He doesn't visit much because he knows you are all busy. Besides, he's better with sheep than folk, as he tends to say what he thinks nowadays and doesn't realize the consequences.' Harriet smiled. 'As for the rest, things are bound to get better. It's just been a bad year so far, so let's hope 1914 will put an end to our run of bad luck.'

'I still can't believe that James cheated on me. I look at him and sometimes I want to slap his face. And what's more, if Madge wasn't already dead, I think I'd want to murder her, for all the hurt she has caused. To think it was going on under my very nose; they were probably touching each other in here.' Isabelle looked around her and started to sob.

'It's not worth tears, Isabelle. She's gone and James is back with you. Just make sure he doesn't wander again.

Stop dwelling on it, and welcome him back into your bed – it's what we women have to do.' Harriet breathed in deeply and looked across at Isabelle, who lifted her head and looked at her.

'But you know nothing about how it feels, to be hurt by someone you love. Danny will never have looked at another woman since he married you. You've no idea of the pain Madge has caused,' she sobbed.

Harriet hesitated. 'No, Danny's always been faithful since we married. But there was a time, just before we were to marry, that I found out he was not being faithful to me, and I never will forget the pain it caused me.' Harriet stopped sewing and breathed in deeply. 'Like you, I didn't know what to do. I loved him so much and didn't want to lose him. I couldn't compete with Amy Brown – she was the talk of the Dales and the sweetheart of all the farm lads, with her easy ways. So I closed my eyes and ears and carried on with the charade of our courtship, in the hope that Danny would see sense some day.'

'You knew about Amy Brown?' Isabelle lifted her head and wiped her face. 'And you still married him.'

'Oh, so you knew, too? I should have guessed, for he always confided in you.' Harriet looked at Isabelle. 'Yes, I knew she was giving him something that I wouldn't until we were married, but I still married him. Unlike Amy, I had my morals. And I knew that was why she was adored by half the male population.'

'I told Danny what Amy was like, Harriet. I told him he was a fool. I didn't say anything to you because I

216

knew you loved him. It was just that Amy let him have his own way.' Isabelle looked across at Harriet, with her head held high.

'I know, you were torn between us. Don't worry, Isabelle, I understand. What I'm trying to tell you, though, is that Madge must not come between you and James. She's done what Amy Brown did to us – given James an easy distraction, and that's all she was. Like Amy, Madge was someone who made him feel he was special when she lifted her skirts. When really it was both of us who loved them more.' Harriet went and put her arms around Isabelle. 'At least you haven't the worry of knowing that a child was born from James's fling. I sometimes wonder if Amy's firstborn could be Danny's, and I hear that he's come back to live at Ragged Hall, which makes me worry even more.'

'Oh, Harriet, I'm sure he won't be Danny's. She married someone from over Slaidburn. He's just come to look after his grandfather while he's unwell.' Isabelle breathed in deeply and blew her nose.

'We'll see, because one day he will turn up like a bad penny, of that I'm sure, and I will know instantly if I'm right or not. Anyway, let's get back to Jane. Bring her to me when she's not busy helping her father and I'll show her how to cut out a pattern. Then we will take it from there. It is what she should be doing: following in your footsteps. Although looking through the store today, I couldn't help but notice how many people are purchasing our finished garments from our suppliers. The fact that people are able to make their own clothing now, too, means that I think our role in life may soon be forgotten, and only needed for very special occasions.' Harriet went back to her sewing and put her head down.

'I'm glad Mother left you shares in Atkinson's, for you are still a part of the family and always will be, Harriet. And don't you worry: Danny loves you and always will. And as for James, well, I've no option but to forgive him, for the sake of our family.'

21

'Well, bugger me, you'll never guess who's just casually sloped back into the yard, with his mattress over his back and two dead rabbits in his hands, as if nothing's happened.' Danny came into the kitchen and looked at his father as he gazed out of the window.

'It can only be Ethan. I told you he'd be back. What did you say to him?' Archie turned around with a grin on his face. 'Welcomed him back with open arms, did you?'

'I bloody well didn't. I asked him where he'd been and said that he'd no right to trail off like he did. I also said that he'd caused no end of worry, both for us here and for his parents.' Danny pulled up his chair and warmed his hands next to the fire. 'There's a touch of frost out there this morning.'

'That's why he's back – summer's come to an end. He's not daft, he knows where he'll be warm and fed. You'll have him now until spring and then he might need another wander. That is if tha wants him.' Archie looked at his son.

'To be honest, I've missed the little bugger. Happen I didn't appreciate him when he was here. He kept the yard tidy and the horse harness was always polished, and the horses loved him. He's a good hand with the two Clydesdales and we will start ploughing that bottom field to plant turnips before long. I should really send him packing, but he's asked if he can talk to me this evening. He looked serious, so he knows I'll not mince my words.'

'This 'un will be glad. Have you heard your father, Rosie? Ethan's turned up, as bold as brass.' Archie grinned at Rosie, with her arms full of washing as she entered the kitchen. 'Tha's had a face as long as a wet weekend in Blackpool since he's been away.'

'What do I care about him? Ethan can trail where he wants. I hope you are not taking him back on, Father.' Rosie stood with her sheets nearly falling out of her arms, secretly feeling her heart flutter as she heard the news. At the same time she was short with her words, for he'd left her in her hour of need and she couldn't forgive him.

'He wants to see me tonight. I told him to go about his work until then. I'll have a think about it. Ethan is a law unto himself, but not a bad worker when he puts his back into it.' Danny looked at his daughter, who seemed flushed. His father was right: since Ethan had been gone, Rosie had been miserable. Happen there was something he was missing here.

'Well, regardless of what Grandpapa thinks, I'm not

bothered if he stays or goes.' Rosie turned on her heels and went quickly to the wash-house with her load.

'Methinks the lady doth protest too much,' Archie muttered.

'I didn't realize you knew Shakespeare, Father.' Danny looked at the old man. 'I do think tha's hit the nail on the head – something that's been happening since that day they both buggered off to Appleby together, now that I think about it.' Danny rubbed his brow.

'Well, we'll have to see what he's got to say tonight – he's been up to something.' Archie looked at his son. Danny had forgotten what it was like to be young, but Archie hadn't.

Rosie quickly pushed the washing into the dolly-tub and started to stir the clothes with the posser. She'd wash the sheets, rinse them and hang them on the line next to the duckpond as soon as she could, regardless of the chill wind that was blowing. She had to see Ethan, before he spoke to her father. She thought of him while she pummelled the clothes. Where had he been, these past few weeks? What had he been up to, and why had he returned now? Happen he did care for her after all.

She swept her hair back from her face and leaned into the dolly-tub. The steam from the hot water hit her face as she lifted the sheets into the earthenware sink to be rinsed. The cold water was icy this morning, and she didn't dally long before she threaded them through the mangle to get rid of the excess water. She swore under her breath as her sleeves and skirt got wet, leaving her

221

arms and stomach cold to the touch. Then she carried the heavy washing basket out of the wash-house, across the yard to the green where the duckpond and clothes line were, sheltered by a small plantation of trees that ran alongside the track down to Austwick. Even there the wind was biting, and Rosie wished that she had grabbed her shawl before setting about her task. Her hands were numb and red as she finally pegged the last of the sheets out and turned to look at them blowing in the breeze. Drops of water fell from them, as if they were white clouds full of rain, as she turned to shoo the goose that was Crummock's guard dog from around her feet. She hated the honking bird; it was never quiet and had a habit of pecking you if you let it get near.

'I see old Napoleon hasn't lost his squawk.' She turned and looked towards the garden gate and saw Ethan leaning over it. 'He doesn't know who his friend is and who his enemy is.' He grinned; the grin that Rosie loved, the one that had made her his, on that fateful day of passion.

'If it were up to me, I'd shoot the thing. Along with a few other things that are worth nowt around here.' Rosie picked up her washing basket and walked over to him. She walked with a swagger, hoping to catch Ethan's eye even more.

'Now, Rosie Atkinson, you are not aiming your words at me, are you? There's me come back specially to be with you, and I could be looking down two barrels, for all you care.' Ethan opened the gate and leaned against it next to her. 'How are you? How are things . . . you know?' He nodded to Rosie's stomach and looked worriedly at her.

'You needn't worry. In fact you need not have come back. I lost the baby, if indeed there was one there at all – I'm still not sure. Nobody knows, I managed to keep it to myself. I lost it through the night and cleaned myself up before anyone suspected anything.' Rosie stumbled over her words. She'd needed him that morning; she'd needed Ethan's arms to be put around her and tell her it was alright and that he loved her, but he hadn't been there. She'd been alone with her loss and hadn't even known where he was.

'Rosie, I'm so sorry, I didn't know. Are you alright? Did you not go to see the doctor? You should have told your mother.' Ethan put his arm around her as she trembled, both with the cold and with the trauma of remembering the terrible night when she had lost her unformed baby.

'What, and have to tell everybody that you were the father and that you had left me? What would that have achieved? We'd both have been cast out by our families. Remember what your father did when we went to Appleby; he'd have been even worse, once he'd found out the baby was yours.' Rosie buried her head in Ethan's shoulder and cried. His tweed jacket and strong arms comforted her as he held her close. She could smell the mountain air on his clothes and realized just how much she had missed him, and how much she loved her wild rambler.

'I've only been living in the shooting hut below Moughton Scar. I had to have time to myself to think things through. To see what I thought about the future for both of us – for all of us.' Ethan put a finger under Rosie's chin and lifted her face up for her to look at him. 'I didn't leave you, Rosie, I just needed time to think. I do love you.'

'But you left and didn't say anything, so what was I to think?' Rosie wiped her eyes clear of tears.

'Aye, but I'm back now, and I was going to tell your father all and ask for his permission for me to marry you. Regardless of who I am. Now, with things like they are, perhaps asking his permission to court you would be a better idea. It'll not be as rushed, and then there's no more sneaking about. Neither of us have enjoyed lying and being secretive.'

'My father would never agree, nor will my mother, especially with you disappearing like you did.' Rosie looked up at him, thinking it was a hopeless request.

'Nay, I don't think they will. But your grandfather knows we are made for one another. I can tell from the way he looks at us when we are just talking together. It's better to marry for love than for money. After all, isn't that what he did?' Ethan held Rosie tight. 'I can but try and, if they are truly against us, then we will continue like we have done, until they realize that we are meant for one another.'

'Alright, but they will both say I'm too young and that I should set my sights higher. I know they will.' Rosie held Ethan tightly; he was everything to her, she had known that when he'd left her on her own in her grief.

'Tonight, then, I'll ask them after supper.' Ethan bent

down and kissed her. 'And yes, I do love you, Rosie Atkinson, and now I can truly say it, as we are under no pressure. I would have married you, if you were still carrying our baby. I would not have deserted you, no matter what.'

'Now then, lad, I suppose you've come to plead for your job back and tell us why you went wandering without leave.' Danny looked at Ethan. For once he looked respectable: his shirt was clean, his corduroy trousers were stainless and his long dark hair was brushed and in place.

'Aye, I'd be grateful if I could keep my job, especially after I tell you why I left. I hope that perhaps you'll respect the dilemma I find myself in.' Ethan looked at Danny and Archie, as they both sat at the polished dining-room table, in a room that was not often used by the farming family. It was one Ethan had never been in before. It was obvious to him that this was just as an important meeting to them as it was to him, and he felt uneasy as he glanced around the room at the oil paintings on the walls and the polished silver upon the dressers. There he stood, a stable boy asking for no less than the hand of the lass that all this would belong to one day, so perhaps he did have ideas above his station.

'Well, go on then, lad, let's be hearing you.' Archie looked at the nervous lad; he'd known Ethan since he was born and, no matter what else was said of him, he knew Ethan never did things without a cause.

'I had to leave. I needed time to think and to see if what I was feeling was right.' Ethan paused and looked

225

at both burly farmers. 'I've been living in the shooting hut below Moughton these last few weeks, because I had to get away from here. I couldn't let my feelings get the better of me until I knew what to do. Rosie has felt the same.'

'Rosie – what has this got do with Rosie?' Danny sat up in his chair and gazed at the swarthy lad, who stood looking uncomfortably at them.

'Let the lad finish, Danny.' Archie pulled on his son's sleeve.

'I, er . . . we, both think a great deal of one another. We can't help it, we are just alike. But I know my father would give me another braying, and I know that I'm way below Rosie's station in life and I shouldn't even be thinking of her in that way. That's why I needed time to think. But I'm hoping that you'll both understand and that you'll give me permission to court her properly.' Ethan blurted it all out. What he'd rehearsed so carefully was nothing like what had come out of his mouth, but at least they knew how he felt.

Danny sat back in his chair. 'I bloody knew it! I've been as blind as a bat, until I saw Rosie's face when I told her that he was back.' He turned and stared at his father. After all, Archie was to blame for making this happen, by bringing Ethan up to Crummock and turning his young daughter's head. 'She pretended not to care, but she cared alright.'

'Hold your noise, lad. It's not the end of the world. Rosie's nearly seventeen, and Ethan here is not a bad soul. At least you know all about him, and he is right: they are alike. Two wild 'uns together. And he's doing the proper thing, instead of sneaking about – give him some credit.' Archie winked at Ethan as he stood, almost trembling.

'But he has nowt, not a bloody penny. I wanted better for Rosie.' Danny sat back and looked at Ethan. 'Oh God, Harriet will not be happy.'

'You are forgetting, lad. I was in the same shoes as Ethan and couldn't afford the clothes on my back, when I fell in love with my Lottie. Then your mother came along and we were happy, but Lottie was always at the back of my mind and I knew she would one day be mine, no matter how poor I was. There's no price on true love, lad, you should know that. Let the lad court her, see how they feel about one another in six months' time. It might come to something or it might disappear like the morning's dew.' Archie smiled at Ethan; he liked the boy's determination and knew he was right for Rosie.

'Bloody hell, Father. Think of what you are saying. He's a stable lad; at least your father had land. I should say no and send you on your way.' Danny looked at the lad who stood in front of him and thought of how un-happy Rosie had been the last few weeks, which he'd put down to her mother giving her extra work, but now he realized differently. 'Rosie is everything to me and I want to see her happy. I can't stand the sullen face we have had the last few weeks. If I say yes, it's on the understanding that you don't get up to anything untoward; no wander-ing hands – you respect her like a lady and you treat her right. Else it won't just be your father that gives you a braying. As my father says, six months and we will see how you still feel about one another. You can join us on a Sunday for dinner and can have the use of the parlour for an hour.' Danny stared at the young lad who had captured his daughter's heart. 'I'll ask Mrs Atkinson to make the room above the storehouse available for you; it'll be a bit warmer than the stable. We were going to have to find you somewhere before the onset of winter, and I've been thinking of that for a while. There's already a bed in there, although you might have mice as company.' Danny looked at the lad, who was now trying to hide his happiness and couldn't believe his luck. 'You treat her right, otherwise God help you.'

'I will, Mr Atkinson, I will. Thank you.' Ethan beamed.

'Now go on, get your arse out of here. I expect hard work out of you and no loitering about, looking at our Rosie. God knows what her mother will say!' Danny shook his head. Harriet wouldn't understand. She had wanted Rosie to be a lady all her life, but Rosie had always had other ideas, he'd known that. She loved the land.

Rosie lay in her bed. She could hear her mother and father talking through the wall that divided them, and knew she was the subject of discussion. She'd gone to her room early that night, avoiding any contact with Ethan and the conversation that would follow between her parents. But now she found herself unable to sleep. She imagined the disgust of her mother, at her setting her sights as low as the gypsy stable boy. She recalled all the times Harriet had sighed and said she wished Rosie was more like her cousin Jane. Jane would never do that, Jane would always be a lady and would marry into higher society, so long as everyone forgot her mad moment of fighting for the suffragette cause.

No matter. Ethan had broken their silence, and no doubt she'd be confronted by an irate mother in the morning. It was a pity it wasn't Harriet's day helping out at Skipton, for she would have to endure her mother lecturing her all day as she helped her. Whatever happened, her mother must never find out that they had already been intimate with one another, and the terrible consequences it had caused. That would always be her own and Ethan's secret; no one else must ever know. Rosie pulled her bedclothes up to her chin and tried to sleep, tugging her pillow around her ears. Tomorrow would be hell, but Ethan was worth every minute, she thought, as she gazed into the darkness of the night.

'I swear this place would go to the dogs if I wasn't here. I'm gone just a few days a week, and then this happens behind my back. And your father seems to have no more sense than he was born with – saying yes to Ethan! For heaven's sake, Rosie, you are only sixteen and, of all the lads in the dale, it's Ethan that takes your eye. Could you not have set your heart on the lad from Woodend or Sowermire? At least their fathers own some land.' Harriet looked across the table at her young daughter.

'But they are not the same, Mother. Ethan and I get on so well; we both have the same love of the countryside, and we are happy in one another's company.' Rosie lowered her head. She'd had earache from her mother all morning – lecture after lecture on how to behave, and on setting her sights higher than a common gypsy.

'Well, I suppose I'll have to make the best of it. Your father says Ethan's not a bad lad, and your grandfather seems to be relishing the thought of you two walking out together. Even told me he was looking forward to a wedding, instead of a funeral. I personally hope it doesn't come to that – wedding indeed! You'd better both behave yourselves, for we are not having the embarrassment of a hurried wedding in the family, so don't be lifting your skirts, my girl, else I'll wipe my hands of you.' The bread she was making got the pummelling of its life as Harriet vented her frustration on the dough.

'No, Mother, we would never do that.' Rosie blushed and passed her mother the greased bread tins, hoping to be out of her earshot soon.

'You can go and sweep out the feed-room and make up Ethan a bed in it. Take them old sheets that the Irishmen have been using, seeing as your father has said Ethan can sleep in there. I'm just glad he's not let him into the main house. I'd never have slept for listening for him and you sneaking about the place. Because that's what he'd do, I just know it.'

Harriet looked across at her daughter. She'd wanted better for her, but Rosie's happiness was the main thing and she was in better spirits this morning.

'Take that old piece of gingham that's in the bedding box at the end of my bed – it'll make him some curtains. And I don't want to see him with next to nothing on in a morning, when I'm off about my work. There's two old

230

chairs that Archie brought with him and a table in the outhouse; take him those as well. We'd better give him a better standard of living, if he's to walk out with you.' Harriet watched as Rosie grinned at her. 'You can grin, my lass, but you behave with him! Just until we know what he's about. And time will tell us that – if you're still on his arm this coming spring.'

Rosie stood back and looked at Ethan's new living quarters. The room smelled of the barley, wheat and corn maize used to feed the hens and pigs, stacked in one corner. But it was warm and dry and quite homely now. The spare bed, which had been there for any travellers and drovers, was now made up with clean sheets, and Rosie had hung the red gingham curtains around the windows and whitewashed walls, as her mother had suggested. In the corner she had placed the old kitchen table and two chairs from Windfell, which had once been in her grandfather's kitchen at Butterfield Gap. They had found a home, just like Ethan, she thought, as she placed a jam jar of late-flowering Michaelmas daisies on the table to brighten the room up.

Ethan was gradually being made welcome at Crummock Farm. Perhaps it was a blessing that she had lost her baby; this way everyone would know that both of them were serious about one another. It didn't matter that Ethan was a stable boy. Anyway he wasn't any more; he could say he was the farm man now, and he'd hopefully have an even better position in the future.

Rosie smiled as she closed the paint-worn door behind

her and climbed down the stone steps that led into the farmyard. Ethan had made it this far and, with her love, he'd get even further with her beside him, of that she was sure. Sunday could not come soon enough, and in six months' time hopefully they would be able to marry.

22

'Seen any tarts on bikes, lately, Fox?' Geoffrey Brunskill, the school bully and prefect, hit Luke hard around the head as he walked down the dormitory, checking that all was in order for night. 'Oh no, sorry – your father just kills them, I'd forgotten.'

Luke hung his head and then pulled his covers back to climb into bed, watching as Brunskill left the room. How he hated him. Since his father's accident Brunskill and his little gang of followers had made his life hell.

'Take no notice, Luke, he's a bastard.' Bill Palmer looked across at his best friend, who he knew was upset about events at home and the fact that he'd been sniggered about for weeks. 'Nobody else even gives a damn about what they heard. Besides, he's only having a go at you tonight because you've received your rifle badge so quickly. It took him ages, and he still hasn't received his red star and fully qualified as an NCO. I bet you get there before him – he's too thick to become an officer. I'd like

233

to know what his parents are like. He's only from Bradford, and they can't be that posh.'

'I'm just a little tired of him constantly having a dig.
One day I'm going to get him and make him pay. But at
the moment it's not worth it.' Luke got into his bed,
before giving another glance at the uniform that was
now hanging up, adorned with the newly awarded rifle
badge on the left arm. He was proud of himself, so Brunskill could say what he wanted.

'Lights out, no talking. Especially you, Fox, I can hear
you and that rat-like Palmer.' Brunskill hit the side of his
leg with the newly acquired silver-topped swagger stick
that all the cadets had been given, for parade purposes.
But in Brunskill's case it was an extra bullying tool, one
he did not hesitate to use.

Luke and Bill went quiet, waiting until the gas lights
had been turned off and the bully had left them in darkness.

'It's feels strange with half the dorm missing and in
the sanatorium,' Bill whispered.

'Yes, have you had German measles, like me? Mother
said I'd had them when I was just over five, but I can't
remember,' Luke whispered back.

'Yes, I've had them, and you can't catch them again.'
Bill looked at the empty beds in the darkness, devoid of
their inhabitants, who had either been sent back home or
were being looked after by matron elsewhere, in isolation
from the rest of the pupils.

'I can see our visit to camp being postponed; they
won't be sending a load of spotty, ill lads anywhere. God

forbid if half the War Office developed German measles because of Giggleswick School,' Luke whispered back. 'Still, it's drill parade in the morning and instruction lecture after tea. We'll probably find out more tomorrow.'

'Now that will annoy Brunskill, as he'll be hoping for his red star and his proficiency certificate to say he's assured of a commission, if we do go to camp. His brother got both at Bordon Camp last year, and he needs to keep up with him. God help us, if we don't go.' Bill sighed.

'We can't do anything about it. I'm tired, Bill – sorry, I'm off to sleep now.' Luke pulled his covers up around his face and thought about the camp he had so wanted to attend. There he would have mixed and made friends with other cadets from around the country, and they would all have the same patriotic feelings that he had. Then his thoughts wandered to home and his mother and father, and the stony silence there had been on his last weekend visit. He hoped things had improved, but now his sister had written to him telling him of her escapades, the fool. Between school and home, there wasn't much to like, but the cadets made him feel special, especially now that he had reached a first-class honour. The military was the life for him and he'd give it all that he'd got.

'Now then, men, I'm afraid I have some bad news for you. As you know, we were due to go to camp next week, but in view of the outbreak of German measles, I'm afraid it has had to be cancelled.' The Commanding

Officer stood in front of the cadets, after putting them through their paces on the square outside the historic school rooms. 'Now I know that you were particularly looking forward to this event, so for those of you who are well enough, I suggest that we have a few days up at Attermire Scar on the practice ranges. The miniature range under the cloisters has poor light, though it serves some purpose, but I propose that we march through Settle and then camp out on the fellside in readiness for using the ranges.' The CO watched and listened as a mumble of discontent ran through the cadets on parade. 'There's always next year, and as you know we will be going to Hagley Park in Staffordshire, so set your sights on that event in late June.'

'I bloody well knew it.' Luke walked back into the school with Bill next to him.

'Well, at least we get a few days off at camp on the side of Attermire, that's better than nothing. I wasn't looking forward to more than a week in this weather anyway, it's gone so cold of late.' Bill patted his mate on the back.

'You'll never make a soldier, you are too soft,' said Luke.

'I don't intend to. Politics is more my thing. I'll make the bullets that you will fire on my behalf – that way it's a lot safer. Isn't that what all politicians do?' Bill laughed.

'Too bloody right; it's them lot that cause half the wars in the first place, but you won't catch them on the battlefield.' Luke sat down at his desk and grinned at his mate.

'No, they've more sense. I'll leave it to the likes of you, if there's ever a war. It's best I sit behind a nice warm desk and let the others do the fighting.' Bill looked at the blackboard, and at the teacher coming in.

'Coward,' Luke whispered.

'Too true, but at least I'll still be around to tell the tale.'

Luke looked around him, stopping to catch his breath as the steep track rose in front of him out of Settle, leading on towards Malham. He turned round to see down to the market town of Settle, and a little further afield he could see the majestic copper dome of Giggleswick School chapel. It rose above all else, stating its importance before the students and school below it. Further to his right, he could just make out the rooftop of his home at Windfell. He looked at it for a brief second, before putting his best foot forward as the CO yelled at them all to keep marching. He missed home, but had decided a while ago that the army was to be his life.

They had marched through the centre of Settle, past the ancient Shambles and up through the market towards the narrow cobbled street of upper Settle, turning all the locals' heads as they swung their arms and walked in time together. Over their shoulders were their trusted rifles and on their backs were their backpacks, filled with what they would need for their two nights on the wild fellside. Luke was quietly looking forward to staying out in the wilds. He knew that he did not excel in his studies, so he devoted his time to becoming a soldier and to one day serving the King. It was what he most desired. And two days of scouting and shooting practice were right up his street; anything to get away from the musty-smelling oak-clad rooms of the ancient school, which his mother had thought he would be happy in.

The troop marched onwards to the winding Stockdale Road, high above the market town of Settle on the remote landscape leading over to Malham. There in front of them stood the high limestone crags of Attermire Scar, and the rifle butts were just visible at the bottom of the crag known as Warrendale Knotts, nearly half a mile from the road. Luke remembered when he had been at the site with his father on Whit Monday, when he taken part in the full-day shoot known as the 'Tradesman's shoot'. The shops in Settle and the surrounding district donated prizes for the best shot. His father had donated and awarded a clock to one of the local boys from the TA and had patted Luke on the back, then turned to him saying, 'Next year it could be you, son.' At the time Luke had doubted it, but now he had progressed with his skills and was certain that the prize would be his in the coming year.

'Right, men, we are staying in the field over the road. Sort yourselves into two groups. Group one needs to erect the tents, while group two will dig holes for the latrines and find some kindling and wood to build a fire. And look lively.' The CO bellowed as Luke and Bill Palmer decided which group to be in, and finally opted to be the ones digging the latrines and gathering firewood.

'Shit attracts shit,' Brunskill laughed as he pushed his way past Luke and Bill, carrying the tent poles into place.

'Piss off, Brunskill,' Luke shouted to the well-known bully. 'Shove your pole up your arse!'

Brunskill glowered at him, and then grabbed Luke by the shirt neck, quickly letting him go as the CO looked his way. 'Go and dig your hole and bury yourself in it,' he whispered as he strode off with his followers on his heels.

'Don't annoy him, Luke. He's not worth it. And we might have to sleep in the same tent as him.' Bill picked up his shovel and made for the wall side, ready to dig.

'I hate him. I'll make him think twice about picking on us, one day. He's nothing but a coward anyway.' Luke walked off, with Bill following. He would get even with Brunskill. He might be older and larger than him, but one day he'd regret being such a bully towards him.

Unfortunately Bill had been right, and the first night of camping neither Luke nor Bill hardly slept, conscious the whole time that a few feet away from them lay Brunskill and his mob of friends. They'd kept themselves out of the way of them all evening, as they had been made to tramp up and down the scar with laden backpacks to improve their fitness. But when night-time had come, they had had to put up with the jeers and mockery of Brunskill as they settled down to sleep. Now Luke was trying to keep awake, frightened that Brunskill would do something to him or Bill while they were asleep. He rubbed his eyes and listened to the snores coming from everyone else, and felt his head getting heavy as the night slowly crept into morning. Then sleep eventually got the better of him.

'Wakey-wakey, sleepy Foxy.'

Luke woke up feeling the warm, foul-smelling liquid being poured over his head and the sound of a voice coming from the person he hated.

'I couldn't be arsed to go out to the latrine, so I've given you a morning wash instead.' Brunskill kicked him slightly and then buttoned up his trousers as he put his dick away.

Luke lay in his bed as he realized that Brunskill had urinated over his head. The smell of pee made him want to be sick. 'You bastard!' He got out from under his soaked grey blanket and was about to confront the laughing Brunskill when the CO entered the tent, on hearing all the commotion.

'All of you, out across to the range in ten minutes. A spot of breakfast is to be served in the wooden hut next to the wall and then practice will begin. Fox, get up and get dressed, and tidy yourself up, man.' He turned and left the group and walked out of the tent.

'Yes, you stink, Fox, anyone would think you'd pissed the bed.' Brunskill swaggered as he led his followers out of the tent, leaving just Bill hunched up in a corner, looking shame-faced at his best friend.

'Sorry, Luke, I couldn't stop them.' Bill watched as Luke emptied his billy can of water over his head, trying to get rid of Brunskill's smell from his hair and his skin.

'It's alright, Bill, I know. But I'll not let this lie, believe me.' Luke made himself tidy and put his uniform on while his best friend watched. He vowed to get his revenge and show up Brunskill for the bully he was.

Bill and Luke ate their breakfast in silence. Luke watched as Brunskill sniggered across at him, making his friends laugh as he held his nose and commented about the smell around the table.

As soon as breakfast was over, the troop went out to the range, which was tucked away under the limestone scar. Raised areas of shooting platforms were distanced at various yards from the targets – one hundred and fifty yards being the easiest and the hardest being set at the lane edge, a distance of eight hundred and eighty yards. Only the most proficient shot could manage to hit the target from there. The six-foot target on a rotating iron axle was only a speck in the distance.

The group started off at the shortest distance and everyone hit the target. Captain Pierce, who had joined the group that morning, was keeping score.

'This is bloody easy – I wish we could get a move on,' Luke complained, as everyone lined up to take shots at the first three distances.

'It might be easy for you, but I missed the target altogether last time. There is no way I'm going to manage the last two distances.' Bill looked around him. He was beginning to wonder why he had bothered entering the Officers' Training Corps, for he was not military-minded, but his father had told him it would make him more of a man, so he'd agreed to give it a go.

'You don't concentrate enough. Hold your gun steady and gently squeeze the trigger. Like the CO says, you've got to treat your gun like the most precious thing in your life.' Luke and Bill walked towards the platform set at seven hundred and fifty yards from the target. In their footsteps came Brunskill, who overheard their conversation.

'Perhaps he's not like you. He's got more precious things in his life. Unlike you, who's not even loved by your family – boarded out, when your family only live two miles away from the school. Let's face it, nobody wants you,' sneered Brunskill.

'They are busy, they work hard, so shut your mouth, you.' Luke stared at Brunskill. How he hated him.

'Aye, we know exactly how busy your father was, especially on that bike of his.' Brunskill sniggered as he walked off and lined up to position himself at the next platform.

'Don't let him get to you.' Bill pulled on Luke's sleeve, holding him back from tackling Brunskill. 'He's not worth it.'

'I'm going to show that bastard he's not perfect. I'm sick of him picking on me and my family.' Luke lined up along with Bill and took his next round of cartridges from the CO before loading his gun, his face set, determined to outshoot Brunskill, if nothing else.

'Right, men, whoever hits this target will go on to try the platform furthest away. This will really test you all,' shouted the CO, as the cadets looked at the distance and knew what was being asked of them.

One by one, each cadet stepped up to the platform, taking his time to line up his scope and fire. All the cadets missed, bar Brunskill, who boasted about his victory. Bill stepped up and did as Luke had told him to, but to no avail, for he was no marksman and he knew it. Then Luke stood behind the wooden platform, resting his gun solidly and holding it firmly within his hand. He squeezed the trigger. He stood back and grinned as the bullet sped to the centre of the target, and Captain Pierce waved the white flag to say the target had been successfully hit.

'Well done, Luke. That means there's just you and Brunskill to try the next platform.' Bill patted his mate on the back and looked at the anger on Brunskill's face as they made their way across the wild grassland to the platform next to the wall. Brunskill's mob was cheering him on and he was full of himself as he opted to shoot first, when given the choice.

The cadets went quiet as he posed himself, taking time lining up the small speck in the distance. Bang! The shot was fired and all eyes turned to Captain Pierce as he rotated the target, and it looked as if it had been hit. But his arm rose and waved a red flag to show that the target had not been damaged, and a gasp of disappointment was heard from Brunskill and his followers.

'Good luck, Luke,' Bill whispered, as the rest of the cadets watched him.

'Aye, good luck, mate,' one of the group shouted as Luke took his position.

He licked his lips and twisted his cap round. Looking through his sights, he lined up the target as best as he could, aimed and fired! It seemed an age before the target was turned round and examined by Captain Pierce, and Luke couldn't believe it when a white flag was raised and a cheer went up from all the cadets. They patted him and congratulated him, swarming round him like bees around a honey pot.

'Right through the bloody centre, Fox, a pure bulls-eye.' Captain Pierce came running up with the paper target showing the impact of his shot. 'Good man.'

Luke grinned and was speechless. He turned and looked at a downcast Brunskill, whose friends seemed to have deserted him. Luke held his hand out to him and watched as Brunskill couldn't quite take in his act of comradeship.

'Hard luck, Brunskill, better luck next time.' Luke shook the hand of the lad who had been a bully to him for so long. He'd no need to prove his worth to him any more. He'd been shown to be the better shot, and now everyone knew it.

Brunskill was silent as he shook Luke's hand. He knew he had to look like a gentleman, but he also knew that his days of being top dog among the cadets were over. No one was even giving him the time of day as he went and sat down behind the drystone wall and lit a cigarette. Bloody Luke Fox – his sort always won.

23

'Really, Harriet, I'd have thought that you would have set your sights a little higher than Ethan, for Rosie.' Isabelle looked across at her sister-in-law in amazement at the news she'd just been told.

'I did – I said anybody but Ethan. There's so many more suitable than him, but it is as Danny says: they are both happy with one another, and that counts for a lot. Besides, they are both young; we are hoping that it will come to nothing and that their so-called love for one another will dwindle. I don't think Ethan has even told his parents. He won't dare, as Jethro would have something to say about it, so he can't be that serious. I just hope he doesn't break Rosie's heart in the process.' Harriet looked up from her sewing and noticed Isabelle scowling.

'Well, I certainly expect better of my Jane, even though she is trying me to within an inch of my patience at the moment. There's plenty of young eligible men in the dale and she's older than your Rosie, so she needs to get a move on. I keep encouraging her to attend socials and the local dances, but with no luck. I think we will have to have a Christmas Ball this year at Windfell, just like Mama used to have, and then perhaps I can invite someone who's suitable along for her. Besides, it will do the family good and will disperse any rumours about James and me having a failed marriage.' Isabelle stood back and admired the dress that she had been finishing off for a customer and smiled. 'If Jane wore something like this, she would have no end of admirers.' She pulled out the long skirts of the deep-red velvet ballgown and sat back in satisfaction at her work. 'Mrs Capstick is a very lucky lady. I hope her husband appreciates her keeping up appearances.'

'I'm sure he does, I've never seen a more devoted couple.' Harriet smiled. 'Should Jane not be with us by now? I was going to watch her as she cut out the pattern for the blouse that Amelia Hall ordered. I thought it was a good one to start with.'

'She's just doing an errand for James; he needed some ink to be collected from the printer's. He barely had to ask her and could hardly believe her eagerness, for she usually turns her nose up at errands, but she went straight away. I think she knows that he is still in quite a bit of pain with his leg, although he dare not complain when he's in my company. He knows that he will not get any sympathy from me. After all, he's only got himself to blame.' Isabelle sighed. It would take longer than a few months for her to forgive James for all the hurt he'd caused, and she was not about to show any weakness on her side of the marriage.

'I was hoping you would have advertised for a new seamstress by now. Winter is fast approaching and I don't want to be travelling from up at Crummock to Skipton each day. Besides, I probably won't be able to, for the road soon gets blocked with snow, you know that.' Harriet looked at Isabelle.

'How can I forget, Harriet? Don't you worry – I placed an advertisement in the local paper just last week, as I knew that although you are enjoying your time with us, it would not be practical for you to work here over the winter. Let's say that I have learned from my shameful past mistakes. Hopefully, by spring, Jane will have learned well enough to follow in your footsteps anyway. Then, if you wish, you can join us as and when you please, as it is a joy to be working with you again, dear sister.' Isabelle walked over to her sister-in-law and hugged her tightly. 'Are you doing anything special for Rosie's birthday next week? It's not every day a girl is seventeen.'

'No, she says she doesn't want any fuss, she just wants a quiet day. No doubt Ethan will come into it somewhere along the line. He seems to have replaced us in her affections. I just wish she wasn't so young, for there will be time for men in her life, and he's the first one she's known.' Harriet looked up at Isabelle and then decided to keep her thoughts to herself. Isabelle was being very understanding, but she was no doubt hiding her true thoughts about her niece's love affair. She remembered the caustic remarks about Ethan the last time he had come up in conversation. Still, she was glad that Isabelle had placed an advertisement for her position, for during the winter she was better up at the farm, which was where she belonged the most and where she would be needed, if snow came.

'Ethan, these are absolutely beautiful. I can't believe you have made them yourself.' Rosie smiled as she admired the miniature set of drawers that Ethan had lovingly made for her birthday present. They both sat outside on the stone steps that led up to his new lodgings in the feed-room. They sat as close to one another as they dared, given that Rosie's father kept walking across the yard as he went about his work, before the family tea that had been arranged for Rosie's birthday.

'I thought they could be put towards our home, when we get wed. They'll look good on top of the mantelpiece. That is, if we can ever afford a home.' Ethan kissed Rosie quickly on the cheek, hoping not to get caught in the act. 'I love you – you do know that. I was just frightened when you said you were with child. I'd have stood by you.'

'I know, and I was frightened too. It was perhaps a good thing I lost it. It makes days like this more special.' Rosie opened the small drawers that could hold various bits and bobs, and looked at the handles that Ethan had fashioned out of offcuts of brass from around the farm and from old brass curtain rings. 'I've been thinking that if we do wed and need a home, I could perhaps persuade Grandfather to let us live in his Great-aunt Lucy's cottage in Austwick. It's been empty for years and needs a lot of repair, but it would be lovely for just us two.'

'I don't think your mother will agree. She doesn't seem to think that I'm good enough for you, but I aim to prove her wrong. There's not much I can't turn my hand to, and your father keeps saying what a good job I'm doing, now I've decided what's important to me in life. I don't want to be just the lad that mucks out the stable and cleans the harness – I can do better than that. Where's the cottage at? Should we go and have a look at it, when we can get away together?' Ethan had decided it was time to show his commitment to Rosie and to prove to her parents that he was a worker, now that he had something to aim for. He didn't want to be excluded from the family as the outcast that he currently felt he was.

'It's down on the back green, just set back a bit off the main road. The garden's overgrown, but the roof is alright and so are the doors and windows. Should we go and have a look at it on Sunday? We are both allowed time together then.' Rosie looked excitedly at him.

'Aye, we can do that. I like Austwick and it would be just right, as you say. Plus, your grandfather is always right with me. I've a lot to thank him for, as it was him who brought me here.' Ethan smiled and wanted to hug Rosie again, but quickly put thoughts of that to one side as her mother came to the garden gate opposite them.

'Rosie, come on in now – tea is on the table and, as it's your birthday, I've made a trifle, so you'd better get yourself in before your grandfather eats the lot of it.'

Harriet looked across at the two love-birds sitting on the step. She remembered how she used to look at her Danny that way, and her heart melted a little towards Ethan. 'Are you coming and all? After all, there's no show without Punch, and it'll make our Rosie happy.' Harriet folded her arms and waited, watching the disbelief on both of their faces. 'Aye, get yourselves in. I might not be suited with this courtship, but I'll not have you miserable on your birthday.'

'Thank you, Mother. It is kind of you to ask Ethan in. Look what he's made for me.' Rosie passed the miniature set of drawers to her mother to inspect, as Ethan took his cap off and walked quietly past her.

'Not a bad job, lad. They are right bonny. I wouldn't mind some of them myself.' Harriet passed the miniatures back to Rosie. 'You're not as daft as you look.'

'Thank you, Mrs Atkinson. I'll make you some, if you want.' Ethan grinned.

'Aye, you can – in your own time, though. You've enough on this next week or two, gathering the fell with Mr Atkinson and bringing the sheep down for winter. He's decided to give you a few more responsibilities.' Harriet passed Rosie the set of drawers back and smiled. 'Now get yourselves in for some tea; there's salmon sandwiches and a present waiting for you, Rosie, because no doubt you'll be expecting something.' Harriet watched the two of them enter Crummock. Her eldest was no longer a little girl; she was a woman, and she'd have to realize that.

Ethan felt uncomfortable sitting at the table in the

dining room of Crummock Farm. He looked around him at the fine china that embellished the oak plate-rack and didn't quite know what to do with his hands and arms, as Harriet sat down opposite to him, giving him a knowing glance.

'Pass Ethan a sandwich, Rosie. Do you like salmon or would you have preferred something else?' Harriet looked at him as he gingerly took a sandwich from the gilt-edged plate, then watched as everybody else helped themselves and started to eat.

'Aye, tuck in, lad – fill your boots. Make best of it while there's stuff on the table.' Archie grinned; he'd been in the same position, the first time he'd sat in the exact same spot and not been wanted by old Father Booth, as he'd eyed his daughter.

'Yes, I like salmon, but what I've caught from the beck is nowt like this.' Ethan looked at the red-coloured fish, which showed barely any resemblance to what he usually caught.

'This is tinned salmon – a real delicacy. We only have it on special occasions, birthdays and Christmas. I thought it would be a treat on Rosie's birthday.' Harriet looked across at Ethan, who didn't appear that impressed.

'Mam, why is Ethan eating with us? He's usually out in the stable,' Ben spouted up as he looked at Ethan, while hiding his bread crusts under his plate edge.

'Because he is – that's all you need to know for now.' Harriet smiled at her young son. 'Now eat your crusts up, they'll make your hair curl.'

'I don't want curly hair. I know why he's here. I saw

him kissing our Rosie in the cowshed last week. They didn't see me because I kept quiet; they are always kissing. Blaaa . . .' He put his tongue out and pulled a face.

'You shut up, our Ben, you don't know anything. You are nothing but a peeping Tom.' Rosie kicked her brother under the table and glared at him.

'Now you make Ethan welcome at our table. Him and your sister are courting, and we will have none of your cheek, Ben Atkinson.' Danny looked across at his son and stirred his tea. 'Else you can go and join Georgina in a sleep upstairs in your bedroom.' He looked across at the two lovers and saw Rosie's cheeks blush. 'I'm off down to Windfell tomorrow, Ethan, do you want to come with me? We can see your mother and father, and then we can tell them how things are between you and Rosie. They've a right to know and, if I tell your father that we are somewhat happy with the situation, he should treat you right.'

Ethan bowed his head. 'I expect my father will bray me again. I shouldn't even be looking at Rosie, let alone walking out with her, in his eyes. But I'll come, and then both my mother and father will know what I'm about. If you'd back me up, Mr Atkinson, I'd appreciate that.' He lifted his head up and looked at Rosie and smiled.

'Right, we'll go first thing. I need to call in at the blacksmith's in Settle, so it will give you a bit of time to be alone with them. But I'll tell your father to behave himself while I'm gone. I'm not having you the worse for wear, just for the sake of setting your eye on our lass.' Danny looked across at his father and hoped that he'd want to come with them both. But Archie said nothing, as he was too busy watching Harriet dishing up the sherry trifle that had been made earlier and passing it to everyone, before she reached for the two parcels that were on the sideboard.

'This is from me and your father.' She passed the larger of the two brown paper parcels to her daughter. 'The smaller one is from your Aunt Isabelle and Uncle James.' She watched as Rosie's eyes lit up with excitement as she pulled on the string bow of the large parcel, unfolding the paper carefully.

'Oh, it's beautiful, Mother, but when will I wear it? It's too grand for everyday use.' Rosie pulled away the paper and pushed her chair back, standing to hold the beautiful dress that had been concealed within the package.

'Now, that is a picture. Aye, lad.' Archie grinned as Ethan looked at Rosie holding her present of a blue taffeta ballgown up next to her.

'Yes, sir.' Ethan looked at the girl he loved and felt unsure of himself for the first time. Perhaps his father was right: he shouldn't be aiming for a girl like Rosie. She was far too high above him, and he should know his place.

'Well, you are old enough to go to one or two of the local dances now, and Aunt Isabelle is going to hold a Christmas Ball this year, so you'll be needing it for that, I'm sure. We can't have you letting the side down.' Harriet looked across at Ethan and noticed his face starting to cloud over. 'Open your other present – that was Aunt Isabelle's doing.'

Rosie's face was beaming as she placed her new dress down behind her chair and quickly tugged on the string of the other parcel, pulling back the paper to reveal a blue-and-silver beaded evening bag. 'Oh, I've never seen anything like it.' She ran the beaded fringe that hung from the bag through her fingers and looked around the tea table at everybody.

'And here, lass, I'm no good at buying presents, but I thought you could make use of this.' Archie passed Rosie the money he had put in his pocket specially for her.

'I couldn't take that, Grandpapa, it's a pound – that's more money than I've managed to save up all year.' Rosie went round the table and hugged him and tried to give it back, but Archie shook his head and thrust it back in her hand. 'Tha'll need it someday, lass, I'm sure it will come in handy. Besides, I'd rather see you happy while I'm still here to see it, than when I'm six foot under and no good to anyone.'

'That's a long way off yet, Grandpapa.' Rosie kissed Archie on the cheek and looked at Ethan, who looked as black as thunder and had not touched the trifle in front of him.

'I'm sorry, but I've things to do. The calf pen wants mucking out, and I need to go and clean the horse harness.' Ethan got up from the table, taking everybody by surprise.

'But you've not had your trifle, and I thought we could go for a walk after tea,' Rosie exclaimed.

'No, I've too much to do. I thank you all for asking me, and I'm glad that you've had a good birthday, Rosie. Now please excuse me, I'll be away.' Ethan pushed his chair back while the family watched him walk off. Rosie was nearly in tears. As he left, he looked at the miniature set of drawers that it had taken him hours to carve and make. They were rubbish; he could never compete with her family and he was a fool even to have thought it. If Rosie started attending all the social events in the district, her head would soon be turned. Perhaps that was what her mother was hoping, when she had given her that fancy dress and the posh evening bag. He was a fool to think she would ever be his, and he was sure his father would say the same to him in the morning, if he went.

'Ethan! Ethan, wait!' Rosie got up from her chair, dropping her precious gifts to the floor, and rushed to be with him as she heard him close the kitchen door.

'He takes after his father, does that 'un.' Archie looked across at Harriet. 'Doesn't like to think he's been shown up or outdone.'

'I wish we'd never invited him in. And yes, I'm not ashamed to admit that if Rosie goes to the dances and balls coming up, in that dress, I hope she'll meet somebody a lot better suited to her than Ethan Haygarth.' Harriet looked at the untouched trifle and sighed.

'Be careful what you wish for, and don't try to alter the path of true love, for you'll only get hurt.' Archie looked across at Danny. 'What does thou say, lad?'

'I'm not saying owt. But he seems nowt but trouble, does that lad,' Danny said.

'Ethan, what's wrong? Why have you come out here? You know full well that you've done all there is to do for today.' Rosie strode across the farmyard. Her skirts billowed in the wind that had suddenly sprung up, making the last of the autumn leaves cascade around her, and her hair lash her face.

Ethan turned and looked at her. 'I'm not good enough for you, Rosie. Go and find somebody else – somebody with more brass, somebody with land and that's been brought up the same way as you. I've come from nowt, and my father's right: I shouldn't even be setting eyes on you, let alone touching you.'

'Why are you saying this now? What's changed from an hour ago, when we were going to look at the cottage in the village and were making plans for our life together?' Rosie stood in front of him and held back the tears.

'I've realized how little I have to give you, that's what's changed. I've nothing, and never will have, and you deserve better. I could never buy you fancy clothes and bags, and go with you to society balls and dances. They would all look at me and whisper behind my back, "He's the gyppo that the Atkinsons let court their daughter." I can hear it now. You deserve better.'

'Well, let them talk, I don't care. I want only you, and I'm not bothered about fancy clothes and snobby social balls. We'll go to the local dance down in the village hall – everyone goes to that, and nobody stands on ceremony there. As long as I have you, I don't care.' Rosie put her arms around him and hugged him close to her. 'I love you, Ethan Haygarth, and only you, so stop being so bloody proud, and go and see your father tomorrow.

He'll have to take it in his stride, if my father tells him that he must.'

Rosie looked up at Ethan, whose black hair was blowing in the wind and whose eyes were dark and as wild as the weather.

'We don't need anything or anybody, if we have one another.' Rosie took his face in her hands and kissed him. 'My wild rover: that's what you are and always will be, and that's why I love you.'

'So, you've finally decided to show your face. Do you know how much worry you've put your mother through? I suppose you've been trailing around looking for your grandfather again. When I told you to bloody well forget about him.' Jethro scowled at his son and spat out a mouthful of saliva as he watched Ethan drive up to the stables and stop next to him, with Danny beside him on the buckboard.

'Now then, Jethro. Ethan landed back the other day and I've told him to come and make his peace with you and his mother, but I need a word before you set into him. That's why I'm here, stopping off on my way to see the blacksmith at Settle.' Danny looked at Ethan. He had been quiet all the way to Windfell. He knew Ethan was not looking forward to confronting his father. 'Let him go into Windfell and see his mother first, while I have a word with you. I'm sure she will be glad to see him.'

Ethan climbed down from the flat wagon and watched as Danny walked into the stable, his hand on his father's shoulder, talking quietly; he hoped that was the way it

257

would stay, as he tied up the team of horses to the metal ring outside the stable, before making his way around the back of Windfell Manor. He stopped just outside the kitchen door as he plucked up courage to face his mother, Mazy, thinking of the fuss she would make of him, now that he had returned, and of the shock she would show at his confession of love for Rosie.

'Hey up, young Ethan! Now you are a stranger, but I know someone who will be glad to see you.' Ruby the cook turned to see who was entering her kitchen as she stirred the year's last batch of blackberry jelly on the stove. 'Mazy! Mazy, look what the cat's dragged in,' she yelled through to the pantry, where Ethan's mother was checking the supplies, ready for winter.

'What are you yelling at, Ruby? I'm only here, not a mile away?' Mazy stepped into the kitchen and stopped in her tracks as she saw her son standing in the doorway. 'Ethan, you are home! Thank God for that. Where have you been? I've missed you so much.' She rushed to his side and hugged him as he put his arms around his mother.

'I'm sorry, Mother, I should have come earlier, but I . . .' Ethan put his head down, not wanting to say that he hadn't forgiven – and couldn't – his father for the braying he'd been given, and that he'd missed her so much.

'Shh . . . I know, your father shouldn't have lost his temper with you. He should have known better.' Mazy held Ethan's face in her hands and kissed him on the cheek. 'You are home now and that's all that matters.' She sniffed and wiped her nose and pushed away the tears that were falling. 'I just didn't know where you were, and if I'd ever see you again, when Mr Atkinson said you'd gone missing. And you know what your father is like; he wouldn't let me come up and see you when you were at Crummock. He said that it was your duty to come and see us.' Mazy breathed in deeply.

'I'll leave you two together. The kettle's nearly boiling, and you know where the teacups are.' Ruby pulled the pan full of boiling jelly off the heat and watched as mother and son sat down together, wanting to make up for lost time in private, as she made her way out of the kitchen.

'I'm sorry, I seem to be good at causing upset and worry. And I'll be making more this morning, when Mr Atkinson finishes telling my father what I'm about.' Ethan dropped his head and looked down at his hands.

'What's up, Ethan? You're not in trouble, are you? Is that why you disappeared?' Mazy reached for her son's hands and held them tightly as she looked at him with love and concern.

'It depends what you call trouble, and if Father is going to lose his temper again.' Ethan sighed. 'I'm hoping that you will both give me your blessing to court Rosie – that's why her father is here with me. He's outside with Father, telling him that they have concerns, but they are happy for us to walk out together on certain days, rather than sneak behind their backs. We can't help it, Mother. I love her and she loves me – we can't stop it. That's why I went away, to see if I could stop thinking about Rosie, but I couldn't and she feels just the same about me.' Ethan looked at his mother and at the shock on her face.

'Oh, Ethan, she's way above us. It's Miss Rosie you are talking about, Master Archie's granddaughter. She's not for the likes of us.' Mazy looked at her son and sat back in her chair, taking in the news. 'Your father will be saying just the same. He'll be going mad, you know he will, despite what Master Danny says. And you say the Atkinsons are alright about it? I just can't believe that. You are a grand, lovely lad, but you can't keep Rosie in the lifestyle she's used to – we have nothing.' Mazy sat back and looked at her son, taking in his news and remembering all the times the Atkinson and Fox children had been part of Ethan's life and realizing that perhaps the inevitable had happened. He'd always thought a lot of Rosie and was better off loving Rosie than Jane, who was way out of his reach, and Mrs Fox would not even be happy if he so much as looked at her.

'I'm sorry, but we do love one another,' said Ethan, without hearing the kitchen door open and his father step in.

'Love! What do you know about love, lad?' Jethro stepped in and stood in front of his son. 'You only bloody hurt folk – not showing your face to us for weeks on end. Making your mother cry of a night and making her wonder whether you were dead or alive. And all for some slip of a lass that you should not be looking at, let alone thinking you are in love with. I thought you'd have learned your lesson after I gave you that braying, but no, you've brought more bother to our door.' Jethro stood in front of his son, while Mazy pulled on his arm to try and hold him back from hitting their son.

'Leave him be, Jethro, don't you hurt our lad,' she shouted.

'I'll not bloody hurt him. Danny Atkinson has warned me off him. But he does deserve his arse being kicked, with him thinking himself something that he isn't and setting his cap at Rosie Atkinson. He should know his bloody place,' Jethro snarled.

'Just like you had to? Don't you realize I know that you worshipped the ground Charlotte Atkinson walked on? I used to watch you helping her with her horses and doing anything you could for her. She could have asked for the moon and you would have tried to get it for her. It's no good lecturing our Ethan; he's only doing what his father wanted to do, and courting the lass from Crummock.' Mazy stopped short; she hadn't meant to say what she had, but over the years of her marriage to Jethro it had become clear to her that he secretly loved his employer. But now it was out, she realized that's why he had vented his wrath on their son so much, for Ethan had done what Jethro had never dared to.

'You are talking daft, woman. I never thought anything about her. I married you, didn't I?' Jethro looked blackly at his son and wife as they stood together, ready to take him on. 'Do what you bloody like. You always have hidden behind your mother's skirts, and if Danny bloody Atkinson has no more sense than to let you see his lass, then I'll have to be bloody quiet. It'll all end in nowt anyway, but don't think you can come trailing home again, because I'll not make you welcome.' Jethro turned and walked towards the door. 'Behave your bloody self and don't bring us any shame.' He grabbed the door handle and slammed the door behind him, leaving both Mazy and Ethan looking at one another.

'Don't fret, he'll come round. You know what he's like.' Mazy reached for the teacups and kettle.

'I thought he'd bray me again.' Ethan breathed in deeply.

'Nay, he won't do that, not if Mr Atkinson says that he is alright with you courting Rosie. Now, we never mention what I said to your father – it's not to be talked about ever again, and I only said it because I knew if he'd have been in your shoes now, he'd have done the same. You enjoy your time with Miss Rosie and leave your father to me.' Mazy poured the tea and smiled at her beloved son.

Ethan looked at his mother, trying to understand his father's secret love for his employer, and the love that his mother must feel for Jethro. She'd been second best all her married life, and had only just now let his father know that she was aware of this. That was no marriage; he and Rosie would be more secure than that – of that he was going to make sure.

'We could make this look lovely. Just look at the garden, Ethan, we could fill it with vegetables. And it looks like there are two bedrooms. Room enough for a family, if we are ever so lucky again.' Rosie blushed and felt a pang of sadness for the trauma and worry that she had been through, while thinking of the future and hoping for better times ahead with Ethan by her side.

Ethan looked around him at the overgrown garden and the ivy-clad walls of the unoccupied cottage. 'Aye, I reckon we could make something of it. But I daren't dream too much about it. Your grandfather might have plans for it and he may not even agree to us living here.' He looked at the excitement on Rosie's face as she peered through the peeling, paint-cracked windows into the kitchen and small living room.

'Grandpapa would only be too happy to let us live here – it's always been empty. He used to say that he would live in it sometime, but now he's happy to be back with us up at Crummock.' Rosie stood back next to Ethan and put her arm through his. 'I'll wait a bit longer and then I'll ask him, once we have proved that we do love one another and that we are serious.' She squeezed Ethan's arm tightly and smiled. 'Our own little house – just us two, where no one can tell us what to do. Won't that be fine?'

'It will, Rosie. In fact I could make a start on the garden in my spare time. I can clear the weeds over this winter, cut back these brambles and give the garden gate a lick of paint. Then everyone will know we are serious about each other. It'll not do the cottage any harm any-way, as it looks so uncared for.' Ethan looked around him. He would give the garden his time, as and when he could. 'I hope that when the time comes your grandfather will agree, because it is, as you say, the perfect home for us. A home that we will cherish between us. We'll do this, Rosie. Despite whatever obstacles they put in our way, we will show them.'

Ethan held Rosie tightly and looked around him. It was a lot of responsibility, but Rosie was worth it. That spring he had been a young lad without any cares. Now he had grown into a man, and he aimed always to be there for his Rosie.

24

'Jane, you might as well make yourself useful today, while Harriet and I interview the new seamstress. You can go into Settle and give Lambert's my instructions for the invitations that I need printing for our Christmas Ball. There's no need for you to come into work, Aunt Harriet won't have time for you and nor will I.' Isabelle looked across at her daughter as she spread marmalade on her second slice of toast. 'Have you any need of Jane today, James?'

James was engrossed in his morning newspaper and didn't realize that he was being talked to, as he read about the latest divisions between the Triple Entente of Britain, Russia and France and the Triple Alliance of Germany, Austria–Hungary and Italy. The division between the two military camps was beginning to make him more aware and anxious that all was not well in the world. Especially with the Irish Home Rule movement insisting on Irish self-government. The world was not a safe place.

'James, are you listening or am I talking to a brick wall, as usual?' Isabelle put her knife down sharply.

'Sorry, my dear, I was just reading about the worries of the world. It will only take a small spark to throw the world into chaos.' He sighed and folded his newspaper. 'Now, what did you ask?'

'Do you need Jane today or can she have the day at home?' Isabelle looked disdainfully at her husband. All he did was worry about world affairs, and consequently she had lost count of the times he had condemned her compliments about Luke excelling in the cadets at school, as he feared that war would soon be rearing its ugly head.

'No, no, I don't think so. I've quite an easy day today. But she can join me in the Leeds branch tomorrow, and then she can keep an eye on me. I'm sure you'll be happier if she does.' James looked sharply at Isabelle, knowing full well that she still didn't trust him.

'You never told me that you were interviewing today. Could I not take the interviews with you, instead of Aunt Harriet – surely it would be more fitting?'

Jane looked at her mother. She still wasn't being included fully in the running of Atkinson's and resented the fact.

'You will get your chance in time, Jane, but at this moment leave it to Harriet and me. She has the experience, and it is her position they will be filling. She does tell me, however, that you are showing promise in your sewing and cutting skills. She was quite impressed when I spoke to her about you.' Isabelle sipped at her tea. 'Now, are you willing to walk into Settle and take my instructions to the printer's? It would be a good help, and the weather is quite pleasant for the first day in November.'

'I suppose I could. I'm obviously not needed in the store.' Jane looked across at her father. 'Am I really to come with you to Leeds tomorrow? Will I have time to look around the arcades and perhaps do some shopping?'

'If your mother agrees, I don't see why not. You haven't been for a while, and it won't hurt the staff there to meet you and realize that you are the future face of Atkinson's.' James smiled at the excitement his daughter was showing. 'And I suppose you will be wanting some spending money – so I'd say "yes" to delivering your mother's invitation instructions. Although I can't say I'm looking forward to a ball. Opening our house to half the dale does not fill me with pleasure.'

'I don't know what to do regarding the invitation to Harriet and Danny and their family. Harriet told me the other day that Rosie is walking out with Ethan – Mazy and Jethro's son. Now I don't want to sound a snob, but I do hope they don't bring him along as part of their family. Imagine, the stable boy coming as a guest into our home on such a grand occasion. What would people say?' Isabelle breathed in deeply and shook her head in disbelief.

'Rosie is walking out with Ethan?' Jane squealed.

'Has she no pride? I wouldn't be seen dead walking out with him, he's so common.'

'Keep your voice down, Jane, Mazy will be able to hear you.' Isabelle quietened her daughter quickly.

'He's not a bad lad. I'd have thought Rosie might have set her sights higher. It will suit your stepfather, Isabelle. I can't see your problem. Just ask them all as a family and then, if Ethan comes with them, he does; and if not, you have no problem.' James smiled to himself. Jane was so much like her mother.

'I just hope he doesn't. It could be quite embarrassing. Now, come with me, Jane, and I'll give you the instructions for the printer, before your father and I catch the train into work. Make sure you ask to have them printed for the middle of the month. I want us to be the first in the district to announce our intentions. I want to get one ahead of the Fosters at Anley Hall. Mary Foster is always bragging about how grand her Christmas Ball is, so let's better her this year.' Isabelle got up from the table, leaving James thinking how mother and daughter both had attitude; if they thought themselves far better than the rest of society, they were heading for a fall.

'My mother would like two hundred invitations to be delivered no later than the fifteenth of this month to us at Windfell.' Jane stood next to the counter, looking at the printer with his blue ink-stained hands.

'Two hundred, you say, with envelopes?' The printer looked up over his glasses at Jane and waited for a reply.

'Yes, and my mother asked if you could place a design

around the invitation, something tasteful, like bells or holly?' Jane looked around the small printing-press room, whose walls were covered with posters and wooden printing blocks, with all different typefaces and designs upon them.

'Perhaps you would like to have a look at some ideas, while I see what this young man behind you is in need of? I'm sure he won't take long to serve.' The printer looked over Jane's shoulder at the young blond-haired man who stood waiting his turn, then reached for some Christmas prints for the decoration on the ball invitations.

'Yes, I suppose I could.' Jane turned to look at the customer behind her as she moved to one side to choose the decoration. She stopped for a second as she glanced up at the young man. He reminded her of someone, but she couldn't quite think who. She smiled at him as he stepped up to the counter while she made her way to the side of the office.

She listened in to the conversation between him and the printer as she looked slowly through the selection.

'So that's fifty funeral cards to be picked up by yourself tomorrow. We can deliver them for you, but that will of course be extra,' the printer said quietly.

'Nay, I'll deliver them myself. My grandfather would have liked that and it's only right that I do so,' the young man said.

'Right you are, sir, they will be ready for you by midday tomorrow. May I give you my condolences from all at Lambert's? We will be thinking of you and your loss.' The printer passed the details over to his young apprentice and watched as his customer left the shop.

'I think we will have this one, Mr Lambert, it looks very seasonal and I think it will be tasteful enough for Mama.' Jane pointed at a print of a holly swag with a silver bell in the centre. 'It's very eye-catching and should look good on our invitations.'

'That's a good choice, Miss Fox, it is very popular.' Mr Lambert folded the corner of the print down to remind him of her choice and put it to one side. 'Anything else, Miss?'

'Erm, no. Well, yes, there is! Can I ask who the young man is that you've just served? I thought I recognized him, but his name escapes me.' Jane peered at the old man while he answered her.

'That'll be old Bill Brown's grandson, Daniel. He's just lost his grandfather and was ordering his funeral cards. Your grandfather will know them – they farm over at Ragged Hall. No doubt he'll be delivering an invitation to your grandfather, as all the farmers in the district knew and respected the old gent.'

'Oh, I didn't think I knew him. I just thought his face looked familiar. I must be thinking of someone else. However, you are correct in thinking that my grandfather will have dealt with his grandfather, if they farm.' Jane picked up her posy bag and looked at the printer.

'Aye, he might not know Daniel Bland, for he's just come to live with the old man, from what I hear. He's been keeping him company in his hour of need. It's a sad day for him.' Mr Lambert shook his head as he turned away from Jane.

'Indeed, Mr Lambert. I should have given my condolences to him as well. I do hope he calls in at Windfell so that I may do so.' She looked sympathetically at the printer. 'Good day, Mr Lambert.'

'Aye, good day, lass. I'll see to your invitations for you.' The printer watched as Jane made her way out of the shop.

She walked up through busy Duke Street, her head held high as she acknowledged fellow shoppers and neighbours. But her mind was on the good-looking man who had stood behind her at the printer's. What a pity he would probably be taking the funeral card to Crummock and not to Windfell, for she would have liked to have seen more of him and introduce herself. He had seemed strangely familiar, but at the same time she had never seen him before in her life. She smiled to herself as she thought of the mop of blond hair and the blue eyes; he was a good-looking man, that was for sure.

'So, you enjoyed your day with your father?' Isabelle looked at her daughter as Jane flicked through the pages of *The Lady*, seemingly uninterested in the contents, just as she was in the *Weldon's Ladies' Journal* that had been discarded to one side, as she decided that she couldn't be bothered to read either magazine on this quiet Sunday morning.

'Yes, it is so different from here. Leeds is so full of life, and the shops . . . well, our little shopkeepers in Settle just can't be compared to the bustling arcades in Leeds. The ladies are more fashionable and the gentleman are that well groomed, I swear even I must have stood out like a country bumpkin.' Jane sighed.

'I'm sure you didn't. As you know, you and I keep well abreast of fashion. It's just that the ladies who attend our Leeds shop are wealthy, as with most of the shops in the arcade. Step a few streets back and you would see another side of Leeds – the poverty and the slums that townspeople still live in. So you must think yourself fortunate, Jane. You have been born into a privileged lifestyle. Did your father have a good day?' Isabelle wanted to quiz her daughter. It had been James's first day back in Leeds since the fateful crash, and she had done nothing but wonder how the Leeds store had reacted to his return.

'Yes, he was busy all day. He had a queue of people wanting their picture taken, so we were both kept on our toes. We barely had time for lunch, let alone anything else. I was hoping I would have had time to browse in a few shops, but all I managed to get was this magazine at the station. And this is full of what the perfect wife and mother should be, and it doesn't keep my interest.' Jane flung *The Lady* to one side. 'Did you find a replacement for Aunt Harriet – one you both agreed on – without my input?'

'Yes, we did, thank you. She's called Margery Sutcliffe and lives in Skipton, so she's ideal. Her seamstress skills are excellent, and she comes highly recommended by her previous employer. I think you and she will get on well.

She's a bit plain in looks, but perhaps that is not a bad thing. She dresses well, and that's more important.' Isabelle pulled on her gloves and looked at her daughter, who didn't look happy, knowing that she had not been trusted to interview the new seamstress. 'Come to church with me and your father. You know you should attend, no matter how much you despise going. The walk there will do you good, and will stop you from brooding.'

'I'm not brooding. I just dislike Sundays. Perhaps Luke will come and brighten up the day, although all he thinks about is how to shoot his gun and how smart he looks in that uniform of his. Stupid idiot!' Jane sighed again. 'But church is one step worse, so I'll find something to do. I'll write a letter or two in the morning room and tell my friends about the ball at Christmas, then they've time to plan their dresses.'

'Suit yourself, my lady. But going to church shows your standing in the local community, and it doesn't hurt to be seen there. We will be back for lunch, so we won't be long.' Isabelle walked over to the doorway and left her daughter in the morning room, reaching for pen and paper from the desk next to the window. Jane was in a mood and was best left alone.

Jane watched her mother and father walk down the drive and past the beech trees that were blowing in the northerly wind. Her mother was holding onto her hat, despite the hat pin keeping it in place, and Jane shook her head, wondering why they hadn't taken the trap instead of walking the half-mile to Langcliffe.

She reached for her pen and looked at the blank pages of paper in front of her. She didn't feel like writing, but as usual on a Sunday that was all there was to do – that and a gentle walk, as her mother had reminded her. She breathed in deeply, sat back in her chair and looked outside: a walk or letter writing? Both were equally boring, she thought, as she picked up the pen again and dipped it in the inkpot. She stopped when she heard the sound of horses' hooves as they disturbed the pebbles on the drive outside the window. She looked out, but could see nobody, so presumed it was Jethro or someone visiting him, or one of the staff, as she couldn't hear the doorbell being rung and answered. She picked up her pen once again and started to write.

She stopped quickly, almost knocking her inkpot over, as there was a knock on the morning-room door.

'Enter,' Jane shouted, as she looked at the words written half-heartedly on the nearly blank piece of paper.

'Begging your pardon, Miss, but there is a gentleman here. He came to the back door, wanting to see your grandfather. I've told him that he no longer lives here, but once he explained what his business was, I thought that perhaps you would like to save him the bother of travelling all the way to Crummock. Our Ethan will be calling on us this afternoon, and he could take the card back with him.' Mazy looked at Jane and waited, with the visitor standing patiently behind her.

'The card?' Jane looked up.

'Yes, Miss. Mr Bland here is delivering his grandfather's funeral card.'

Jane got up from her desk and looked past Mazy, ignoring her question.

'Mr Bland, how good it is to make your acquaintance. Please do accept my deepest condolences, on behalf of myself and all my family, on the loss of your grandfather. I'm afraid it is as Mazy says: my grandfather is now living at Crummock with his son. But, as Mazy is suggesting, we can make sure the invitation reaches him safely later in the day.' Jane looked up at the blond-haired young man she now knew to be Daniel Bland, and was even more taken with his striking features.

'I thank you, Miss Atkinson. That would take a few miles off my journey, so I am most willing to accept you and your maid's suggestion.' Daniel smiled at both of the women, who were staring at him in a most bemusing way. 'Who do I give the invite to?' He looked at both and waited for an answer.

'I'll take it, Mr Bland. My son will take it back to Crummock with him this evening – he works for Mr Atkinson.'

'Thank you.' Daniel gave the invitation to Mazy and turned to go.

'Mr Bland, would you like to join me in a drink of coffee? I must confess, I was about to put pen to paper, but cannot be bothered with writing this morning. My parents are at church and I could do with some company. I'm sure some warm refreshment would be just the thing for you.' Jane looked at Daniel and then at Mazy, noticing that she too couldn't keep her eyes off the visitor.

'I would not say no to that. Especially as I can see that

275

you have a grand roaring fire.' Daniel smiled at his host and walked past Mazy, who stared at him as he made his way into the morning room.

'Coffee for two, please, Mazy, and perhaps some of Cook's rock-cakes?' Jane quickly dismissed the gawping housekeeper and joined her visitor in a chair next to the fire. She looked him up and down, noting how tall he was, at least six foot; and although he was dressed like any other local farmer, in a shirt and waistcoat with corduroy breeches and jacket, he carried them with a swagger. His high cheekbones and blue eyes, framed by his blond hair, made him a most handsome man – and one that Jane found quite fascinating.

'I feel I'd better introduce myself, Mr Bland. I'm not, as you called me, Miss Atkinson, but Jane Fox. Mr Archie Atkinson, your late grandfather's friend, is my mother's stepfather and she took the Atkinson name when her own father died, until she married my father, James Fox. So we are in no way related, although my grandfather – as we have always called him – is loved by me and my brother and is just as good as a true grandfather, of that I'm sure.'

'Families can be a terrible mix-up. I know that myself, but I'll not bore you with mine just now. It is far too complicated.' Daniel looked across at Jane and thought how good-looking she was, with her long auburn hair; it was nearly how he remembered his mother, Amy, when she was young – before years of living with his so-called father and four brothers had taken their toll on her. She too had been beautiful, until all life's dreams had been

276

beaten and wrung out of her by her husband and his family. He'd hated leaving her over at Slaidburn so he could look after his grandfather, but knew he could not stand living at home another minute. He knew that his mother was better off without him there, as a reminder of her free-living past. It was a thorn in the side of her husband, who frequently reminded both Daniel and Amy of the differences between Daniel and his other sons. He was different; he was not his father's child and all the world knew it, it was that obvious.

'It is as you say. I doubt anything would shock me, when it comes to families, but we have said enough about our family, I'm sure.' Jane smiled. 'When is your grandfather's funeral, and will you be leaving us and going back to Slaidburn when he has been buried?'

'It is on Friday, at Rathmell, at two p.m. And no, I won't be going back to Slaidburn. My grandfather left his farm, Ragged Hall, to me, so I aim to stay there, build the farm into what it used to be before my grandfather took ill.' Daniel looked into the fire as Mazy entered with a tray laden with coffee and rock-cakes. She bobbed a curtsy as she left the young couple helping themselves.

'Mazy's son will deliver your card – you've no need to worry on that score. I'm sure my grandfather will attend, and also his son, who shares your Christian name, although we call him "Uncle Danny". We never use his "Sunday name" of Daniel, as he calls it.' Jane smiled at her guest as she poured him his coffee and passed him a rock-cake. 'He has the same-coloured hair as you, too – strange, that!' Jane paused and then bit into her rock-cake and watched Daniel's every move, as she realized that it was her Uncle Danny that her guest reminded her of.

'Aye, well, we are all Dales folk around here. All inter-related, one way or another, and folk often look alike.' Daniel bit into his bun and looked at his hostess. 'Were you not in the printer's when I ordered the cards? You were looking at some fancy designs.'

'Yes, I was. That's how I recognized you, when Mazy introduced you. My mother had asked me to go to Lambert's to get some Christmas Ball invitations printed. I was look-ing at what I thought she would like printed on them, while you were placing your order.' Jane breathed in, wondering if she dared say the next line. 'You must come as my guest. I know it will be a little soon after the death of your grandfather, but I'm sure he would approve. And I know Grandfather Archie would like to see you there. It's on Christmas Eve, at eight p.m. I'll send you an invitation, to remind you.' She blushed. She had never been that for-ward before, but Daniel Bland was so good-looking and he was about to get his own farm, so her parents could not complain.

'Aye, I might just do that. My grandfather would want me to. His dying words to me were to get on with life, after his day, and not mope about. You remind me, with an invitation, and I'll be here.' Daniel smiled across at the young woman who had made him welcome; he'd like to see a bit more of her, now that he knew who she was.

'It's a deal then.' Jane laughed.

278

'That it is, but now I'd better be on my way. Thank you for the drink and the warm-up. I'll get on with the business of handing out my cards and telling everyone my bad news. It's going to be a long day, if everyone I meet invites me in for a drink and to get warm. My grandfather must have been well liked.'

Daniel rose from his chair and looked at the young woman in front of him and at the house she lived in. It was a million miles from the hovel he'd been brought up in, and yet he had been told by his mother that this house was where his true father had lived nearly all his life. His true father, whom he had yet to meet.

25

'Well, that's another bugger gone. There's hardly any-body left that I played and grew up with.' Archie looked at the funeral card that Ethan had just handed him.

'The devil looks after his own. You'll be with us for a good time yet.' Danny patted his father on his back as he stared at the notice of Bill Brown's demise.

'I suppose I will have to show my face at his funeral. Now, are you going to come along with me? It could be awkward for you. You'll get to see the lad, though.' Archie looked at his son and knew this was the moment that perhaps Danny had been waiting for: a glimpse of his former lover and their son, both of whom, he knew, must have been playing on his mind.

'Well, you can't go without me really. I'll come, but I'll keep a low profile and sit at the back of the church, away from the family.' Danny glanced quickly at his father. The old bugger knew him too well; he knew exactly what he was thinking.

'I wonder what's to become of Ragged Hall. Will Bill have left it to his lass, or perhaps her lad will have been given it? He's the one that deserves it – he was there when he was needed.' Archie leaned upon the kitchen table and looked out of the window, deep in thought. 'Ragged Hall's always been in the Brown family. Bill will not have wanted it to go to any of that lot over in Slaidburn. I bet your lad's got it.'

'Father, he may not be my lad. Just because he's blond, it means nowt,' Danny snapped.

'Tha'll see for yourself. He's yours alright, and he's back where he belongs. A cuckoo never falls far from its nest. He'll be back at Ragged Hall, I'll bet you my last penny.' Archie grinned.

'Now, we can't have you looking like that. Here, let me straighten your tie. And keep your trilby on if you can, at the graveside, as your hair needs cutting.' Harriet fussed over Danny, making sure he looked respectable for the funeral that both he and his father were attending. She turned to Archie and straightened the white handkerchief in his pocket. 'Now, don't worry if you are late back for milking. Rosie and Ethan have it in hand. We all know how these funerals drag on, especially with you farmers. You'll be discussing the price of sheep and what the weather is doing, while poor old Bill's grave is filled in and he's already forgotten about.'

'Nay, lass, we will try and be back in good time. Now Bill's gone, his family doesn't have anything in common with us.' Archie smiled at Harriet and then glanced quickly at Danny. 'Right, lad, let's be away. It's only a little chapel at Rathmell and I need a seat, as my old legs won't be able to hold me up through the full service.'

'Bye, Harriet. We should be back before milking, so don't worry. As you say, the time we get back will depend on this old gasbag and who he gets talking to.' Danny leaned forward and kissed Harriet on the cheek. He rarely did this and Harriet knew exactly why he had done it today, as she watched father and son leave the warmth of her kitchen.

She sat down and glanced out of the kitchen window, looking out over the Dales and watching Danny and Archie going down the road from Crummock on their way to Bill Brown's funeral. She breathed in deeply, trying to control her thoughts as she watched the horse and buggy carrying father and son disappear over the hill on their way down into Austwick, and then on to the sleepy hamlet of Rathmell. Today Danny would see her rival, for the first time in nearly twenty-five years. Yet she could not suppress the jealousy and hatred she felt for the woman who had nearly stolen her man from her, albeit briefly, all those years ago. She held back the tears that were threatening to fall and looked out to the fells in the distance. 'God help you, Amy Brown, if you look at my man the way I know you did all those years ago. He's mine now. We have a family and a home, and I would fight you with every breath of my body this time, if you tempt my man again,' she whispered to herself. Then she let her tears fall, as she remembered the hurt she had once felt – a hurt that had nearly destroyed them.

*

'I knew there'd be a lot of people here. Bill was highly thought of.' Archie sat next to Danny in the pew that was one back from the last row, in the small chapel in the centre of Rathmell. 'He was well respected, had damn good sheep in his day,' whispered Archie, as they stood when the vicar could be heard entering the chapel, followed by the coffin and the mourners.

'I am the resurrection and the life. Whoever believes . . .' The vicar walked slowly in front of the grieving family and stood before the coffin, which the pall-bearers rested next to the altar in the small chapel.

Danny caught his breath and looked at the grey-haired, weeping woman who stood behind it. That couldn't be Amy – not his Amy. Then four dark-haired men joined her in the front pew, after following the path of the coffin. Danny looked at the onetime love of his life and couldn't believe his eyes. Where was Amy's thick auburn hair and the spring in her step, and the smile he had loved so much? He knew it was her father's funeral, but he'd expected Amy to look just as beautiful as he'd remembered her to be. Instead, she was an old woman. Her once-vibrant hair had turned grey and was pinned up in a bun under her black mourning hat, and her face was tanned and covered with lines, showing the hard life she had endured since her marriage.

Amy's sons and husband sat next to her, like black crows, hanging on every word the vicar spoke and guarding her from prying eyes. Their dark hair was slicked back, covering the white collars of their shirts and blending with the blackness of their suits, making the pew look like one of death and grieving. Seated on his own on the other side of the chapel was a lone figure, quite the opposite of those in the adjacent pew. There sat a man with blond hair, his black suit showing it off as if a halo shone around his head, as he listened intently to the vicar reading the life story of Bill Brown.

'Let us rise to sing psalm number twenty-three, "The Lord is my shepherd",' the vicar called out and the congregation all stood.

'I told you – he's your lad alright. Just look at him,' whispered Archie to Danny. 'He's not one of them, anyway.' He nodded in the direction of the pew containing Amy and the rest of her family.

'Quiet, Father, folk will hear you.' Danny looked ahead of him and sang. He looked at the lad who was singing all alone. His father was right: there was no doubting the fact that he was a cuckoo in the nest and that he had come home, whether Danny himself liked it or not. It was obvious to one and all who his father was.

'You are home soon, did you not go to the funeral tea?' Harriet stood back and looked at both of her men as they came back into the kitchen.

'No, we didn't even go to the graveside. My father was struggling with walking and it looked like rain, so we just did the service.' Danny threw his trilby on the table and pulled the black tie from around his neck, placing it on the back of the kitchen chair. 'Come here, you bundle of rubbish.' He reached down for baby Georgina and held her on his knee, as Harriet placed the kettle on the hob.

'We didn't want to impose on the family. And besides, I don't ken the lad that Bill's daughter married, but he looks a moody bugger. Plus she's changed out of all recognition, and she didn't bother looking to the side we were on. So we didn't stop.' Archie pulled up the other chair next to his son and smiled at his youngest grandchild as she played with the teaspoons on the table.

'Oh, so there was no gossip or anything? That's not like you two.' Harriet poured out two cups of tea and took Georgina onto her lap, to hold her tightly next to her.

'No. I don't suppose we'll have much to do with Ragged Hall again, now Bill's gone.' Archie sipped deeply from his cup and sat back in his chair. 'It will no doubt be put up for sale, unless one of his grandchildren farms it.'

'Well, perhaps that would be for the best. Their home will be Slaidburn, after all.' Harriet smiled and sat back, content with the news she had been given. There was no need to worry about Amy Brown; obviously time had favoured herself, for keeping her looks, otherwise Danny would not have returned so quickly. He was still hers, and always would be.

26

'Close your eyes. No peeking.' Ethan held Rosie's hand and guided her across the back green to the garden of her Great-aunt Lucy's cottage. 'You are cheating – keep your eyes closed. Here, stop there and I'll tie my neckerchief around you and then I know you can't see.' Ethan stopped Rosie in her tracks and undid the red-and-white spotted neckerchief from around his neck. He tied it securely round her eyes, making sure she couldn't squint through it. 'There, that's better. Now I know you definitely can't see.'

'But why do I have to close my eyes? What is there so special to see?' Rosie held out her hands, grasping Ethan's as he guided her over the green and through the garden gate of the small, dilapidated cottage. She held tightly on to Ethan as he guided her up the path to the back door and then turned her round, before untying her blindfold.

'There, what do you think? I've cleared all the brambles and dug the flowerbeds ready for spring, and I've taken the ivy off the walls of the cottage. At least you can see into the rooms more easily now.' Ethan stood back and watched Rosie's face light up.

'Oh, Ethan, you've even made a birdtable?' She rushed over to where a birdtable stood in the middle of the paved garden area, and looked at the workmanship that had gone into it and how tidy the garden looked. 'It looks lovely, Ethan.'

'Snowdrops are already beginning to show. I told them to keep their heads down for a while longer yet, as we are only just into December. And there's a Christmas rose over here by the back door – it will flower shortly. Your Great-aunt Lucy must have known her plants.' Ethan grinned. 'It's a grand garden and there's enough room for a veg plot round the side, so we'd never go hungry.'

'Now we've just got to convince everybody that we are serious; that it's not just "puppy love", as my mother keeps calling it.' Rosie walked over to the cleared windows and peered in. 'I could see us two living here. It would be ideal, and we'd be away from my family and yours, in our own little home. Although you'd still have to work for my father or find something else.'

Rosie turned and looked at the lad who had stolen her heart. She was going to have to speak to her grandfather. He understood her and had always stood by her, no matter what her parents had said.

'I'll ask my grandfather for the key, just to have a look around at the moment. And then I'll ask if he'd give his blessing for this to be our first home, if we are still together in the spring. Which, of course, we will be. I know he wouldn't approve of us going behind his back.' She smiled and held Ethan close to her as he kissed her and ran his fingers through her long hair.

'I love you, Rosie Atkinson. I always will. Spring is only like a day away to me. This cottage will be ours – I'll wish it so. Just like I wished for you.' Ethan held her tightly and kissed her passionately as they stood outside the back door of the old cottage, hoping their dreams would come true and that one day they'd wed and live there.

'I wish that too, Ethan. I don't want anyone else, just you.' Rosie held him tightly. She knew that if her parents had their way, they would prefer anyone other than Ethan, for he just wasn't good enough for her in their eyes. But they didn't know him like she did.

'I don't know, Rosie, your father won't be that suited.' Archie looked with concern at his granddaughter. 'I know the cottage is empty and could do with a bit of attention, but I don't think your father would be happy if I was encouraging your affections for Ethan.'

'But, Grandfather, we only want to have a look around. We wouldn't get up to anything while we were there. Please . . .' Rosie at her grandfather looked like an appealing puppy as she tried to get her own way.

'Oh, alright, I suppose a quick look round is not going to get you into any harm. Now you take care and behave yourselves, else I'll be out on my arse if your mother finds out I'm encouraging you both. I'll give you the key and I expect it back later today. You just look round, and you say nowt to your parents. Otherwise I'll not be welcome living here no more, and I'll need the cottage.' Archie scratched his head and went over to the drawer in his desk. 'My Aunt Lucy will be looking down and laughing at me. She always used to have a soft spot for me and Charlotte, and now I'm in the same situation with you and Ethan. I know true love when I see it, even if you are both too young.' He looked at Rosie. 'Now you do nowt you'd be ashamed to tell me of and you return this key to me tonight, and then I'll say nowt to nobody.'

'I promise, Grandfather, and thank you. I knew you'd understand.' Rosie took the key and kissed Archie on the cheek. She hesitated before leaving him to walk down into Austwick with Ethan. 'I do love him, Grandfather.'

'I know, lass, just be careful. I'd hate to see you hurt.' Archie sat on the end of his bed and sighed as he watched Rosie nearly skipping out of the doorway. She was only young – too young to be wanting a home and family of her own, especially with raggle-taggle Ethan, even if they were made for one another. Anyway, it might all come to nothing. Time would tell.

'It's perfect Rosie. I know it's only got two bedrooms, but that's all we'd need for a start.' Ethan looked around him.

'For a start, Ethan Haygarth! How many children were you thinking of us having? I might not want any.' Rosie looked out of the window at the limestone scars of the fell called Moughton and smiled to herself. Then she remembered the night when she had lain alone with her worries and her pain, bringing a pang of uncertainty back to her.

'I'm sorry, Rosie, I should think more of what I say.

But I'd love a big family. And after a good paint with whitewash, and new homes found for the various spiders that seem to be everywhere, I think we could not wish for anything better for a brood of our own.' Ethan put his arms around her waist and kissed her neck as she looked out of the window. 'We could be really happy here.'

'I know, Ethan, but I'm scared,' Rosie whispered.

'Don't be scared. I'll always be by your side, I promise,' he whispered as he held her tight.

'I can't help it, not after . . .'

'Shhh. If I'd known what had happened, I'd never have gone away. I'm sorry for the hurt, Rosie.' Ethan kissed her again. 'We will always be together, I promise. Now let's get the key back to your grandfather, so he isn't worrying.' He smiled. He'd found a spare key hanging up in the back kitchen, and now he felt for it in his pocket. He would keep his find a secret. Over the winter he would secretly put every hour he could into the cottage, because come spring Rosie would be his, and he aimed to have a home ready for them both.

'I hope you can all make it?' Isabelle passed to Harriet the newly printed invitation to her Christmas Ball.

'Oh, Isabelle, it'll be like old times. Your mother gave such grand balls in her time. I was in awe of them and inspired by the grandeur. It was the special part of Christmas – an excuse to dress in your finest clothes. I felt like a queen, when I had Danny on my arm and we were dancing in the hall.' Harriet looked lovingly at the invitation and smiled, remembering the good times when she was younger.

'I'm surprised he didn't cripple you – he's always had two left feet, our Danny. Knowing him, he'd stand on your feet more than lead you in a dance.' Isabelle looked at her sister-in-law and wondered how to word the invitation for Rosie, but not for Ethan, without offending her.

Harriet interrupted her thoughts. 'Is Rosie included? She can wear the new dress I made her. It matches the evening bag that you gave her. I hope you will include her in the invitation. I need her to see what she is missing, and to stop making a fool with herself with that Ethan. He's not good enough for her. I don't know why Danny and Archie make a fuss of him.' Harriet looked at her sister-in-law and recognized a look of relief, as she talked yet again about her unhappiness with her daughter's courtship.

'Rosie is invited, but I would prefer it if Ethan didn't attend. It just wouldn't be right, with Mazy being our housekeeper and Jethro being the groom. He would be so out of his depth and it would be embarrassing for us all.' Isabelle breathed in deeply and waited for Harriet's comments.

'I just wish Rosie was not so infatuated with him. Do you and Jane know a few eligible young men who might catch her eye and encourage Rosie not to lose her way with Ethan? Anybody would be better than him.' Harriet put down her sewing, as she admitted her despair over the love affair that was unfolding between Ethan and Rosie.

'Leave it to me. We both know a few young men who

might take her fancy. There's the Knowles lad at Feizor, and the Robinson lad at Horton. He's just been left some land by his grandfather – he would be a good catch. And let's face it, your Rosie is a good-looking girl. Dress her up and I'm sure, by the end of the night, we will find somebody more suitable.' Isabelle smiled. 'Now about work: when do you want to call it your last day? Do you agree with my choice of Margery Sutcliffe? I think she was the most adept of the bunch and, between you and me, she is too old and set in her ways to turn James's head. I've learned by my mistakes, Harriet, I really have.' Isabelle looked thoughtful as she thought back to the flighty Madge, and then of the woman she had just employed. 'Plus, Margery will be a steadying influence on Jane to learn the skill of dressmaking, and it looks like she will not take any nonsense when it comes to her work.'

'She's a bit stern, but she does have very good skills. So, yes, you have made the best choice. If she is to start next week, as you have agreed, I'll finish working here the following week. We seem to have caught up with the orders now. Another week here will give Margery time to settle in, and time for me to spend with Jane, although she is showing great promise in her skills. I don't think you will have any worries with Jane. She seems to have settled down and realizes now, after her silliness with her so-called suffragette friend, just how much she thinks of this wonderful shop. Especially as she knows that one day it will be hers. I wish Rosie had as much sense. I'm sure she is going to ruin her life, if she doesn't see sense soon. The more I moan at her, the more she digs in her heels and swears undying love for her Ethan.'

'Oh, Harriet, it will work out alright; she'll see the error of her ways eventually. I'll ask Jane to make a fuss of Rosie at the ball and to introduce her, as I say, to some of the eligible young men in the district. Hopefully she will return home with her eyes open and realize that Ethan is not for her. Now, once winter is over, and if you are not too busy on the farm, you must come back and keep your hand in at Atkinson's. After all, you are a part shareholder and you should have your say in the running of the stores. We could have tea together, if there is nothing to discuss, and it is just good that we are close again. Mother would be so happy that we are no longer at loggerheads with one another.' Isabelle smiled at her sister-in-law; she had missed Harriet over the years and was glad of her being there now for support.

'I will. It is just the travelling to Skipton this winter that will keep me away. The nanny has been perfect with Georgina, and Rosie is good with her, too. And as for Ben, well, he's growing up quickly, so I would like to come back in spring, once the worst of the weather has gone. I've enjoyed my time here with you, albeit brief and under terrible circumstances.' Harriet bowed her head, thinking of all the hurt James had caused with his fling. But at the same time she was glad that the misfortune had brought down the barrier between her and Isabelle.

'Well, what he did to me still hurts me and the family, but hopefully it will make us stronger. He chose his moment, though, didn't he? Just after my mother dying – a time when

I was at my most vulnerable. It will take me a long time to forgive him. And I think a lot of Jane's behaviour lately is a result of his stupidity and his actions. Thank heavens Luke is away from it all at Giggleswick.' Isabelle sighed. 'Still, some good has come out of the bad, and just look at us two: thick as thieves once more, and for that I'm thankful.'

'Yes, me too. We were both young and foolish, and you think only of yourself at that age. We should not forget that when chastising our own children. Even though we want the best for them.' Harriet looked around her and remembered the time when Atkinson's was just starting out, and all the excitement there had been in the air. Her mother-in-law had been dressed to the nines, and she and Isabelle had taken orders and fittings for dresses and clothes that no one in the district could compete with. Now things were changing. Some working-class house-holds – the ones that could afford it – owned their own sewing machines and bought ready-made patterns in different sizes, to make their own clothes more easily. Coupled with the new ready-to-wear range that Atkinson's now had in store, tailor-made clothes would soon be solely for the few, with alterations perhaps being the most that Atkinson's seamstresses could offer. Times were changing, and the economy was more austere. She couldn't help but think that the best times for Atkinson's had perhaps been and gone now. Anyway, time would tell and she could do nothing about the ways of the world, even if she wanted to.

27

Windfell Manor was thronged with staff getting the hall ready for Christmas and the coming ball. The kitchen was especially busy, as they prepared for the many meals that would be expected of them.

'I'm rushed off my feet. I don't know how the mistress thinks we can cope,' said Ruby. 'She's not offered any extra staff, or told me yet how many guests we have at this ball. I haven't even got Lily any more; she used to help, if she thought we were busy. But you won't find Dorothy getting her hands dirty down in the kitchen. Oh no, she's far too much up her own arse to come down here too often. Too busy making sure everyone's wardrobe is correct – as if that takes much doing in this house!'

Turkey feathers filled the air as Ruby and Nancy plucked the four birds that Jethro had brought in from Settle market.

'You'd think Jethro would have plucked these birds

for us, but no, he's too busy faffing about with his horses and moaning about his lad. I don't know why he's so bothered about Ethan. I say, "Good lad." There's nowt wrong with aiming high, and Rosie is a grand lass – unlike our snooty Miss Jane.'

'I can understand Jethro not being happy about it. Ethan should know his place. Although I'd never say so to Mazy – her lad can do no wrong, in her eyes. We should never mix with them above us; it only ends in tears. Think of that flighty bit that turned Master James's head.' Nancy picked up the meat cleaver and aimed it at the feet of the turkey she had just plucked and came down hard with it onto the chopping block, before moving on to cutting off the crinkled pink-and-blue wattle. 'I don't mind plucking the birds, but I hate cleaning them.' She went over to the kitchen sink and put her hand down the turkey's neck to remove the crop, which was filled with the remains of the turkey's last corn supper. 'It's the smell.' Nancy retched as the odour hit her nostrils.

'You have never had a strong stomach.' Ruby turned round quickly and shook her head at Nancy. 'Thank heavens Christmas is only once a year, and at least I can prepare quite a bit in advance. But I'm sure it was never this chaotic in Miss Charlotte's time, and she'd have been down here making sure we were alright. Mistress Isabelle just says what she wants and doesn't think of the consequences – she's always been like that. Always wanted her own way and never thought how it affected anybody else. Miss Jane is just like her; she'll have to learn by her mistakes or it'll be the worse for her.' Ruby examined her plucked turkey. 'I'll have to singe this fine down off. I'm tearing the skin, trying to pluck it off.' She walked over to the mantelpiece and got a spill from the container above the fire and lit it. Holding the turkey up in one hand, she ran the lit spill over the fluffy down on the turkey's neck and chest, watching it brown and curl up and disappear, while filling the kitchen with the smell of burnt feathers and acrid smoke. 'I can't hold this bird much longer, it'll have to do.' Ruby looked at her handiwork and then put the heavy turkey down on the kitchen table. 'Open the back door and then clean me this one, Nancy. At least we've done half of them. It's coming up to lunchtime, I need to put the cock-a-leekie soup on the stove.'

Nancy opened the back door wide, letting fresh, cold air into the kitchen, before returning to cleaning the turkey. 'I don't want any dinner.' Her stomach churned as she looked at her next victim and thought of the chicken in the soup that she usually enjoyed, but not today.

'You don't know what's good for you, lass. You've got to eat,' grinned Ruby, as Nancy retched again and gave her a look that said everything.

'I know I do, but the thought of any fowl in anything makes me want to be sick. You could have made mushroom soup – or anything other than what I can envisage running around a farmyard.' Nancy breathed in and took courage as she picked up her carving knife to operate on the dead bird.

*

'Now, doesn't that look beautiful?' Mazy stood back and admired the decorated pine Christmas tree that stood proudly in the hallway of Windfell.

'It certainly does. I do love Christmas.' Dorothy Baines stood next to her with an armful of mending and cast-offs from the Fox family.

The tree looked magnificent; glass baubles shone and tinsel glittered in the light of the chandelier that had recently been hung in the entrance hall. The tip of the tree was finished off with a sparkling golden star reaching halfway up the staircase from the base on the marbled hallway's floor.

'The mistress has really gone to town on things this year. I thought it would be a quiet Christmas, after she lost her mother this spring and after the scandal that hit the family, but it seems it has not affected her Christmas plans.' Mazy looked at Dorothy, knowing that she was her mistress's ears when it came to the staff.

'I think that is exactly why she has planned such a big event. To show that there is new life in Windfell, and to make her and Mr Fox look strong. You can't mourn forever – life goes on.' Dorothy balanced her pile of clothes over her arm and watched as Eve wrapped a long garland made of holly and fir around the iron handrail of the stairs. She smiled slightly as she watched Eve stop and nearly swear as the holly pricked her, in defiance of being twined around the banisters.

'You've got an armful of mending, I'd better not keep you.' Mazy had tried to make friends with Dorothy, but she found her hard work and even though she knew it was not Dorothy's fault that she had replaced Lily as lady's maid, she couldn't forgive her for filling her shoes so readily.

'Oh, most of this is to be thrown out. It mainly belongs to Mister James. The mistress says he should have a new dinner suit for the party, and Miss Jane goes through clothes like nobody's business. In fact let me give them to you, and then you can give them to the rag-and-bone man when he comes again.' Dorothy held each item up, passing nearly all of them to Mazy as she did so, before going into the morning room to sit and mend the few items she had kept.

Mazy looked at the armful of garments that Dorothy could have taken to the outhouse herself, to await the weekly rag-and-bone man's visit. She was so lazy, thought Mazy. But she knew Dorothy didn't want to show her face in the kitchen, realizing that she would probably be given a job to do. Mazy picked through the garments one by one: the pretty silks that had once adorned Jane, the frills and fancies of the best quality. On the bottom of the pile was a perfectly good dinner suit, which Isabelle had decided was not good enough for her unfaithful husband, with a bow tie still attached. Perhaps she was getting rid of it because he had worn it with his lover, Mazy thought, as she held it up and looked at it carefully. Whatever the reason, the suit was too good to give to the rag-and-bone man. Neither of her two would ever wear anything like it, but she could sell it to the second-hand shop in Settle and boost her pay a little. Snooty-drawers Dorothy need never know it had not gone to its rightful place, she thought, as she moved to put the contents of her arms in a secret location in the stable, to be taken home later. The money was better in her purse than in the kitchen funds, where it would have gone if the rag-and-bone man had bought them, she thought, as she walked back smiling into the kitchen.

'Been to see your Jethro, have you? Did you tell him it's nearly lunchtime, if he fancies joining us in this kitchen that's in disarray?' Ruby looked up from stirring her soup.

'He's not here today; he's gone to the blacksmith's to shoe two of the horses.' Mazy glanced at the red-faced cook, who looked as if she was going to burst with heat and stress from running the busy kitchen.

'There you go – nobody tells me anything. I've made enough soup for an army and there's only going to be the four of us having it, because madam here says she doesn't want anything, and Thomson has gone into Settle to pick up Master James's new shoes. I suppose he will have gone in with Jethro, when I think about it. Those upstairs will have to have cock-a-leekie for their starter tonight, and they'll just have to lump it.' Ruby placed the bread board down on the table in front of Mazy and looked at her face. 'Aye, and you needn't pull that face – that's what we are having, despite the smell of turkey guts. If your Jethro had cleaned them, then my kitchen wouldn't smell like it does.'

'He's busy as well, you know. You are not the only one who's rushed off their feet. He's been told to collect people all over the dale, for this ball at the weekend, and he's busy with Christmas jobs just like the rest of us.' Mazy was holding her own with the angry cook.

'Busy poaching pheasants off the Maudsley estate, I suspect. I don't suppose he's got a spare brace, has he? I could do with one, if he's some spare. Only if he has the time, of course,' blustered Ruby.

'Here, I'll make your life easier and take Dorothy her dinner. She won't be able to sit in here with this smell, you know what she's like. Yes, I'll tell Jethro you need a brace of pheasants – he's got some hanging already, if you need them with a bit of taste. They should just be right for Christmas Day.'

Mazy reached for a tray and placed a cruet set, spoon, bowl of soup and plate with buttered bread on it. 'That should do Her Ladyship Dorothy. Not that she'll show her face anyway, because she knows you are busy in here and she's in the morning room, mending clothes as usual. I'll give Eve a shout – she's busy in the hall seeing to the decorations – before I'm on my way to serve madam.' Mazy lifted up the tray and left Ruby and Nancy shaking their heads in disbelief at how one of their group could get away with doing nowt.

'Is your Ethan coming to the ball? He should, you know, if he's courting young Rosie.' Ruby sat down next to Mazy, on her return, and sipped her soup, waiting for her to reply.

'Oh no. It's not his place to be with the family. Mistress Isabelle won't want him there. After all, he'll be bringing the Atkinson family along in their carriage, and it wouldn't

301

be right.' Mazy shook her head. She was proud that Ethan was courting Rosie, but knew his father did not agree with his son's love for her and thought Ethan should know his place.

'I don't see why he shouldn't. Miss Jane will have asked plenty of her friends. It's not like it is a formal occasion, it's only Christmas celebrations, and everyone should be welcome,' said Eve as she enjoyed her soup, oblivious to the smell, which had dissipated into the cold air.

'Nay, his father would not approve. Besides, what would he wear? You know how they all dress up on occasions like this. He'd only be embarrassed by looking out of place.' Mazy thought about the dinner suit she had hidden; it might be a bit on the large side, but she was adept with a needle and could alter it to fit her Ethan. Perhaps Eve was right: he should attend; he should be with Rosie and be proud to be seen there.

'Well, if I were him, I'd be there. Poor Miss Rosie is going to be lonely without him. And Miss Jane will not help, as she always seems to be slightly jealous of Rosie. Although I don't know why; she has everything she needs in her life and always will have, while poor Rosie has always had to be more grounded and is more like us.' Nancy leaned back next to the sink and watched the others eating their lunch. 'I bet he scrubs up well, your Ethan; under that long, wild hair there's a good-looking man hiding.'

'Nancy, hold your tongue – he's half your age.' Ruby looked at her second-in-command and shook her head.

'I don't know how you can even think about him like that. He's Mazy's son, and perhaps she's right: them and us shouldn't mix. Only thing is: Miss Rosie is not one of them, she is more like us. So there's no wonder Ethan has taken her eye. Still, it's a shame he'll miss dancing to the Beresford Band. Especially when they are coming all the way over nearly every dale in the area. I just hope the weather is good for them and that there's no snow. I might have a dance myself, down here in my kitchen, if I can interest that miserable Thomson.' Ruby sat back and laughed. 'Tell your lad to come and dance with me in the kitchen; he can't sit out in the stable feeling sorry for himself all night. Nancy will make him smile, by the sound of it.'

'I'll see. Perhaps he should attend. He is Rosie's beau.' Mazy looked around her at the faces she knew supported her.

'Aye, tog him up smart and sneak him in, just for Miss Rosie. It'll make her night.' Nancy turned round to start plucking her next turkey, making feathers fill the kitchen again.

'I'll see. He might be asked yet anyway, and then there is no need to sneak him anywhere.' Mazy stood up and cleared her dish.

'Nay, he won't, not with Mistress Isabelle, but you can dream.' Ruby pushed her chair back. 'Here, Nancy, I'm plucking, you are cleaning. Wash these dishes up, while I finish plucking your bird. I know just how much you can't wait to get your hands into that bird, and I wouldn't deprive you of the pleasure.'

Nancy got hold of the half-plucked turkey and watched Ruby nearly swear as she did so. Bloody birds, she thought, they were nowt but work, and these are just the first of many to be eaten over Christmas.

It was the Sunday before Christmas, and Rosie sat with her mother next to the kitchen window, looking out on the frosted landscape while having a quiet family moment. Georgina was lying asleep on her mother's knee and Ben was laid out in front of the open kitchen fire, reading his latest copy of *The Boy's Best*, occasionally letting out a chuckle as he read about the character's latest exploits.

Rosie concentrated on the darning that she had been given and felt content in the warmth of the kitchen. The smells of Christmas filled it, as the plum pudding steamed on the stove top and the scent of pine from the newly erected Christmas tree in the parlour drifted through the whole house.

'It's nice to have you back home all the time, Mother. We've managed, but in all honesty we have missed you when you have been at Skipton.' Rosie looked up at her mother and smiled; it was a rare day when all was quiet at Crummock. The cattle were in for winter, the sheep were down from the fells and the two blazing fires were keeping the long farmhouse warm throughout.

'Yes, I'm best at home in this weather. Come spring, I'll give them a hand again. I think your Aunt Isabelle enjoys me participating a little in the business, and you all seem to cope without me for at least two days of the week. It's good to be back in my kitchen, though, with-

304

out wondering what exactly is going on at home. Speaking of which, will Ethan be joining us this afternoon, as usual on Sunday? We will have to stir them two sleepy heads, if you need the parlour to yourselves.'

'No, Mother, it doesn't matter today; he's gone down to see his mother and father this afternoon and we've arranged to see one another later, after supper. I can tell him to join us for Christmas dinner, can't I, Mother? I want him to share Christmas with us.' Rosie blushed. She still found it hard to display her love for Ethan openly, knowing that her mother did not approve of her choice.

Harriet shifted slightly in her chair as Georgina weighed on her arm. 'He can come to Christmas Day dinner, but he does not join you at the Windfell ball. Your Aunt Isabelle has requested that, as a family, we come alone and said that Ethan will not be welcome. You can see her point of view; there will be dignitaries and people of all standing there, and she will not want a simple stable lad there on your arm.' Harriet looked across at Rosie and waited for the temper that was about to erupt from her daughter. She saw her face turn from smiling happiness to a dark scowl. She was a creature with plenty to say.

'How can she? If I'm going, Ethan is going. What's she going to do when I marry him? Because that's what I'm going to do. Tell her, Mother, or I will.' Rosie threw the darning down and stood up, scowling in front of her mother and watching as baby Georgina awoke as she vented her wrath. 'She's nothing but a snob, and so is Jane. Well, she can keep her Christmas Ball – I'm not going.'

Rosie stormed out of the kitchen and up to her bedroom and lay sobbing on her bed, staring at the unworn ballgown that she had been admiring since her mother had given it to her, as she waited for her first ball at Windfell with the love of her life on her arm. If Ethan wasn't welcome, then she wasn't, either, and wild horses would not drag her there.

28

'I'm so glad you've seen sense, Rosie. Just look how beautiful you are – you deserve to go to the ball. Ethan will understand; he would only feel uncomfortable, because – let's face it – he will have tethered the horses of most of the guests and he's bound to feel inadequate around them.' Harriet stood back and admired her daughter, who was all dressed up for the Christmas Eve Ball at Windfell. 'Isn't she beautiful?' Harriet turned and looked at Danny and Archie, wanting them to give Rosie the same assurance.

'Aye, a right bonny lass. You'll put everybody else to shame.' Archie looked up at his granddaughter and smiled; she was the spitting image of her grandmother and, being so, was especially dear to him. 'Never mind, lass, Ethan's not going anywhere. He'll be happier sitting in the kitchen with his mother, and you could always go down and visit him there. They'll probably be better company than half of the buggers upstairs.'

'Father, think on what you say! It's a big night for Isabelle – she needs to prove her standing in society, and show that she and James have recovered from his wanderings.' Danny looked at his father as he pulled a face and tugged on his collar and bow tie. He hated these sorts of event, and the fact that he had to toe the line and be polite to people he didn't normally have time for.

'It's nowt but a bloody sham. Folk are still going to remember James for being the first to have a motorbike in this area and killing his lover on it. Despite how big the show is tonight. And as for her ladyship not inviting Ethan, she's wrong. If he makes our Rosie happy, he should come with her.'

'Just keep your thoughts to yourself, Father. Remember the children's carer is in the next room.' Harriet looked sternly at her father-in-law as she pulled on her gloves and put the fireguard up to safeguard the kitchen fire, after filling a small metal-lined wooden box with warm ashes to keep them warm in the carriage.

'It's alright, Grandfather. Ethan wasn't too worried and, who knows, I might just enjoy myself with whoever may be there.' Rosie smiled at her grandfather. He always fought her corner for her, no matter how annoying it was to her parents.

'Right, if we are to get there in time, let's go. Ethan is outside with the carriage and team, and at least it's a fine frosty night. The weather is in our favour, albeit a little chilly. Have you all got everything?' Danny looked at the two women in his life and thought how fine they both looked. 'Mrs Atkinson, would you care to take my arm?'

'Why yes, sir, it would be a pleasure.' Harriet smiled and linked her arm through her husband's.

'That means you are with me, lass. Never mind – I'm the one with the brass. You remember that.' Archie winked at Rosie as she took his arm.

'I'd love you if you hadn't a penny to your name, Grand-papa. Money isn't everything.' Rosie kissed his cheek and took his arm as they walked out into the crisp winter's evening and towards Ethan waiting with the team.

'Good evening, so glad you could join us.'

Isabelle smiled at each guest as they entered Windfell, with James by her side in a show of unity. The hallway and ballroom were filled with well-to-do locals and dig-nitaries and their wives, and were awash with the bright colours and glitter of precious jewels.

'I don't think even Mama had as many guests as this. I don't even know everyone who is here. I think some are friends of Jane's, and of course there are some masters from Giggleswick School. It was only right that Luke asked them. It will do his standing at the school good. I do wish he had worn his dinner suit, though, instead of his cadet's uniform,' whispered Isabelle to James as he stood next to her, shaking hands with each guest and guiding them towards the drinks and food, which were being served by all the staff of Wind-fell.

'Just how many people have you invited? And tell me, do you recognize the tall blond lad who's with Jane? She keeps batting her eyelashes at him and I haven't a clue who he is. He's not in a dinner suit, so he can't be one of yours.' James smiled yet again at the incoming guests and glanced across at his daughter and her companion.

'I haven't got a clue who he is, but he is quite good-looking, although not well dressed. I'm just glad that she's entertaining him, instead of sitting like a wallflower or telling everybody the virtues of the Suffragette movement.' Isabelle smiled yet again and then looked out onto the driveway as the carriage from Crummock drove up. 'Here's the rest of the family. I hope Archie doesn't speak out of turn, and I do hope Harriet has told Rosie that Ethan is not welcome.

'Harriet, Danny and Papa, how lovely that you have joined us. And just look at you, Rosie, aren't you beautiful – quite the young lady. You'll be fighting the young men away from you.' Isabelle kissed Harriet on the cheek and smiled at her family.

'You've put on a good show, Isabelle; we could hear the band playing as we came past Stainforth. I hope you've invited your neighbours.' Archie kissed his step-daughter.

'Yes, the neighbours have been invited. The Maudsleys are mingling somewhere, so you can catch up with them, Father, and I'm sure you will know more people than I do. Rosie, Jane is over there in the corner, if you wish to join her. Although she seems to be giving all her attention to a certain young man, who I must admit seems familiar, though I'm sure I don't know him.' She smiled at Rosie, who struggled to reply to her and wasn't looking at where Jane was. Isabelle looked at Harriet, realizing that her request that Ethan did not attend had

310

not been popular with her niece. 'I'm so glad you could all come. It's quite like old times.' She smiled as Harriet passed Thomson her wrap and put her arm through Danny's.

'Indeed it is. Let's hope this is the beginning of a wonderful Christmas, full of magic.' Harriet put her arm around Rosie and pulled her close to her. She noticed Rosie glance at the lad who was talking to Jane, with his back towards them, and saw that he was not well dressed, so Ethan would not have looked too out of place. She guessed Rosie was thinking the same thing.

'Go and enjoy yourselves. Just shout when you want a drink and Thomson will serve you. There's cold platters laid out in the dining room and, as Archie says, there's the Beresford Band playing in the ballroom. They would have been a bit too racy in Charlotte's day, but we've moved with the times.' James patted Danny on the shoulder and watched as the family walked into the throng and were made welcome by the other guests.

'Please excuse me, dear; most of the guests have arrived now and I want to have a talk to the officer who is standing next to Luke and his friend. Just to get an idea of how he thinks our country stands in these turbulent times.' James smiled at Isabelle. He'd done his duty, standing like a stuffed dummy, meeting and greeting while some of the so-called ladies looked at him and then giggled as they walked away, and their husbands chastised them even for looking at him. It would be a long time before his transgression with Madge Burton was forgotten, of that he was sure. Nobody forgot anything in the Dales, especially when it came to a scandal.

'Certainly, dear, I'm about to mix myself and make everyone welcome to our home. Isn't it wonderful to have the manor filled again with so many people – we must do it again next year.' Isabelle picked up her champagne flute and made a beeline for Jane, as she needed to know who the mystery guest was that was keeping her daughter so enthralled.

'The world is in chaos, sir. Every country has its eye on another one, and before long the alliances between countries will be tested beyond belief.'

Captain Pierce looked sternly at James as he stood alongside Luke and his best friend, Bill.

'The decline of the Ottoman Empire when the Balkan League captured the Ottoman lands in south-eastern Europe has been a major factor in the unrest. Those Russkies thought it would be a very useful tool to access the Adriatic Sea; and as for Germany, it is busy building a railway between Berlin and Baghdad through Istanbul, so it can't afford to fall out with anybody yet. I'm just thankful that the London Conference this year resolved the conflict in Serbia and formed an independent Albania. That was one less conflict. But it's only a matter of time – the world is a powder keg, sir. That's why we need stout fellows like your son here to fight for his King and country.'

'That's what I am afraid of. It's alright playing at soldiers in the grounds of Giggleswick School, but I would not want to see my son go to war. I'm glad that he is the age he is; at least he is too young for action yet.' James looked across at Luke, whose face showed that he thought otherwise.

'A war, if it came, wouldn't last long. No country can afford it, and most countries are in an economic mess. But as for playing soldiers, I beg to differ, sir. I train my cadets better than any of the officer classes of the Duke of Wellington Brigade. They are officers and gentlemen by the time they leave Giggleswick and my care. My training and values will be with your son all his life and he is one of our leading cadets, especially on the firing range. Something you are proud of, I'm sure?' Captain Pierce slapped Luke on the back and looked at James for his response.

'I am indeed proud of him, but I'd have been even prouder if he took my stance on life and didn't believe in war, for it only brings death and despair. There are other means to ensure peace.' James looked at the captain and then at his son.

'Father, please!' Luke sighed.

'You are not one of those conscientious objectors, are you, sir? With no backbone, and someone who would rather see other people die in their place than fight for their country?' Captain Pierce stuttered.

'No, but I'm not one for needless war and the slaughter of innocents, especially when one of them may be my son. Now, please excuse me. I'm afraid my wife is urging me to mingle and I've wasted enough of your time.' James looked at the man whose whole life revolved around fighting and war, and who had influenced his son far too much for his liking. He needed to make his excuses and speak to Isabelle regarding taking Luke away from the school, which acted as an army recruitment centre, before it was too late and the war that was threatening broke out.

'Now, Jane, who is this? Are you not going to introduce us?' Isabelle touched the arm of the young man who had captivated her daughter. 'I don't believe you made yourself known to me as you entered Windfell.' She caught her breath as he turned to smile at her.

'Mother, may I introduce Daniel Bland. He is the grandson of Ragged Hall's Mr Brown. I met him when he came to inform Grandfather of Mr Brown's death. I hope you didn't mind me inviting him this evening.' Jane beamed at the handsome young man who stood next to her.

'Delighted to meet you, Mrs Fox. My grandfather spoke often of your family and was insistent that I made myself known to you and your brother.' Daniel looked at Isabelle and recognized a change in her manner as she studied his features.

'Please accept my condolences on the loss of your grandfather. He will be missed by the local community. I know my stepfather and stepbrother knew him very well. Tell me, Mr Bland, are you his only grandchild? I have quite lost track of your mother and what family she has, since she moved over to Slaidburn.' Isabelle fished cautiously for what she already knew was the answer. It was

clear to her who this young man was – and who his
father was, for the likeness was uncanny.

'I'm the oldest and I have left four brothers back in
Slaidburn. However, I'm afraid I have fallen out of
favour with them, as my grandfather left me Ragged Hall
upon his death. My father is not happy that he did not
see fit to will it to my mother, for some reason. There is
nothing stranger than families, but I was always there for
my grandfather, and he was there for me. I seem to be
the odd one out in the family, but blessed when it comes
to luck.' Daniel smiled, knowing full well what Isabelle
was thinking.

'So, will you be staying in the area? I'm sure it would
have pleased your grandfather to know that his farm is
in good hands and will be remaining in the family.' Isabelle looked at Jane, who kept glancing at her companion.
She was smitten by him, even though he was improperly
dressed for the occasion and of little standing in the community.

'Yes, it needs a lot of work and a great deal of time
spending on it. But I'm willing to give it both, so you won't
be seeing the back of me quite yet.' Daniel grinned. Isabelle
knew who he was, and his grandfather had told him that
the stepsister and brother were very close. She knew that
he was Danny Atkinson's son – something his mother had
told him when he was old enough to understand.

'Well, I wish you well, Mr Bland. Jane, I know you
are enjoying Mr Bland's company, but don't neglect our
other guests.' Isabelle gave a tight smile as she stepped
away from the young couple.

'Please, Mrs Fox, my name is Daniel. In future, please call me Daniel – I'm sure you know why.' He caught her arm.

'Oh yes, I know why. I only hope you are not here to cause trouble or hurt any of my family,' whispered Isabelle out of earshot of Jane, thankful that the band was extremely loud.

'No, I simply want to meet my father, and this is one way to do it. My mother loved him, and still does, but I'll keep that to myself. There's been enough hurt in my life, without causing it in somebody else's. I'll take care.'

Daniel looked earnest as he watched Isabelle make her way to her husband and then on towards her step-brother, and then lead Danny away from his wife and family. He didn't want to hurt anyone, not in the way he had been hurt in his life; he just wanted to fit in. The more he had talked to Jane, the more he knew he was where he belonged, and that this was his true family. The family his mother had wanted to be part of, but had never had the chance.

29

'I can't be down here long, Ethan, they will miss me.'
Mazy stood back in the bustling kitchen of Windfell and
looked at her son. 'Heavens, you look different. Nancy's
done a right good job of cutting your hair and shortening
the trousers – I couldn't have managed without her. I feel
real tearful, just looking at you: my son dressed up like
a gentleman. A handsome one at that.' Mazy bit her lip
and stood back to look at her son, dressed in the evening
suit that had been discarded for the rag-and-bone man.
He looked handsome, clean-shaven, his black hair slick
and neat; a match for any man on the dance floor.

'Aye, I don't think Rosie will look at another bloke
once she sees me. I may have no money, but even I'm surprised at how well I scrub up.' Ethan looked down at his
black trousers and at the work shoes that were just hidden
under the length of them. 'Pity he wasn't throwing out
some shoes as well, but you can't have everything.'

'Yes, your feet are too small for anybody's cast-offs

– I did try. Well, you had better get yourself up our stairs and make a quiet entrance; don't be too flash. If Miss Rosie's meeting you by the Christmas tree, I'll stand there with you and serve drinks, to support you both. Mistress Isabelle won't dare make a scene, once you are both up and dancing, as she won't want her night spoiled. So she'll just have to accept you.' Mazy looked at her precious son. He was good enough for anybody, in her eyes, and she would walk through hell to protect him.

'Thank you, Mother. You know how I feel about Rosie, I had to be with her tonight.' Ethan kissed his mother and held her tightly.

'Aye, well, your father will have something to say to us both in the morning no doubt. But it'll be worth it, just for the pair of you to turn a few heads and to let them know nothing's going to stand between you.' Mazy wiped her eyes with her hanky and led the way up the servants' stairs, weaving through the crowds to where the Christmas tree stood.

'She's not here yet. I can see her father talking to Mrs Fox, but I can't see Rosie, nor her mother.' Ethan gazed around the room at all the well-to-do guests and tried to hide behind his mother, as she picked up a tray of full champagne glasses from the dresser and offered them to passing revellers.

'She'll be here, don't fret. She keeps her promises, does Rosie – not like that Jane, who seems to be occupied with a young man. Although her mother and Mr Atkinson don't seem that happy with her, by the look of the glances they are giving her and the young man.

318

Happen you won't be the scandal of the evening after all.' Mazy smiled as her tray started to empty to all the partygoers.

'Ethan! Ethan, I'm here.' Rosie tugged on his jacket and pulled him towards her into the relative quiet of the drawing-room doorway.

'I couldn't see you. How do I look – swanky, eh? Not so much a stable boy now.' Ethan grinned. He held his hands and arms out and looked himself up and down. 'Do you think you can afford to be seen with me, Miss Atkinson?'

'Oh, Ethan, I wouldn't be bothered if you were still in your old work clothes, as long as we are together. But yes, I'm right proud to be on the arm of such a good-looking man. Let's see what they do about us now.' Rosie grinned.

'Could I interest you in a dance, madam? I do believe the band is playing a waltz and, as that is the only dance I can do, we had better make a move and show them how it is done.' Ethan winked; he was going to enjoy himself, just like everybody else.

'Do you think we should? My mother will have a fit when she sees you. She's been trying to introduce me to eligible young men all evening. The only one she hasn't bothered with is the one Jane is talking to, and although Mother says she doesn't know him, she keeps looking at him strangely.' Rosie took Ethan's arm as he led her onto the dance floor, feeling excitement and a little fear as she realized that people were looking at what, in their eyes, was a handsome young couple making the most of Christmas at Windfell.

'That's our Rosie. Who's she with? Oh my Lord, it's Ethan. Just look at him, he's in a suit. You can hardly tell it's the same boy that drove us down here tonight. Oh, I could die with embarrassment!' Harriet turned to Archie and then looked around her, at the faces watching the couple as they glided around the room. 'Where's Danny? Has he seen? What will Isabelle say about this? Oh, heavens! She'll never talk to me again.'

'Stop getting yourself flustered. Just look at them, they are the bonniest couple here tonight, and they know it. You should be proud of them, especially Rosie – she loves that lad, you know. And you can't say you haven't been there yourself, because you have. My lad had money, and you didn't have much, so how do you think we felt when you became part of the family? It didn't worry us, and it shouldn't worry you now. Just look at them, they are as pretty as a picture.' Archie leaned on his stick as he sat at the edge of the ballroom and watched Rosie and Ethan holding one another tightly as they waltzed around the room. Rosie's face was full of love, and Ethan looked so proud as he concentrated on his footwork. 'Bonniest couple in Yorkshire, that's what they are.' He sat back and shook his head as Harriet pushed her way through the crowds in search of Danny and Isabelle, to reassure her sister-in-law that she had known nothing of Ethan and Rosie's plans.

'I know – I've seen him, he's here!' Flustered, Harriet broke into the conversation that Danny and Isabelle were having. She didn't notice the look of worry on both their faces when she spoke to them, and was nearly in tears as she saw the anger on Isabelle's face.

Isabelle looked shocked at Harriet's words.

'Oh, Harriet, I'm sorry. I had no idea he was going to attend. I didn't know Jane had invited him, otherwise I would never have allowed Daniel Bland to come. I'm sorry, it must be deeply upsetting for you. Danny knew nothing about him until just recently, I can assure you. But how long have you known? Please don't upset yourself; it is only us who knows who he really is, after all.' Isabelle looked at Harriet, distraught, and then pleadingly at Danny, who now had to face his wife and then make himself known to his illegitimate son.

'Harriet, I'm sorry you've had to find out this way. You do know that I loved only you, and that Amy was just an easy distraction – there was never anything between us.' Danny tried to put his arms around his wife, who looked puzzled by their responses.

'What are you both on about? Who is Daniel Bland, and why are you mentioning Amy Brown? At least I presume it is Amy Brown, considering that I told you, Isabelle, that I knew Danny had been unfaithful to me all those years ago. Don't look so shocked, Danny, you made it so obvious at the time, and I've always known I was second best.' Harriet looked at brother and sister and knew something untoward was in the making, with this so-called Daniel Bland. 'I was referring to the fact that Ethan is dressed up to the nines and is parading our daughter around the dance floor, for all the world to see.

So whatever it is that I'm not supposed to know and will be so shocked by, tell me now.' She breathed in and looked at them both. It must be bad, as neither of them had blinked regarding the news of Ethan and Rosie's escapade.

'I think I have a son! That's who Daniel Bland is. And he's caught the eye of Jane; she's been with him all night. That's what Isabelle was telling me when you came over to us. I'd no idea – I'm so sorry Harriet, I must have hurt you all those years back, and now for you to have all this thrown in your face. He's not thought of his actions.' Danny reached for Harriet's hand, but she pulled it away from him.

'He's not the only one who hasn't thought about his rash actions, is he? Where are they? Does he know you are his father?' Harriet gazed around the dance floor. Her eyes flitted from person to person, and the noise of the band and the sight of her Rosie and Ethan making fools of themselves to one and all made her feel quite faint.

'They are over there by the window. I am sorry to say that when you look at him, I don't think there is any doubt about his parentage.' Isabelle put her arm around her sister-in-law, feeling her body shake and seeing tears well up in her eyes.

'And does he know that Danny is his father?' Harriet spotted Jane and Daniel standing together, lost in conversation. 'He is more like you, Danny, than any of our children are, so I'd say there is no doubt whatsoever.' Harriet pulled her handkerchief out of her pocket and held it against her mouth, stifling a cry.

'I think so. From the way he talked, I believe his mother has told him who he is and that he is named after his true father.' Isabelle breathed in deeply. This was not the night she had planned. Yet again family scandals were being played out under the roof of Windfell Manor.

'I'm sorry, Harriet, I'm so sorry. I was young and I was foolish, and when Amy got married to the fella from Slaidburn, I thought that would be the last I'd see or hear of her.' Danny tried to put his arm around his wife, but she pulled away.

'You mean you hoped that your sins would not be found out! Well, he's standing there and looking every inch like you. And there I was, worried about Ethan showing us up with Rosie. At least they are not sneaking about with their love; they are proud to declare it to the world.' Harriet looked across at Daniel and then at Danny. 'No wonder you didn't stay long at Bill Brown's funeral. You and Archie realized then. You both had nothing much to say about how it went, because you had seen Daniel and noticed the resemblance and knew instantly that he was your son.'

'Oh, Harriet, if only you had said that you knew about Amy. I've been carrying the guilt for years.' Danny looked at his wife. All around him people were enjoying the festive season, but his world was falling apart.

'Guilt – you know nothing about guilt. Remember that I was to blame for the death of our two boys. It was my fault I put my work before them both. I lost my first-born, while Amy kept her son and your heart.' Harriet looked across at Jane laughing and flirting with Daniel.

323

'You make it right by him; go and tell him that you are his father, and then he has no hold over us.'

'I can't. How do I do that?' Danny looked at the hurt in his wife's eyes. Their marriage had been tempestuous, but now he knew why, for Harriet had always known about his love for Amy and had kept it her secret. A secret that had eaten away at her, every year she had been married to him. Every time life's trials went against them, she had questioned his love for her and it had gnawed away inside her.

Isabelle put her hand on Danny's arm. 'I'll distract Jane. It is best if Daniel gets to know that his secret is out. Take him into the drawing room and speak to him, find out what he is about. Although it sounded to me as if he just aims to farm Ragged Hall and is not here to cause trouble.' Isabelle looked at her brother and sister-in-law. Her perfect evening had been spoilt, but that was of little consequence compared to what Harriet and Danny were going through. She stepped through the crowds, passing Ethan and Rosie lost in one another's arms on the dance floor. Both stopped in their tracks as they watched Danny and Harriet following Isabelle over to where Jane and her admirer stood.

'Looks like Jane is in more trouble than we are.' Ethan smiled as Rosie watched her parents looking distressed, while following her aunt.

'No, something is wrong – my mother's nearly in tears.' Rosie let go of Ethan's arms and walked to her parents' side.

'Go back to Ethan, Rosie.' Danny glanced round at

his daughter as Harriet stepped in front of Isabelle, intent on getting to Jane and Daniel first.

'No, let her stay, she should hear this. In fact everyone should hear this; it is yet another dirty secret that has made itself known tonight,' yelled Harriet, making everyone around her fall quiet as she strode up to Daniel and Jane. 'Yes, yet another scandal – more for you all to talk about.'

Everyone looked at Harriet acting so strangely.

'My daughter is courting a stable lad, and now my husband has another son in our midst. Is that not right, Daniel? For is my husband and the father of my children not your father, too?' Harriet stood in front of Daniel Bland and the startled Jane, as tears flowed down her cheeks.

Daniel put his head down and looked at the faces of the revellers. The band had stopped playing and all eyes were on him and Jane, and the Atkinson family.

'I believe so. That is what my mother has always told me, since I was young.' Daniel looked at his father. 'Although I had no intention of making my parentage so public. I didn't come here to make trouble, just to see the family that my mother had talked about for as long as I can remember.'

'Harriet, lass, come here to me, don't get yourself so upset.' Archie made his way through the crowd and put his arm around the hysterical woman, whose heart had been broken once more. 'Come on – come over here with me, away from these folk. Rosie, you and Ethan go and tell Jethro to take us back to Crummock. I don't think

325

your mother will want to stay and see Christmas in with these good folk.'

'Yes, Grandfather.' Rosie looked as bewildered as everyone else, as she and Ethan ran to fetch Jethro to take her mother home. The man who was with Jane was her own half-brother? Where had he come from? Who was his mother? Rosie glanced back as she watched Archie and her mother walk steadily out of the hallway, her mother in tears; and then the crowds of guests turned their attention to her father, standing with his namesake. There was no doubt in anybody's minds that Danny Atkinson had another son, and Rosie a half-brother.

'I'm sorry, good people, please don't let this outburst spoil your evening.' James stood on the band's platform and tried to draw attention away from Danny and his new-found son, as they made their way into the drawing room of Windfell. 'Families, eh, who would have them?' He was trying to make light of the situation. 'Come on, we've still got a few hours until Christmas Day. Enjoy the band and food, and forget your worries, because compared to ours they will be nothing.'

James grinned and instructed the band to start playing again, as he looked across at his wife and daughter. He was not the first in the family to fall from grace and he certainly wouldn't be the last, he was sure of that. Right now, he hoped that Danny was doing right by his new son, but also that he would return to Crummock and tell Harriet just how much she meant to him and that he had always loved her. He knew that, like his own fling with Madge, it must have ensued from the thrill of the moment, but unfortunately a son had been born from Danny's forbidden passion.

'Thank you, James. Isn't it all a mess?' Isabelle linked her arm into James's and looked at Jane, standing alone and aghast, until Rosie reappeared without Ethan on her arm, making her way to where her father and her newly announced brother had been standing with Jane. Luke was moving through the crowd to join them, not wanting to be disassociated from the breaking scandal. 'You try to protect your children from hurt and then you, as a parent, do more damage than you could possibly dream of,' said Isabelle regretfully.

'What do you expect? It's been the year from hell. It is only fitting that we end it on a high note – or should that be a low note? Did you know about Danny's affair and that he had a son?' James looked at his wife and noticed how shaken she seemed.

'Yes, I've always know about his love for Amy Brown. He nearly didn't marry Harriet because of her. Poor Harriet, she doesn't deserve all this worry.' Isabelle stopped short as Jane, Luke and Rosie came to join them both.

'Rosie, are you alright? Would you like to stay with us at Windfell tonight? I know it's Christmas Eve, but perhaps your mother and father might appreciate you staying here. Ethan would be more than welcome to stay with his mother and father tonight – I'm sure Mazy would like that. You can see him first thing in the morning and then go back with him to Crummock in the evening.' Isabelle's eyes had been opened; it didn't matter about your standing in the world; it was love for one another that mattered.

'I don't know, I'll see. Ethan has taken my mother home, along with my grandfather. It seemed only right that he took her home. I should have gone with her, but Grandpapa said I had to stay here and wait for my father. Ethan's father will take us back to Crummock, when my father is ready.' Rosie looked at her cousin Jane and Luke, and for once they looked sympathetically at her.

'Well, this must have been a shock for you, too. A brother you knew nothing about, being made so public. Your poor mother was distraught. Now, if you do stay, I'm sure you will be able to find a few presents under the tree with your name on. Won't she, Jane?' Isabelle gave her daughter a knowing look, to acknowledge that what was to have been hers might have to be reallocated.

'Yes, of course, and you can help me out by listening to the boring conversations about the cadet school at Giggleswick with this one.' Jane glanced at her brother and put her arm around her cousin. 'I didn't know who he was, Rosie, else I wouldn't have invited him. I didn't mean any harm.'

'I know. It's just been a shock to my poor mama.' Rosie glanced over at the closed drawing-room doors.

'Don't worry, Rosie. Your father still loves you just as much. Your mother will calm down, and life will carry on as normal.' Isabelle kissed her niece's brow as she tried to ease the worry that the night had caused.

'It's very strange to find out that I've got a big brother I knew nothing about.' Rosie smiled.

'Well, at least you haven't been fluttering your eye-lashes at him like I have all night. I had no idea who he really was.' Jane looked at her mother.

'That's typical of you. No more sense than the day you were born on,' Luke teased his sister. 'Desperate – that's what you were!'

'Why, you cheeky devil!' Jane scalped her brother with her hand. 'Come on, let's go outside and get a bit of fresh air. It will stop all these folk from looking at us as if we are exhibits in a showground.' She looked at her mother and father.

'Christmas sky tonight, let's see if Saint Nick is on his way.' James laughed, for the magic of Christmas could not be forgotten.

'I hope he's put his hand in his pocket this year. Nuts and sweets are alright, but I wouldn't mind a surprise or two.' Luke grinned.

'You'll get what you are given,' said Isabelle. 'Now go on, get some fresh air while we make sure all's calmed down among our guests.' Isabelle watched as the three of them walked arm-in-arm out of the ballroom and hall-way into the winter's evening.

'They are growing up, James. They are no longer chil-dren.' She sighed.

'I know, and I fear for their futures. We can but be here for them. We can't tell what 1914 will bring, but if it's anything like this last one, we are all going to have to be strong.' James kissed Isabelle, before stepping out with her on his arm to mingle with their guests. War was coming, of that he was sure. But for tonight he would try and forget, and would be there for his family.

'Just look at those stars.' Jane looked up to the star-studded sky. 'Listen, you can hear the church bells in Settle.'

All three children looked up at the sky over Windfell.

'I hope my mother and father will be alright, and that the appearance of Daniel Bland does not cause even more upset in the family.'

'I know. Let's make a wish all together, a Christmas wish to the stars – as Father said, it's bound to come true.' Jane put her arm around Rosie.

'I know what I'm going to wish for. My red star, so that I can become an officer,' said Luke as he closed his eyes and made his wish.

'Shush . . . you shouldn't tell us,' Rosie said, as she closed her eyes and wished for herself and Ethan to be allowed to wed, and for peace at home.

'Well, I'm not telling you mine, but it is hopefully going to come true, if I have my way.' Jane closed her eyes and thought of Daniel Bland, despite the scandal he had brought with him.

All three stood on the gate leading to Windfell Manor, lost in their thoughts, until Danny's voice was heard calling down the drive.

'Rosie! Rosie, come here and meet Daniel.'

Rosie breathed in deeply. She looked at her cousins and didn't say a word as she walked back up the drive to her father and the tall blond-haired young man she now knew to be her brother.

'Rosie, this is Daniel. Although he has a different mother from you, he is my son and your brother, and I want you to make him welcome in our home.' Danny put his arm around his precious daughter and looked at Daniel.

'Hello, Rosie. I've always wanted a sister, and now I have one.' Daniel smiled at her.

Rosie looked up at his open face. He was the image of her father – a father she loved so dearly. She wanted to vent her wrath on him for being unfaithful to her mother, and then she remembered her own love and passion for Ethan. She could have been like Daniel's mother: alone and pregnant and desperate to find a father for her child, if she had not lost her baby. She thought of the fear and the scandal there could have been. She bowed her head and then lifted it to look at her new brother.

'Welcome to our family, Daniel. A big brother for Christmas – now that's different. Better than any present I could have wished for. Happy Christmas, Brother.' She linked her arm through Daniel's and her father's, and looked towards where Ethan stood waiting with the horses to take them home. Ethan was the main love of her life, the one whose love made her strong. Unlike her father, she would marry her wild rover, regardless of the scandal. She knew that her Christmas wish would come true.

30

'Harriet, I love only you, and have done since the day we met. My fling with Amy Brown was just that. We both were young and stupid. I knew you were the only one for me, but she was just too much of a temptation.' Danny lay next to his wife as she sobbed, with the bedclothes pulled up around her.

'But you have a son, and you have brought him home! How am I supposed to feel and deal with that?' Harriet turned and faced her husband with tear-filled eyes.

'I'd hope you would deal with it like you always do with our children. I know he's not yours, but he is mine. My son, who I've just found. And by the sound of it, he has had a very bad deal in life up until now.' Danny sighed as he held his wife close to him.

'Do you think I care about his upbringing? I hated Amy Brown and everything she stood for – she was wild and uncaring, while my mother always groomed me to behave like a lady, to find a good man and settle down. But just as I had done so, Amy came along and stole you from me, albeit just for a brief time. She deserved all she got. At least your firstborn is alive, while mine are dead in the grave and I will never see them again.'

'Oh, Harriet, we can't do anything about the past. I loved our sons, too, but we must look to the future. We have both gained a son tonight – if you let Daniel into your heart. He's not come to make any bother. His grandfather's left him Ragged Hall. He'll not ask anything of us, except recognition of him as my son.'

Harriet looked up at the husband she loved. It was true that she could not alter the past, and she had always known about Danny's affair with Amy, so a child from the dalliance should not come as a shock. 'It was the way I found out – I made such a fool of myself. I was more worried about Rosie and Ethan dancing together, and then Isabelle looked at me like I was mad, not realizing I knew nothing of Daniel Bland's presence.'

'Surprisingly, Isabelle handled it well, and so did James. However, I wish Daniel's arrival into the family could have been a little less public.' Danny smiled. 'On the way back home, he and Rosie talked as if they had known one another all their lives.' He ran his fingers through Harriet's long hair and kissed her brow. 'Forgive me, and make our black sheep welcome into our fold.'

Harriet nodded her head, before turning over in bed and keeping her thoughts to herself. Daniel was Danny's son, and she would grow to love him. In the morning another two places would be laid at the Christmas dinner table: one for Ethan and one for Daniel. Her family was complete once again. They would celebrate Christmas with the living, and would look to the future.

Archie lay in his bed with the bright moon shining down through his bedroom window, the ghostly ribbons of light illuminating the room and making him unable to sleep. It was his first Christmas without his beloved Charlotte next to him. He thought of her laughter, and of her love of Christmas and her family. What would she have made of Daniel's appearance? he wondered. He pulled the blankets up over him, trying to keep warm against the hard frost that was being laid down in the outside world.

'God bless, and happy Christmas, Charlotte, my love,' he whispered as he closed his eyes and dreamed of Christmases past, and of the love that he and Charlotte had shared. 'One in, one out,' he muttered as he drifted off to sleep, thinking of Daniel sitting at the Christmas table. What the future held, they would have to wait and see, but whatever it was, he knew he'd never love another like his Lottie.

'Noel: Christmas Eve 1913'
by Robert Seymour Bridges

A frosty Christmas Eve
when the stars where shining
Fared I forth alone
where westward falls the hill,
And from many a village
in the water'd valley
Distant music reach'd me
peals of bells aringing:
The constellated sounds
ran sprinkling on earth's floor
As the dark vault above
with stars was spangled o'er.
Then sped my thoughts to keep
that first Christmas of all
When the shepherds watching
by their folds ere the dawn
Heard music in the fields
and marvelling could not tell
Whether it were angels
or the bright stars singing.

Now blessed be the tow'rs
that crown England so fair
That stand up strong in prayer
unto God for our souls
Blessed be their founders
(said I) an' our country folk

Who are ringing for Christ
in the belfries to-night
With arms lifted to clutch
the rattling ropes that race
Into the dark above
and the mad romping din.

But to me heard afar
it was starry music
Angels' song, comforting
as the comfort of Christ
When he spake tenderly
to his sorrowful flock:
The old words came to me
by the riches of time
Mellow'd and transfigured
as I stood on the hill
Heark'ning in the aspect
of th' eternal silence.